IN YOUR EYES

CHRONICALLY IN LOVE
BOOK 1

MOLLY MCCARTHY

CONTENT NOTE

This book contains strong language and sexual content. The following topics are mentioned in some capacity: chronic illnesses (specifically Sjogren's and Lupus), cancer, SIDS, loss of a sibling, loss of a child, infidelity (in the past, not one of the main characters).

For my twenty-year-old self, who was newly diagnosed with Sjogren's and worried she would never live a fulfilling life. Honey, it won't be perfect, but it will be better than you could have imagined.

CHAPTER 1
HANNAH

People don't look like they're drowning until they go under and never come back up. That was what being diagnosed with a chronic illness felt like. I fought and resisted the symptoms as they came, trying my best to stay above water, until one day I couldn't fight anymore. You can only tread water for so long.

My fingers hover over the keyboard as I let out a cleansing puff of breath. Writing always helps me organize my thoughts and feelings into something more tangible. It helps me take the complicated tangle of facts, stories, and emotions floating through my mind and turn them into a presentable product. I guess I'm pretty good at it, considering I've been able to make a living talking about my experience with chronic illness online.

Although, when I say "making a living," I suppose I really mean "getting by." I make enough to pay rent, buy groceries, and drive a semi-decent car, but that's about it. It's not like I have a body that allows me to go out drinking every weekend or spend money on other such things people my age do anyway. So long as I can afford my daily iced caramel latte, I'm set.

Rolling out my aching wrists, I return to typing.

It's also not uncommon for people who try to save others from drowning to wind up drowning themselves. Maybe that was why all my friends abandoned me when I got sick. They were so afraid I'd drag them down with me into the chronic illness pit of despair that they cut and ran. I can't really blame them. It sucks here.

Damn, this blog post is getting depressing fast. I'm coming up on my five-year anniversary of being diagnosed with both Lupus and Sjogren's—two autoimmune diseases that irrevocably changed my life. I wanted to write a reflection post on what it was like being diagnosed at age twenty, having to leave college, losing friends and, frankly, my entire identity. But now that I'm sitting down to write it, it feels a bit too heavy.

Shutting my laptop, I shuffle off to my bedroom to get dressed for the day. I'm taking my mom to a follow-up appointment at her orthopedist this morning. She shattered her knee in a freak line-dancing accident three weeks ago, and she's been in a full leg cast ever since. There's a lot she can't do these days, including driving herself anywhere, which is how I wound up waking up bright and early on a Monday to take her to the hospital.

Although I've driven in and out of Longwood Medical Area in Boston countless times, I still dread it. Unlike the well-planned metropolises of Washington D.C. or New York City, there's an urban legend that Boston's streets are paved over cow paths. I think it's just a rumor, but I honestly wouldn't be surprised if it was true. The layout doesn't make sense, and there's always a ton of traffic and obnoxious drivers who have no clue where they're going.

Despite my aversion to Boston's roads, I buckle up and take my mom to her appointment because no one else will. She has to ride with the passenger seat pushed all the way back, her casted leg resting in an awkward position before her. It looks uncomfortable, but she doesn't complain.

The appointment goes by quickly, with me furiously scribbling notes the entire time. I learned a long time ago that taking notes during medical appointments is key. Even if you think you'll remember everything the doctor says, chances are some things will slip right past you. Having someone to be a second set of ears accompanying you doesn't hurt either.

"How much longer did he say I need to wear this thing again?" Mom asks on our way home, knocking her fist on her hard cast.

"Two to four weeks," I reply as I smoothly cross over two lanes to make my turn. "It depends how your x-rays look at your next appointment."

The doctor said it would likely be the full four weeks, but I don't want to break Mom's heart by reminding her. She's determined to get back to her weekly line-dancing event. Before the injury, she hadn't missed a single one in over a year, save for the week she had Covid and was forced to quarantine. She asked if she could attend in an N-95 mask and a face shield, but they turned her down. They ended up striking a compromise by setting up a laptop at the front of the room and allowing her to attend via Zoom. Thank goodness, because otherwise she probably would have forced me and my siblings to go over to her apartment and learn the steps so she could still get the full group line-dancing experience.

"Thank God you remember this stuff," Mom says, waving her hand as if the details of her medical condition are a complicated math equation instead of a very routine course of action.

"I wrote it all down for you too," I say. Mom has always been a bit of a free spirit, more worried about keeping track of her line-dancing events and what obscure indie concert she's attending next than practical things like how to care for an injury. If she'd been able to drive herself today and attend her appointment alone, she probably would have walked away and told everyone, *"The cast comes off in two weeks! I should be back on the floor soon. I just have to take it easy on the triple steps."*

Mom reaches over and pinches my cheek. "You're my angel, Hannah."

I give her a small grin. It would be easy to resent her for relying on me to help in times like these instead of asking my younger siblings to step up, but she always makes sure to voice her gratitude.

I pull into a guest spot at Mom's apartment building and grab her crutches from the back, rounding the car to open the passenger side door. She stands shakily on her good leg, and I help wedge the crutches beneath her armpits. Then we begin the slow trek to the elevator.

"I just have a couple things I need help with today," Mom begins as we meander along. "I need to get the electric frying pan down from the top shelf. I usually go up on a ladder to get it, but I figure I can't do that on one leg."

"Good thinking, Mom," I say as we enter the elevator, and I push the button for the fourth floor. "I can get it down for you, but how are you planning to use it? You can't balance well enough to stand at the counter."

"Oh, I'll figure something out." Her gaze turns toward the ceiling of the elevator. "Maybe I'll put it on the kitchen table and sit in a chair while I cook."

"What are you planning to make?"

The elevator doors open, and I step out, putting my hand in the door frame to keep it open while Mom crutches her way out.

"Hawaiian stir fry," she replies as we near her apartment. "I'm having my book club over for dinner tomorrow night."

I shake my head. "Only you would entertain guests while in a full leg cast."

Mom *tssks*. "I won't let this damn thing hold me back from having a little fun."

As we arrive at the apartment, she voices her second request. "I hate to ask you this, Hannah, but would you mind helping me clean the bathroom too?" she asks as she plops into a chair and drops her crutches on the floor beside her. "It's getting pretty grungy. I tried to clean the toilet yesterday, but I almost fell into it."

I release a long sigh. "Of course I'll help you with the bathroom. You should have asked me before trying to do it yourself. You have to be more careful."

She shrugs as she pulls over another chair to elevate her foot. "I hate asking you to do all this, but I wouldn't know who else to call."

Annie, I want to say. *Owen.*

My younger twin siblings live nearby like me. We grew up in a suburb of Boston and all ended up back here despite going to various other places for college. I headed to Ithaca in upstate New York for their writing program, Annie went to the University of Pennsylvania because she's a certified genius, and Owen was recruited by Clemson for football. I wound up back at home midway through college after the proverbial shit hit the fan, but Annie and Owen both decided to return to Massachusetts after graduating this past spring. Annie got a job at one of the "Big 4" accounting firms in Boston while Owen became the assistant football coach at our old high school.

Even though they're both nearby and able-bodied, Mom would never think to turn to either of them for support. I don't know if it has to do with my job being more flexible than either of theirs, or with the fact that I've simply always been the one everyone in this family turns to in a crisis. I'm the eldest sister, and with that comes a set of unspoken rules and expectations.

I learned this at a young age, when my parents got divorced and I had to be the "strong" one for my siblings. I had to act unaffected while I worked to keep them calm and convince them everything would be okay, which luckily turned out to be true. Mom is thrilled with her single life and barely has time for dating amongst all her other commitments, while Dad is happily married to his old college roommate whom he reconnected with after the divorce. They settled in Alaska, where my dad became a park ranger at Denali National Park. We don't see him much, but we talk a lot, and when we make family holidays happen, everything is quite civil.

I truly don't mind the role I'm in. I love knowing that my siblings feel safe enough to come to me for anything and that my mom trusts me with things like her medical care. I know the twins are busy getting their post-grad lives off the ground, and they deserve to be able to do so without needing to play nurse-maid to their mother.

But it's not like I sit around all day doing nothing. I may live a smaller life than anyone else in my family, but it's still a *life*. And despite my limitations, I think it's a pretty damn good one. I have a job—albeit a nontraditional one—a small group of friends, and an apartment that I turned into my own personal oasis. Living alone means I'm responsible for all the cleaning, cooking, laundry, and other household tasks, all of which take not only time but also energy, which is already limited for me.

Being here today to help my mom takes away from all of that. It means I'll get a late start to my work and may have to reschedule my usual Monday-night viewing of *The Bachelor* with my best friend, Rhiannon, to meet my deadlines. It means I probably won't have the energy to go to the grocery store later like I had planned to, and my laundry will likely go undone for yet another day.

But it's okay because Mom needs me, and there's no way I wouldn't show up for her.

After getting the electric frying pan down and setting it on the kitchen table, I grab the caddy of cleaning supplies from the closet.

"It really doesn't look too bad," I say, relieved as I inspect the bathroom from the doorway. I'd expected much worse, but it looks like all it will take is a quick scrub down of the toilet, sink, and tub. The tile floor is spotless, and the mirror has barely more than a single fingerprint on it. Hopefully, this won't take too long. Then I can be off to Waffee, the coffee shop where I do most of my work.

"Make sure the tub is super clean, Han," Mom calls from her throne in the living room. "I'd like to take a bath one of these days."

I bite back a groan as I drop to my knees in front of the toilet. "Mom, you can't take a bath with a full leg cast on," I shout back.

"I can be creative," she retorts.

I shake my head but don't bother to reply. Once Mom has an idea in her head, it's rarely worth it to argue with her. If she wants to try taking a bath with one leg hanging over the edge of the tub, more power to her. I'm not going to waste my energy talking her out of it. Instead, I get to work scrubbing the toilet bowl.

CHAPTER 2
HANNAH

Fifteen minutes later, the white porcelain bathroom appliances are gleaming, and my duties are done. I kiss Mom goodbye, go back outside to my used Mazda CX-5 —the very first major purchase I ever made with my freelancing money—and head to my favorite place to get some work done.

At first glance, Waffee may look like your run-of-the-mill coffee shop. It has a long marble counter filled with glass cases that house various bakery items, a monstrous commercial espresso machine adorned with an overwhelming number of gleaming silver knobs and handles, and a rotating crew of hipster millennials manning the register. You could probably find a place that looks just like this in every major city and most of the suburbs too.

What makes Waffee stand out is that every food item they sell —yes, every single one—is put through a waffle press. Not only do they serve delicious Belgian waffles with every mix-in you could possibly imagine, from berries to chocolate chips to bacon or sausage, but they also serve waffled cookies, brownies, cinnamon buns, and all sorts of other pastries. You can get waffled banana, zucchini, and pumpkin breads. Waffled French toast. Waffled hash browns. Waffled avocado toast, which is a piece of waffled brioche with mashed avocado stuffed into every little pocket, sprinkled with salt and red pepper flakes. And it doesn't stop at breakfast food. You want a panini? Sure! But instead of a panini press, it will be put through a waffle press. You can grab a waffled quesadilla (the pockets are great for holding a nice chunky salsa) or a waffled grilled cheese. You can even get a Caesar salad with waffled croutons. That one's a bit of a cop-out, since the lettuce can't possibly be waffled, but everyone lets it slide because the waffled croutons are to die for.

My personal favorite thing is when they pull out the seasonal waffle presses around the holidays. Nothing screams Merry Christmas like devouring a Santa-shaped waffle. At Halloween, you can get your treat waffled into a ghost or a pumpkin, and around Valentine's Day, almost everything becomes heart-shaped. That particular time of year isn't my favorite. I'd prefer my Valentine's Day meals to more accurately reflect my love life. Perhaps a trash-can shape would do. If they could make invisible waffles, that would be even better because my love life is essentially non-existent and has been for the past five years.

Who needs a boyfriend, anyway, when you've got coffee and all the waffled treats your heart could possibly desire right at your fingertips? Waffee provides me with both of those, as well as the perfect space to do my work that's reasonably quiet but still busy enough with other patrons filing through that I feel connected to the world. I may not know what any of these other people around me are working on, or why they're able to be here at 11:42 a.m. on a Monday morning, but I feel like a part of something when I'm here. That's a hard feeling to achieve when you work a solitary job like mine.

When I discovered this place five years ago, it became my haven. A home away from home. After my life burned up into nothing but a pile of ash, a mere sliver of what it had once been, I was so beyond lost that I didn't know where to begin rebuilding. Without school, work, friends, or anything else to give my life meaning, I turned to the only thing that had ever helped me process my feelings: writing. It started out as a few freelance pieces but quickly grew into a blog that took off beyond my wildest dreams.

As I sit here in Waffee, with my trusty iced caramel latte with almond milk by my side, I open my laptop and feel complete peace. That is, until my gaze lands on the checklist I left for myself on Friday. It's full of emails and messages I need to respond to, brands I need to reach out to, posts I need to finish, and photos I need to take.

Some people, including my beloved mother, think being a blogger is a breeze. They don't view it as a real job because it can be done from anywhere, in any chunks of time, and I don't have to report to anyone. But just because I make my own schedule doesn't mean I don't have deadlines to meet. It means I have to create my own schedule and keep myself on task, which is arguably harder than reporting to a higher up.

People also don't see everything behind the scenes that goes into my work. They see a final product, like a blog post full of shiny product photos or a video flawlessly edited to music, and they assume it was as easy to create as it was to consume. That's pretty much never the case. I don't post about the hours of editing I did in my pajamas with my greasy hair up in a bun, fingers coated with Cheeto dust because I couldn't be bothered to make myself a meal. I don't share the moments when I'm crying or want to bang my head against a wall because I can't get something to work the way I want it to.

I can see why some people may think this job is somewhat of a glamorous joke, but despite the difficulties and stigmas that can come with it, blogging has served me incredibly well for the past few years. The flexibility it offers is essential to the way I need to live my life now, and it has allowed me to connect with so many people I never would have otherwise. There is a vibrant chronic illness community online, and I'm proud to be part of it.

After a long sip of my latte, I dive headfirst into my to-do list. I may have gotten a later start than I wanted to, but I'm really hoping to salvage my *Bachelor* Monday date with Rhiannon later, which means working at warp speed.

I've answered a whopping two emails when I hear a deep voice that I can't quite place.

"Hannah? Hannah Reilly?"

My head whips up. Lots of the regulars at Waffee know me by my first name, but I don't give out my last. This must be someone from my past, which immediately puts my guard up. As I focus my gaze, I'm greeted by the sight of a tall, bearded brunet. A tall, *handsome*, bearded brunet. His facial hair is something longer than scruff, but it's not scraggly. Rather, it looks well-kept and neatly trimmed. His brown hair is just long enough that he could probably pull it into a ponytail if he wanted to, but right now it's pushed back behind his ears. His deep, dark-brown eyes are trained on me.

He places a hand on his chest, covering the pocket of his navy-blue Henley. "It's Caleb. Caleb O'Connor."

I freeze, my eyes widening as my lips pinch together. I've never been able to control my facial expressions. What I'm feeling is always written all over my features.

Holy hell. It's Caleb O'Connor. The boy next door from back in high school. The football player with a heart of gold. The neighbor whose little brother was best friends with mine. But this isn't the same Caleb O'Connor I once knew. This one isn't a boy. He's a full-grown *man*.

Caleb was handsome back in high school, but now he's...well...*hot*. Like, *smoking* hot. His shoulders have broadened, his body filled out. He's never been skinny, but he looks even burlier now. I imagine if he put on a flannel, he'd be a dead ringer for a lumberjack.

"H-hi," I stammer, a million thoughts crossing my mind in the span of a single second. Do I stand up? Shake his hand? Give him a hug? A salute? Wait, no, that last one makes no sense.

Caleb makes the decision for me when he reaches forward, gives my shoulder a squeeze, then steps back and shoves his hands into his pockets.

"It's really good to see you," he says with a smile. "It's been a long time."

I inadvertently let out a nervous chuckle. Damn my uncontrolled facial expressions and vocal cords. "Yeah, it really has."

As he rocks back on his heels, I realize I'm making this little reunion incredibly awkward, and I scramble to pull myself together.

"Are you...do you want to sit down?" I gesture to the open seat across from me at the table.

Caleb looks to the chair then back to me. "Would you mind? I'm waiting on my order, and I was hoping to eat it here, but it was looking like that wasn't going to be a possibility."

I follow his gaze as he glances around the space. I hadn't even realized all the other tables had filled up since I'd arrived.

"No, please join me. It'll give me a good excuse to keep my table." I gesture to my latte, which somehow only has about two sips left in it. I must have really chugged it while answering those emails.

I come to Waffee at least three times a week—even more when I'm up to it—and I always order a few items and tip well. The employees have told me they don't mind if I want to take up a table all day, but I still feel bad when I'm sitting there with very little food or drink.

"Awesome, thanks." Caleb folds his body into the chair, his gaze still wandering over the interior. "This place seems really cool."

"It is." I shut my laptop so I don't seem anti-social. "Is it your first time here?"

"Yeah," he answers, his eyes focusing back on mine. "I just moved back."

"I heard you went out to California," I reply.

He scratches at the back of his head. "I did. Got a really good job there. Just got a better one here."

"Congrats," I say. "Are you happy to be back?"

Caleb tilts his head to one side. "I'm...happy to be near my mom and sister again. And happy to be at this new job."

I nod, even though that wasn't exactly an answer to the question I asked. "Where are you working now?"

He settles back into his seat, seeming much more at ease with that question. "It's a really cool tech start-up. A couple of MIT grads got it off the ground last year. It's still small, but they're starting to expand."

"That sounds neat," I reply. "What do you...do? Make? Sorry, I'm not really familiar with the tech world beyond using the products it produces."

Caleb chuckles. The throaty sound sends an inexplicable jolt of heat through my veins. "No worries. We're in the app space, so we're currently working on getting a prototype of our app up and running so we can get it in front of investors. Then, hopefully, we can launch sometime in the next year or so."

"That's awesome," I say. I'm about to ask him more about the app when a barista calls out his name.

He sticks up his pointer finger. "Hold that thought," he says before sliding from his chair and heading for the counter to grab his meal. The dark jeans he's wearing hug what appear to be thighs like tree trunks and a sculpted ass that's too perfect to be wasted on a man. Most women would kill for a butt like that.

My head is still spinning that Caleb O'Connor is back in town. We were pretty close in high school, but we haven't seen each other since we left for colleges in different states. I've thought about him a lot these past few years, wondering how he was doing and what he was up to, but I never quite worked up the nerve to reach out.

Caleb and I were unlikely friends. He spent Friday nights on the football field with the rest of the team while I sat in the stands playing with the band. He had girls falling over him while I was a late bloomer, not dating anyone until college. I spent my free time in high school less worried about boys and more worried about my next piece for the creative writing club.

Despite our differences, we often wound up in the same spheres. His family moved in next door to mine right before the start of freshman year, and that proximity alone meant seeing a lot of each other. We would often catch rides with one another to school, run over to each other's houses to borrow a cup of flour or an egg, and other neighborly things like that.

Our little brothers also became fast friends. Even though football-loving Owen probably had more in common with Caleb, he got along swimmingly with Caleb's artsy younger brother, Matty. With those two attached at the hip, Caleb and I inevitably ended up spending time together. We would often join Owen and Matty if they were just hanging out in the yard or on someone's porch. Sometimes either Caleb or I would be recruited to give the boys a ride to the mall, and we'd beg the other to come along for company. Carting your baby brother and his friend around was so much more fun with a same-aged buddy.

Our families had the occasional dinner together—me, my mom, Annie, and Owen with Caleb, Matty, their older sister, Heather, and their parents. We weren't the types of families that vacationed together or anything, but we were close enough that Caleb and I were some form of friends.

Then my mom and the twins moved a few towns over almost as soon as I left for college, wanting Owen to attend a high school with a better football program to foster his budding talent. Without the previous proximity of our houses, Caleb and I never got around to connecting over holidays or school breaks. We occasionally conversed on social media, dropping a "like" on a photo here or commenting on a status update there, but our friendship didn't stand the test of separation.

Now he's back, and he looks better than ever—which is saying something, considering I used to think he was pretty much the most handsome guy I'd ever laid eyes on. Not only that, but he's *here*, at Waffee, my refuge and the one place I'd carved out for myself where no one knows the old me. I'm a different person than the one Caleb used to know, and I suspect he is too. Despite our time and distance over the past few years, I feel a burning desire to get to know the new him.

CHAPTER 3
CALEB

I'm almost as surprised to be holding a caprese panini in the shape of a waffle as I am that I've just run into Hannah Reilly. I haven't seen her since we graduated from high school, but I think about her here and there. Admittedly, I think about her more than is probably normal for the extent of our relationship.

Hannah was my next-door neighbor throughout high school, and while we were friendly, we were never really *friends*. We gave each other rides when one of us had access to a parent's car and sometimes hung out when our brothers were, but we didn't make weekend plans or anything. It was more of a companionship of convenience.

So, I'm not quite sure why I think about her so much. Maybe it's because so many of my later memories with Matty include her brother, Owen. They were practically inseparable. Or maybe it's because she was always so damn kind, so ready to help out with whatever someone needed. It's hard to forget kindness like that. Plus, I always thought she was beautiful in an understated sort of way. Her ginger hair leans more toward orange than brown, the striking color contrasted by her dark-brown eyes.

I always regretted losing touch with Hannah, even if only

because she was a point of connection to Matty. Seeing her now, I know it's much more than that. I *missed* this girl. No...woman. Hannah is a woman now. Of course she had boobs and a butt and all that other stuff back in high school, but she's grown into them. Even though I've only seen her sitting, I can tell her hips have filled out. Her hair remains that same arresting Titian color, and some strange part of me feels a rush of relief that she never dyed it.

I'm not sure what to make of the warmth that enveloped me when I first recognized Hannah sitting in Waffee, but I know that I'm glad to see her. Things have changed a lot in my hometown, both personally and logistically. Like, we never had anything as cool as a waffle cafe when I was growing up here. Being back is bittersweet, and seeing her familiar face brought me a comfort I hadn't realized I needed.

With my waffled panini and an iced tea in hand, I return to our table and sit down.

"This looks incredible," I say, pointing to where the mozzarella cheese is oozing out the side of my sandwich.

Hannah grins, showing off perfectly straight, white teeth. I remember when she wore the braces that got her those. They were scheduled to be removed the day *after* picture day during freshman year, and she was so pissed about it. I remember wondering why she was so upset. I didn't think they took away from her beauty at all.

Her voice shakes me from the memory.

"It looks like Brendan made that. You're lucky. He's the best at paninis. Mark is better at making coffee, but I see you got tea, which is hard to mess up."

I take a sip and raise a brow. "You come here a lot, huh?"

A faint pink creeps into her cheeks. "A few times a week. For a few years now."

"That's cool. I had a regular lunch spot back in California. It's nice to go to a place where people know you."

She nods, but her eyes take on a faraway look. I don't read

too much into it, instead pushing up the sleeves of my Henley as I prepare to dig into my meal. Hannah's gaze immediately zeroes in on my right arm.

"Those are new." She points to the tattoos running up my arm—at least, the ones that are visible. I have an entire sleeve of them running from my shoulder all the way down the top of my hand. There are still plenty of small spaces to fill in, but there's enough ink to give the impression of a full sleeve.

"Yes," I reply, not sure how much to say. Hannah and I have only just begun to get reacquainted, and I hate to immediately bring the mood down. As I glance at the ninja tattooed over my thumb joint—he's holding a sword that runs the length of my thumb—I realize she might appreciate the significance, so I decide to tell her. "They're all doodles Matty made."

Her gaze shoots from the tattoos to my eyes. "Oh...that's... Caleb, that's beautiful," she finally says, her eyes welling with tears. "I'm so sorry. I... I'm sorry I wasn't at the funeral. I couldn't get away from school in time. I always felt terrible about it. I really wanted—"

"Hannah," I say, desperate to wipe the tears from her eyes and the apology from her lips. "Don't worry about it. I completely understand."

"I"—her voice cracks as she wipes one stray tear from her cheek—"I sent flowers."

I can't stand to see Hannah crying. My hands itch to reach across this table and take hers, or better yet, to pull her into my arms. But all I do is say, "I know."

Her brow furrows, creating a cute little wrinkle above her nose. "Y-you do?"

"Of course I do. You sent the bouquet of tiger lilies, just like the ones that—"

"Ran between our yards," she finishes my sentence for me.

I'll never forget noticing that particular bouquet in the sea of flowers at Matty's wake. The color immediately reminded me of Hannah's hair, and I didn't need to read the note to know it was from her. Even though she wasn't physically there, knowing Hannah had sent those flowers was enough to give my aching heart a bit of comfort.

Long before my family moved in next door to hers, Hannah's mom had planted a row of tiger lilies on their property line. They were immaculate up until our first spring there, when Owen, Matty, and I trampled them playing flag football. Her mom was so pissed that she forced us to buy new ones with our own money and spend an entire day planting them, as well as tending to her other gardens as payback.

The memory pulls a slight grin from me. "As soon as I saw them, I knew they had to be from you."

"I wish I could have done more," she says, that frown still in place. "I know they had a meal train and everything going for you guys, but I was so far away. I just..."

Hannah shakes her head, looking so forlorn over the fact that she didn't rush home and single-handedly save my family from drowning in our grief after Matty died. As if anyone would have expected her to. But that's Hannah—always the first one to pitch in or help out. It must have killed her—bad but true choice of words—not to be able to do anything more than send flowers.

The anguish written on her features is too much for me, and this time I do reach over the table to take one of her hands in mine. That seems to snap her out of her melancholy as her gaze finds mine.

"Hannah." I keep my eyes trained on hers to hopefully drive my message home. "No one expected you to come home from school on such short notice to go to the funeral of someone you hadn't seen in years. Owen was there to represent your family, and I was incredibly touched that you thought to send flowers. *Please* do not feel bad about it."

Matty's glioblastoma, a rare and aggressive brain cancer, took him just a month and a half after he was initially diagnosed. Those six weeks were a whirlwind of doctors, decisions, and tears. Lots of tears. The day he was diagnosed, I got on a plane home. Heather was already living nearby, in her first year of nursing at Mass General, and we both temporarily moved back into our parents' house to help support each other and care for Matty.

We tried to keep things as natural as possible for him, but sleeping in a hospital bed in the living room and having palliative care nurses in and out all day wasn't exactly normal. Even so, getting to be there for Matty in his final days meant everything to us and, hopefully, to him too. We made all his favorite foods, watched his favorite movies, and celebrated every holiday in the calendar year in the span of a single month. Despite the backdrop of intense grief and heartache, we created some really great memories in those weeks.

It became obvious when the end was near, and we held the wake and funeral just a couple days after Matty passed away. We'd already spent six weeks grieving. We didn't want to extend it any longer than we had to. It may have made it more difficult for people who had to travel, but it made it easier for our family, and that was the priority at the time. We certainly didn't hold it against anyone who couldn't make it to the services.

I release Hannah's hand and she brings it toward her mouth, biting her thumbnail between her teeth.

"I just wish I had done more," she says. "I know I'd lost touch with you both, but when I heard what happened...I should have made more of an effort."

I sigh as I lean back in my chair. I can tell she's going to be stubborn about forgiving herself, but I hope what I say next brings her some comfort.

"I've learned that sometimes the most powerful things aren't the ones you expect them to be. Like, I feel most connected to Matty when I'm getting one of his doodles tattooed on my body, not when I visit his grave. I still go once a month, but it doesn't feel as meaningful to me. And I'm telling you...when I saw that bouquet of tiger lilies next to his casket, it meant more to me than the attendance of half the people who were there. You had put special thought into that bouquet, and it brought back a memory of Matty that made me smile on one of the hardest days of my life. I'll always be thankful for that."

A reluctant smile stretches over Hannah's lips. "That makes me feel a little better."

"Good." I finally pick up my sandwich to take a bite and catch a glimpse of the watch on my left wrist. "Shit, sorry to shove this in my face and run, but I have to finish in the next ten minutes, or I'll officially be over my lunch break."

Hannah's eyes widen. "Oh! Sorry. I didn't realize you had limited time."

"No worries," I say around bites. "I'm in the office today, but I work from home a few days a week. Maybe I'll try working from here sometime. I'd love to catch up more."

"Me too," Hannah replies. "I'm here most Mondays, Wednesdays, and Fridays. I don't stick to that schedule stringently, but those days are your best bets. I'd love to see you again. It's been too long."

"It has," I agree as I finish my sandwich, leaving behind only crumbs. I do some quick mental math. "Seven years, right?"

"That's right." She shakes her head. "Gosh, I can't believe it's been that long since we graduated high school."

"Me either. And three years since graduating college."

She nods, but her heart doesn't seem in it. I wonder what that's about, but I don't have time for any more questions. As it is, I'll have to sprint to the office to make it back before my break ends. The guys I work for are pretty cool, but I'm still new and don't want to make a bad impression by taking long lunches right away.

I stand, collecting my trash to dump on my way out, and take one last long look at Hannah. "I'll see you around?"

"You know where to find me."

CHAPTER 4
HANNAH

There's something about sitting in a bustling coffee shop that inspires me like nothing else. Perhaps it's the caffeine coursing through my system, the smooth jazz music playing in the background, or the presence of other focused, hard-working people, but I miraculously finish everything on my to-do list and make it home in time for *Bachelor* Monday.

Rhiannon arrives at my apartment at 7:50 p.m., only ten minutes before the show is set to start, with a fancy bottle of sparkling water in hand. Her long, raven-black hair is arranged in a messy bun on top of her head, and she's in her standard work uniform of black yoga pants and a long black t-shirt.

"Sorry I'm cutting it a little close," she says breathlessly as she races into my apartment, heading for the kitchen. "My characters just would not shut up. I've been having a little writer's block lately, so when they decide they want to come out and play, I have to run with it."

Rhia is a relatively successful romance author. She started self-publishing a few books in college, and by the time she graduated, she was already making a decent living. Sometimes it still baffles me that we were both able to make writing our full-time jobs, albeit in two very different ways. Rhia and I met in the creative writing club in middle school and had big dreams about turning writing into careers. As we got older, we realized how difficult that would actually be, yet we both still managed to pull it off.

"It's okay," I say, pulling two glasses from the cabinet and heading to the freezer for ice. "I have the popcorn in the microwave, ready to go. Just hit start."

Rhia taps the button, and the microwave whirs to life. I bring the glasses with ice to the counter, and she pours a generous amount of sparkling water into each of them. Rhia doesn't drink much because of her anxiety, and I don't drink at all because of the medications I'm on, so we've been on a quest to try every type of seltzer and sparkling water we can get our hands on.

"What's the flavor of the week?" I ask.

"Strawberry clementine," she reads off the label. "Sounds refreshing."

"Totally." I bring our drinks over to the coffee table while Rhia grabs a big bowl for the popcorn. This is our weekly tradition—sparkling water and popcorn while we watch people on TV try to find love. Rhia is a hopeless romantic—if that wasn't obvious by her genre of choice—and I...well... I like to think there's someone out there for everyone, even if it's hard for me to believe that sometimes.

Caleb's face pops into my mind, with his new (at least to me) brown beard, the perfect complement to his espresso-colored eyes. I think about his sleeve of tattoos and how much I'd like to inspect each one. I'm equally interested in the muscles beneath them. He's seriously beefed up since high school, and he's obviously found his own personal style. I wonder if he's found his person too.

"How was your mom's appointment this morning?" Rhia asks.

"It went well," I reply. "She'll probably be in the cast for another month, though."

"Dang," Rhia replies, shoving a handful of popcorn into her mouth.

I nod in agreement, fingers plucking absentmindedly at my lips.

"Anything else going on?" she asks, and I realize she's been watching me. As my best friend since middle school, Rhia doesn't miss a single one of my cues. She can tell how I'm feeling with one look at me, overly expressive face or not.

I'm not sure if I want to tell her about running into Caleb. It was such a brief meeting, and it's not necessarily like we're rekindling our friendship. He might show up at Waffee again sometime, and we might chat some more, but what happened today might not even turn into a *thing*.

Knowing Rhia, if I tell her Caleb is back in town, she'll try to cook up some match-making scheme. The last thing I want is pressure to make our relationship into something it's not. Sure, I would love to be friendly with Caleb again, and sure, there was a time when I wanted to be *more* than friendly with him, but it's like he said today—it's been seven years. I have no expectations that our relationship will turn into anything more than what it has been.

Before I can answer, I'm saved by the voice of the host declaring that this will be the most shocking episode yet.

"We'll talk at the next commercial," I whisper, hoping Rhia will have forgotten about it by then.

The show begins, and I shovel popcorn into my mouth as I half watch and half think about Caleb some more. If he just moved across the country, then he *could* be in a long-distance relationship, but most likely he's single. How long will it take before he's snapped up by someone here? Back in high school, he had his pick of the girls at school. Based on what he looks like now and the fact that he seems just as sweet as he was back then, my guess is not long. The thought makes my stomach fall.

When the show cuts to its first commercial break, Rhia immediately turns her body toward me.

"Okay, spill," she says. "You're beyond distracted over there. I bet you can't even tell me which guy she just went on a date with."

"Uhh... It was the puppy fosterer, right? The guy who built a specialty staircase so his Dachshund could get up on his bed and sleep next to him?"

She rolls her eyes. "Okay, fine, so you were somewhat paying attention. But there's something on your mind, Han, and I want to know what it is."

I sink into the couch with a sigh. "I ran into Caleb O'Connor at Waffee today. He's back in town."

Rhia cocks her head to the side. "Caleb O'Connor? That hunky football player you used to live next door to?"

"That's the one."

"Oh," she coos, tenting her fingers and tapping the pads of them together, already scheming. "That's very interesting news."

"Rhia," I begin, using my parent-preparing-to-discipline-a-child voice. "We only talked for a few minutes. I said I was sorry about Matty. Then Caleb went back to work. Nothing is happening with us."

"Come on," she whines. "You haven't dated since your diagnosis, and now the perfect man from your past just *happens* to waltz into Waffee when you're there. That's like your ideal meet-cute, except you weren't actually meeting him for the first time."

She's not wrong. Running into a handsome man at Waffee has basically been my dream since I first discovered the cute coffee shop. I always pictured that one day I'd be working on my laptop and someone would come up to me, asking for the WiFi password, and the rest would be history. What happened today was *not* that. It was me running into my old neighbor, being slightly awkward, and apologizing profusely for missing his brother's funeral.

I point a finger at Rhia. "First of all, do not talk about this in romance-novel terms. It was not a meet-cute. It was two old acquaintances running into one another. Secondly, the chances of anyone running into me at Waffee are pretty high, considering how often I'm there. So, don't try to say it was some kind of divine intervention. And lastly, there's a reason I haven't tried dating since I got sick. Dating is exhausting, and my health is unpredictable. It's not fair to put that burden on someone else."

Rhia purses her lips and lets out a farting noise, shooting me a thumbs-down. "You could definitely date if it was with the right person. Did you tell him about your illnesses?"

"No." I wag my head. "I told you—we only talked for a few minutes. It's not exactly the first topic of conversation I like to bring up. Though, I guess Matty probably isn't the first topic Caleb likes to bring up, and that's mostly what we ended up talking about."

Rhia rolls her neck side to side as she considers this. "You should tell him next time you see him. See how he reacts."

I lift a brow. "Who said there's going to be a next time?"

"There had better be a next time," she says. "Or I'll go find him and deliver him to your doorstep myself. I have a good feeling about you two."

"Okay," I say, drawing out the *o*. If I'm not careful, Rhia will end up making good on that promise, or she'll write a romance novel featuring characters named Hannah and Caleb, or something else equally heinous, just to force us together.

"How did he look?" she asks in a hushed tone just before the show comes back.

"He looked...really good," I respond reluctantly.

I notice Rhia tapping and scrolling on her phone periodically throughout the next date—this one with a surf instructor who hasn't put on a shirt or shoes the entire season.

At the next commercial break, I send her an accusatory glare. "Now who's distracted?"

Her head snaps up. "Caleb's not on *any* social media platforms. I've checked Instagram, Facebook, Twitter, *and* TikTok." She taps her screen a couple more times. "Oh wait—there he is on *LinkedIn*." Her eyes bug out a little. "He has a beard now?" she practically shouts.

I rub my temple. "Yes, he has a beard now."

She uses two fingers to zoom in on Caleb's profile picture. "That looks like a real pussy-tickler."

I reach over and grab her arm to stop her zooming fingers before all we can see are Caleb's supple lips. "Rhiannon Margaret James, stop objectifying that man right now."

"Oh!" she exclaims, covering her heart with her hand. "You're already protective of him. That is so sweet."

I let go of her arm before standing and heading to the kitchen for more sparkling water. Rhia's footsteps pad behind me, but I ignore her until my glass is refilled. When I turn away from the fridge, she's leaning against the door frame, her eyes soft.

"I don't mean to pressure you, Han. I just love you, and I think it would be good for you to put yourself out there."

"I could say the same about you," I fire back.

She shoves her hands in her pockets. "I'm...working on it. I know dating has seemed too daunting to you these past few years, but maybe this is someone you could try it with. Caleb is someone who already knows your heart. Dropping a bomb like having chronic illnesses might not faze him as much."

I shrug. Everything she said is true, but I still have my reservations. And besides, we *just* reconnected. Rhia suggesting we date is way too premature.

"Why don't we wait and see if he ever even comes into Waffee again, huh?" I suggest. "And maybe we can work our way to being friends again before we dive right into something like dating."

"Friends to lovers," Rhia says. "I like it."

I just roll my eyes again.

CHAPTER 5
CALEB

Pulling up to my childhood home sends a tsunami of nostalgia crashing over me. I've been back here for holidays and such since I moved to California, but it's my first time coming here since moving back permanently. Everything looks the same as it always did on the outside. The house is still light blue with white shutters. It still has a navy-blue door with a stained-glass window on the upper half. There's still a row of tiger lilies running between my house and the one next door.

But inside, I know everything is different because the house lacks Matty's presence.

I was in my last semester of college when he got sick, and my university was kind enough to give me extensions on my work for all my classes. I only bothered to attend graduation because my family seemed excited about it, and we desperately needed something to celebrate. I received a blank diploma until I completed the requisite coursework, which happened midway through the summer. After that, I took off like a racehorse.

After applying exclusively to jobs across the country, I landed a position at a tech company in Silicon Valley. I was grateful for the opportunity to go somewhere far away. Boston held too many memories—good and bad—and I'm big enough to admit that I was running away from them.

Now that I'm back, I'm sure there will be hurdles to get over. Memories to face. But right now, all I can think about is what my mom might be cooking for dinner. She invited me, my older sister, Heather, and her fiancé, Greg, tonight. I belatedly realize I probably should have brought something—a bottle of wine or a dessert, maybe—but I find myself empty-handed. I'm sure Mom won't mind.

I've just slammed the car door shut when the front door swings open, and Heather appears, her brown ponytail swinging as she flies down the front steps.

"Cale!" she screeches. She knows I hate the nickname, but she started calling me that when we were toddlers, and it stuck.

"Hey, Heather," I say, chuckling as I wrap her in my arms and swing her around. She's still in her scrubs and must have just come from work.

"Hey! That's supposed to be my move," Greg calls from the top of the stairs.

I wave a hand in his direction. "Yeah, yeah. Fiancés, and love, and shit. I knew her first. She can divorce you, but she'll always be my sister."

Heather whacks me upside the head for the bad joke. Greg just laughs. He and I have a good relationship, even though I'll never stop worrying about him hurting my sister. He's never given me any reason to believe he would, but that doesn't stop me from imagining all the ways he *could*. After what happened between my parents—a couple whose love I thought could withstand anything—I've lost faith in the sanctity of any sort of romantic commitment.

Heather herds me toward the house, where I stop to shake Greg's hand then slide it back into a fist bump.

"Nice to see you, man," I say, relieved he's still smiling and didn't take my little jab to heart.

"You too," he says as we file through the front door. My

senses are immediately bombarded with the scents of garlic, basil, and tomatoes. I take a deep inhale of the appetizing aroma and pray that it's my mom's chicken parmesan.

"Caleb?" her voice rings out from the kitchen.

"Hey, Ma," I shout back, avoiding looking at the family photos that line the hallway as I make my way toward her.

"Hi, sweetheart!" my mom cries as I come into view. She's standing in front of the stove, stirring a pot of pasta that looks as if it's about to boil over. "Get over here and give me a hug."

I do, narrowly avoiding being scalded by the bubbling water she's standing beside. I reach across the stove to lower the heat slightly.

"It's good to see you, Ma," I say. She's gained a couple of new wrinkles since I last saw her, which was back at Christmastime. I came home for a full week to spend time with family, and that was the last time I was here.

"You too, Caleb," she says as she gives my shoulder a squeeze. She has to extend her arm all the way to reach it. My mom has always been on the tinier side at just five feet two inches tall, but today she seems even smaller. I know it's scientifically proven that people shrink slightly as they age, but I can't tell if that's what's going on or if I'm just projecting.

It's hard to admit that my mom is growing older. Losing Matty did a number on my family, and I can't imagine how Heather and I would fare if we lost a parent. I already feel as if I lost my dad, even though he's alive and well. I can't afford to lose someone else.

Realistically, I don't think there's anything wrong with my mom. I think my brain will always just jump to the worst-case scenario when it comes to mortality. No amount of statistics in the world about lifespan will ever ease my mind. Matty was practically still a kid when he died, and other than the glioblastoma, he was perfectly healthy. He was still playing football until the month before his diagnosis, when his energy began to wane.

"I made your favorite—chicken parm," Mom says, completely oblivious to my wandering thoughts.

"It's my favorite too," Greg adds as he leans against the counter with Heather by his side. She slides a finger through one of his belt loops to pull him closer. The move is so subtle yet so intimate. A pang of jealousy ricochets off my chest because I'll never have that—that intrinsic pull toward a partner. It looks like it feels nice. Heather's face is completely at ease as she snuggles into Greg's side, but I can't fathom trusting someone enough to give my entire heart to them. Not when I'm my father's son.

"Thank goodness. If you didn't like it, I don't think we could invite you to family dinners anymore," Mom jokes. She opens the oven, and the delicious smell almost knocks me over. In this moment, I'm *so* glad I came home and can have access to my mom's cooking as often as I want. No Italian restaurants out in Cali ever measured up to it.

"Everything's ready!" Mom announces as she slides the dish from the oven. "Heather, if you could strain that pasta, I'll plate the chicken, and Caleb, you can grab the salad from the fridge."

"Yes, ma'am," I reply as I head for the refrigerator. We bring everything to the dining room table and dig in.

"Heather, how is the wedding planning going?" Mom asks as she twirls some spaghetti onto her fork.

Heather and Greg are getting married in September up in New Hampshire by Lake Winnipesaukee. My family has had a cabin up there since before I was born, and we went up there many times a year throughout my childhood. It's a special place for us, and we all planned to get married there when the time came.

Heather releases a huge, pent-up sigh. "It's...going," she answers. "There are just so many small details to consider. We've had the venue, caterer, DJ, and photographer booked for months, but we're still finalizing flowers, the seating chart, place cards, centerpieces...that sort of thing. Every time I think I'm getting close to the finish line, I'm reminded of yet another thing I have to figure out."

I have a hard time understanding why anyone would want to go through the whole rigmarole of a big, fancy wedding. It seems like a lot of time, energy, and money for something that only lasts a day. Then again, I have a hard time understanding why anyone would want to get married at all—especially Heather. After what my dad did, I swore to myself I would never make a commitment that huge.

"I'm happy to help with anything you need," Mom offers. "But you know I'm not all that crafty."

It's true. She once hot-glued her finger to a popsicle stick so securely that we had to take her to urgent care to get it removed. It would be best not to let her near any sort of crafting tool with the potential to maim.

"That's okay," Heather says. "I have a plan for everything. I just have to find the time to do it all."

Greg swallows a huge bite of chicken parm. "Who knew something as simple as a seating chart could be so difficult?" he complains. "We were looking at it last night, and it feels like an impossible equation to fill twelve tables with ten people each that all know each other, get along, and won't start World War Three before the toasts."

Heather shifts in her seat. "Actually, I wanted to talk to you both about that." She said "you both," but she's pinning *me* with her gaze. "Are you okay with sitting at a table with Dad, Marcie, and the girls? I've tried working out the seating chart a million different ways, and the easiest solution is to put Dad, Marcie, Taryn, Taylor, you, Mom, and both sets of our grandparents at one table."

I barely contain a groan. I'm planning to avoid Dad as much as humanly possible during this whole wedding-week extravaganza, and I'd really rather not be confined to a table with him and his new family. However, it'll only be for a couple of hours max, and then I can ditch the table and hit the dance floor for the rest of the night.

"Sure." I give her what I'm sure is a tight grin, but it's all I can muster right now. I would do anything for Heather, and she, unfortunately, knows that. We've always been close, but we've grown even closer since Matty died. Losing a sibling makes you grip on even tighter to any that remain. If agreeing to sit with my father makes her life and wedding planning easier, I'll do it.

Heather claps her hands. "Thank you so much, Cale. I know it's not ideal, but I really appreciate it."

I grimace. Not ideal is an understatement, but I'm not about to get into that conversation right now. Everyone in this family knows exactly where I stand.

After Matty died, things were understandably rocky in our household. We'd lost the baby of the family, and everyone dealt with that in their own ways. I focused on finishing my degree; Heather committed herself to becoming an oncology nurse so she could help patients like Matty; Mom leaned heavily into her social circle, constantly having lunch or grabbing drinks with some friend or another; and Dad...well...he dealt with his issues by running away.

At first, Dad just seemed...numb. Whereas Mom sought comfort from socialization, Dad completely isolated himself. He quit his office job for one he could do remotely, stopped talking to his friends, and barely left the house. He walked around the place like a ghost, alive but not really living. It was like he was *there*, but he wasn't. And then, one day, he left for real.

Maybe I should have seen it coming. He'd been acting so out of character, and he'd obviously needed help, but I had been busting my ass to finish my degree and hadn't had much time to think about anyone other than myself. Admittedly, I hadn't had the wherewithal to either. I couldn't carry anyone else's grief on top of my own.

Not to mention that *he* was the parent. Parents are supposed to be the ones checking up on their children, not the other way around.

When Dad left, he moved back to Chicago, where he was born and raised. I was pissed at him for leaving us when we should have all been leaning on one another, but I was *livid* when he started dating Marcie not even three months later. He and Mom hadn't even officially divorced yet. I blocked his number and refused to speak to him at all. I couldn't *believe* he would betray our family in that way.

Despite severing all direct contact with my dad, I still heard updates about his life through Heather. She has a bleeding heart and couldn't bear to lose yet another family member. I, on the other hand, said good riddance.

I had assumed Dad's relationship with Marcie was some kind of grief-fueled fling that was destined to sizzle out, but he wound up marrying her not even a year after meeting her. Marcie is a good decade younger than Dad and had always wanted kids of her own, so they popped out Taryn and Taylor, and within three years of losing Matty, Dad had a whole new perfect little family.

The whole thing disgusts me to this day. And now I'm going to have to see him face to face for the first time since he left.

Everyone is silent as they wait for me to respond with a, "No problem," or, "It's fine. I'm actually looking forward to seeing Dad again," but I say nothing. There is nothing *to* say. I haven't seen Dad since he ditched our family, and now I'm being forced to sit in close proximity to him at an event I'm otherwise very much looking forward to.

"Are you going to bring a plus-one to the wedding?" Greg asks me, clearly trying to shift the subject to something lighter. Little does he know that he's only creating more tension, as my love life—or lack thereof—is another point of contention between my mom, sister, and me.

"No." I take a sip of water to give me a second to come up

with a good excuse. "I want to be able to enjoy the wedding without worrying about a date."

"But having a date would make the wedding so much more fun!" Heather argues, throwing her hands up to emphasize her point. "You would have someone to dance with! And weddings are so romantic. I think you'll regret not bringing someone."

"Who would I bring?" I challenge. "I just moved back, I don't know anyone around here, and I'm not going to risk finding a date on an app and having them turn out to be a serial killer or some kind of kook or something."

Heather rolls her eyes. "That's a pretty defamatory view of dating apps coming from someone who's literally *creating* a dating app."

I slide some spaghetti around my plate with my fork. "Yeah, well, the other apps' algorithms are nowhere near as good as ours. I don't trust any of them. Maybe if our app was up and running, I could use that to find a date for the wedding, but it's not. So, no date for me." I'm spinning my wheels at this point, coming up with whatever word vomit I think might make my family just leave me alone. I should know better. That isn't likely to happen.

"Honey," Mom says gently, and I brace myself for whatever parental concern she's about to unleash on me. "You haven't dated anyone since your brother passed. We all worry about you. We just want you to be happy."

Me not dating has nothing to do with Matty's death and everything to do with my father's actions, but I'm not going to correct her. I hate that she and Heather worry about me. I'm completely fine—better than fine—now that I've started a new job that I'm passionate about. I don't need to date to be happy. I just don't know how to convince my mom and sister of that. I wish there was someone I could take to the wedding, even just as a friend, to get them off my back.

A face flashes through my mind. Orangey-red hair. Dark-brown eyes. A delicate dusting of freckles. Hannah. I *do* know her. And even though we haven't seen each other in years, I have a feeling our friendship could easily pick up where it left off. If I was desperate for a date to the wedding, I'd ask Hannah...but I'm not, so I won't.

I was so slammed the rest of the week that I didn't make it back to Waffee. I feel a little bad about it, and I hope Hannah didn't get the wrong idea about my absence. It's not that I wasn't eager to see her again; it's just that startup life is so hectic. Sometimes there are fires you have to put out that don't afford you much flexibility or personal time. I'm hoping to catch her this week.

"I'm happy, Mom," I assure her. "Really. I'm loving the new job, and I'm glad to be home. I don't feel the need to be dating right now."

Heather slides her hand into Greg's. "We're so happy to have you back, Cale," she says, her voice almost breaking on the last word. She sniffles, and Greg drops a kiss on her forehead.

Despite their pestering and incessant worrying about me, I adore my mom and sister—okay, and Greg too. As I look around the table, a flood of gratitude washes over me. This is my family —what's left of it, anyway—and I love them dearly. I'll put up with their badgering, sit with Dad's new family at the wedding, and do it all with a smile on my face, because I don't want them to worry about me.

I give them a genuine grin. "I'm happy to *be* back."

CHAPTER 6
HANNAH

A lot of chronic illnesses are referred to as invisible illnesses. I have mixed feelings about the term. On one hand, it's true that many of these diseases cause internal side effects that are not as readily apparent as those of certain other medical issues. Many chronically ill people look completely average on the outside.

On the other hand, these illnesses are only invisible if you're not looking closely enough. Our internal symptoms—ranging from fatigue to joint pain—are visible in the way that we have to cancel plans, in the long soaks we take in Epsom salt baths, in our daily medication and supplement regimens, in the grocery delivery services we use to save energy, in the chances we don't allow ourselves to take.

If you're paying enough attention, our illnesses aren't invisible at all.

Although I told Caleb I don't always stick to my Monday-Wednesday-Friday schedule at Waffee, I did last week in the hopes of seeing him again. He never showed, which really shouldn't bother me as much as it does. Each day, I entered the café with a spark of excitement in my belly at the prospect of seeing him again, and then I left with a little pit in my stomach, gnawing at me as I wondered if there was a reason he hadn't come.

When Monday rolls around again, I set up camp at my favorite table in Waffee, fully expecting another solo work session. My table sits right in the corner, so I can have my back to a wall and not worry about anyone reading over my shoulder. The sun pours in through the windows in such a way that it's bright and warm, but at my angle, there's no glare on my screen, and I don't overheat. I have a perfect view of the whole place, and I can watch customers coming and going while I remain tucked into my private area.

I take a long drag of my latte and get to work. Mondays always mean catching up on anything I didn't finish last week, plus completing a normal day's workload. I was able to tie up some loose odds and ends over the weekend, so I'm starting fresh today by putting up a new post on my blog. After I publish it, I'll advertise the post on social media, respond to any new comments on my previous blog or social media posts, and then, finally, dig into my direct message inbox.

Responding to messages is the most draining part of my job. People tend to do a lot of trauma dumping in my inbox, and while I'm glad to be a listening ear, so to speak, it gets exhausting reading about other people's health woes when I have enough of my own. I guess it comes with the territory, but it was an unexpected consequence of choosing this career.

When I first started my blog, it was a place where I could vent about my own experience with chronic illness and connect with others who had been through similar things. I was able to create a community of young women who were dealing with the difficulty of living with diseases that were oftentimes isolating, unpredictable, and overwhelming. The more I wrote about my journey with chronic illness and shared advice based on my own experiences, the more people flocked

to my corner of the internet for information, advice, and solidarity.

Most of the time, when someone messages me with their health saga or asks for specific health advice, I direct them to get in touch with their doctor, and I always put a disclaimer that I am not a doctor and cannot give medical advice. What I *can* offer them is my personal experience and the strategies, products, etc. that have been successful for me.

I scan the subject lines in my inbox to get an idea of what I'll be responding to later. Today, the top message is titled: *HELP!!!!! MY DOCTOR IS INCOMPETENT.* If the all caps hadn't given away this person's urgency, the five exclamation marks definitely would have. If I had to guess, this inquirer is probably a newbie to the chronic illness world, maybe even still in the process of getting a diagnosis.

I release a heavy sigh. I know this messenger's plight all too well. It often takes years for someone to receive a diagnosis, especially a correct one. Doctors are too quick to write off symptoms as "normal," or as "just anxiety," or to give a blanket diagnosis that doesn't actually reflect the person's specific issues. Young women especially are often overlooked or seen as being dramatic when we explain our symptoms. It can take a lot of independent research and self-advocacy to get doctors to truly hear and believe us.

It shouldn't be this way. Patients shouldn't have to do their own research in order to figure out what's going on with their bodies. We should be believed when we tell our doctors our symptoms, and they should be the ones figuring it out. We should be supported when we reach out for help. But until we are, I'll continue making my living by being the support system for people like today's messenger.

Tucking away that annoyance in a back corner of my mind, I navigate over to my blog. I'm excited for today's post. Mondays are when I get to put up personal posts, and other days of the week are dedicated to guest posters. Since I serve a community with a vast array of different illnesses and concerns, I do my best to offer a wide variety of perspectives and expertise. Despite living with a chronic illness myself for the past five years, I'm well aware that there's a lot I don't know. I love educating myself about other illnesses and disabilities, but I want to uplift the voices of those who actually deal with them rather than speak about them myself.

I wrote today's post about my experience navigating my mom's recent medical emergency as a chronically ill person. It was interesting to be a bystander to this medical issue, rather than the patient. I saw how seriously my mom was taken by the doctor because he could physically *see* the problem in the form of swelling and bruising in her knee. As opposed to those of us living with so-called invisible illnesses—though they're not really invisible if you're paying attention—my mom's doctor never questioned that her symptoms were real, because he could see them with his own eyes.

I know this post is going to strike a chord with so many readers. My diagnosis reflection blog post did really well, and I'm hoping this one will be a powerful follow up. As I hit *post*, I'm already looking forward to the comments I'll get. As opposed to my direct messages and emails, which are often a source of stress, my comments section brings me so much joy. It's often full of people feeling so seen and understood—sometimes for the very first time. Plus, rather than everyone asking *me* for help and advice, other readers often respond to commenters. It's cool to see the little community I built helping each other out.

I go on to advertise my post on all my social media channels —Facebook, Instagram, Twitter, and TikTok—and I'm just about to post about it on Pinterest when I hear that deep, husky voice I waited for all last week say, "Hey, Reilly."

Reilly. Hearing Caleb call me by my last name instantly brings back memories from a different time. Sitting in the grass in his yard as I waited for him to jumpstart the old 1999 Honda CRV he inherited from his mom. First it was passed down to his

sister, and then to him, and by the time it got there, it had been through three accidents and sometimes needed a little boost to start up.

Why don't you get off your butt and help me, Reilly?

The smell of chocolate chip cookies wafting through the kitchen as Caleb, Owen, and Matty traipsed through, covered in dirt and grass from playing flag football in the yard.

You make those all for me, Reilly?

I never knew why Caleb referred to me that way but used my siblings' first names. I never asked, and I'm not going to now, because the sound of that old nickname on his lips is like music to my ears.

"Hey, Caleb." I can't help but grin up at him as he towers over me, a black t-shirt stretched across his broad chest and shoulders. Today he's wearing short sleeves, and I can see many more inches of his tattoos. I want to spend hours roaming my greedy fingers all over his arm, asking about each one and looking at all the intricate details. Instead, I add, "Good to see you again."

"You too." He gestures to the empty seat across from me. "Mind if I join you? If you're too busy, I can take a different table. I brought my laptop so I could do some work from here."

"No, sit there." I point across from me. "I'm due for a lunch break before I go back to work anyway."

I shut my laptop and push it to the side as I watch Caleb settle into his seat. It's a task for him to tuck his long legs beneath the table. He rolls his shoulders a couple times and shifts until he finds the right positioning for his burly body.

I arch a brow when I see the drink he's placed on the table between us. "Tea again?"

I swear a bit of a blush creeps into his cheeks as he scratches the back of his neck.

"Yeah, I'm not much of a coffee drinker," he admits. "But I still need some form of caffeine to make it through the work day."

I let out a dramatic gasp and clutch my throat. "Not a coffee drinker? Caleb O'Connor, I don't know if we can hang out anymore."

"I know, I know, coffee is the nectar of the gods. I just..." He mock shivers. "I can't stand the taste."

"Ahhh," I reply. "You've just never had coffee made the right way." I point to the half-empty latte I've been sipping on all morning. It's the perfect brownish-beige hue that tells me there's a healthy amount of almond milk and caramel syrup mixed in with the bitter espresso. "*This* is a caramel latte. It couldn't taste bitter if it tried to. Want a sip?"

Caleb eyes the latte as if it's an adversary then bravely reaches for the cup. As his lips close around the opening in the lid, it dawns on me that his mouth is where my mouth was just moments ago and will be again just moments from now. It shouldn't be a big deal—people share drinks all the time—but the thought of our lips touching by proxy on the coffee cup sends a zing of excitement down my spine.

As his tattooed hand places the cup back on the table, Caleb taps his tongue quickly against the roof of his mouth as if deliberating the taste. He tilts his head to the side. "Not bad."

"Not bad?" I repeat. "Not *bad*? That right there is liquid *gold*. Joy in a cup. Genuine *lifeblood*."

A smile tugs at the corner of his lips. I can tell he's trying to fight it, but he's losing the battle.

"You feel really strongly about coffee, huh?"

"Now you're learning," I reply before taking a sip of my own. I try not to focus on the fact that my lips are basically touching Caleb's by the transitive property. Is that how that works? Math was never my best subject. English all the way.

He shakes his head and takes a sip of his iced tea. "So, what else are you into these days?" he gestures toward my closed laptop. "What do you do for work?"

It's the million-dollar question and one I answer differently, depending on who I'm talking to. If I say I'm a blogger, people will ask for the name of my blog. If I give it to them, I'm basically giving them access to my life story. I usually want to avoid giving away that much personal information right off the bat, so instead, I use my default answer.

"I'm a writer."

Caleb's face lights up. "No way. I remember how much you used to love writing. You were on the school newspaper and the yearbook, right?"

"And the creative writing club," I add.

"Good for you," Caleb says, genuine delight radiating from his smile. "Who do you write for? Or what do you write about?"

"I work for myself, mostly doing freelance pieces for websites, magazines, and news outlets," I say. "My niche is health and wellness, so most of what I write about is in that sphere."

All of that is true. I *do* write freelance pieces about health and wellness from a chronic illness perspective. It's just not the bulk of my job. My blog and social media are how I make at least seventy-five percent of my income. I'm not trying to hide that from Caleb, but I don't think he knows about my illnesses, and I'm not sure I'm ready to tell him yet.

Caleb and I weren't the only ones who lost touch when we went off to college. Since my family moved right after I graduated high school, our parents also mostly severed their connection. It's not like my mom would have told his mom that I got sick in college. I learned about Matty's cancer through Owen, who had remained good friends with him, but my health issues were kept much quieter. A chronic illness is much easier to mask than a terminal one.

"That's great," Caleb says. "I'd love to read some of your work sometime."

"Uh..." I hesitate, hoping he doesn't mean sometime soon. If we keep hanging out, I'll have to tell him the truth eventually, but I'm not prepared for that right now. "Sure," I say before changing the subject. "I want to hear more about what you do. What kind of app are you working on?"

Pink tinges Caleb's cheeks again. It's easy to miss, with his beard obscuring so much of the lower half of his face, but I catch it.

"It's actually a dating app," he answers with a visible cringe. "I didn't choose the content of the app. I just do the coding and stuff for it. But it's actually a really cool concept."

He says the second part quickly, defending his work as if he's worried I'll see it as inferior or silly. Little does he know I often have the same fears about how people will see my own job.

"Tell me more about it," I say. I've never used a dating app, but Rhia has, and she's told me how the platforms differ in terms of how matches are made or how people connect. Sometimes you have to answer specific questions, and sometimes you can choose which open-ended questions you want to answer. Sometimes the women have to send the first message, and sometimes anyone can make the first move.

Caleb leans forward and puts his hands on the table. "Okay, so the app is actually pretty unique. The algorithm we use is based on people's answers to a variety of personality tests. We present a bunch of them, and people can choose which ones to take, but the more they take, the better the potential matches will be."

"Wow, that's actually really neat." I'm not super into personality tests like some people are—ahem, Rhia, who basically creates entire personality profiles for her book characters—but I have used them as tools to learn more about myself in the past. I think they can give people valuable information about themselves, and I can see how that would translate to picking a partner with complementary personality traits. "What kinds of quizzes are involved?"

Caleb ticks them off on his tattooed fingers. "Right now we're working with Enneagram, Human Design, Myers-Briggs, 5 Love Languages, and then also astrology. There are a ton more tests and systems we can add over time, but those seemed like the most popular and relevant ones for a dating app right now."

"That's so cool," I say. I'm only familiar with the Myers-Briggs and zodiac signs, but now I actually kind of want to take the other tests. "Why did you seem embarrassed about it when you first brought it up?"

Caleb shrugs and runs a hand over his beard. "I guess I feel a little funny about working on a dating app, because I'm not a dating app user, nor am I even dating. It feels a bit disingenuous."

Huh. So he's *not* dating. I tuck that information into a file cabinet in the back of my mind.

"Heather thinks it's the coolest thing ever, though," he says with a fond grin. "She's dying to try it out even though she's getting married in a few months."

I chuckle along with him. "How is Heather? I heard she became a nurse."

"Yep. She's currently working in the oncology ward at Mass General. She's doing really well. She and her fiancé, Greg, are getting married in September."

"That's wonderful," I say. I never knew Heather as well as I knew Matty, since she was older than all of us, but I know Caleb has always been pretty close with her.

"Yeah," Caleb replies, but he's fidgeting with his fingers as if there's more to that statement that he's not sharing. I don't push —this is only our first time kind of hanging out on purpose—but I hope there will be more times in the future so I can dig in further.

"Want to grab some food?" he asks.

"Definitely," I reply.

We spend our lunch talking more about Heather, and then Annie and Owen, until we're all caught up on each other's siblings' lives. Caleb mentions that his parents got divorced after Matty died, which I vaguely knew. I tell him about my mom's knee injury and how I'm the one tasked with being her chauffeur and nursemaid. We get up to speed on each other's families but don't talk too much about ourselves, which is more than fine with me.

Chatting with Caleb feels natural and almost too easy. We end up talking for over an hour before realizing that we really have to get some work done. He pulls out his laptop, and we set up across from each other. With Caleb's handsome face peeking over the top of his screen, I have an inexplicable spark of renewed energy to respond to those pesky emails and messages.

CHAPTER 7
CALEB

A knock sounds on my apartment door on Friday morning just as I was about to head out to Waffee. I was hoping to meet up with Hannah for lunch and a co-working session like we had on Monday and Wednesday. Around reminiscing about high school memories, I got a surprising amount of work done. Hannah said she gets her best work done at Waffee, and I'm starting to think I might too.

Hopefully seeing her three times in one week isn't too much. I don't want her to think I'm some kind of stalker or that I haven't been able to make any new friends in Boston, so I'm clinging to her. Talking to her just feels so natural, and in so many ways it feels like we haven't missed a beat since high school. Plus, she's incredibly easy on the eyes. Sometimes I have to remind myself not to stare.

I open the door to find Heather still dressed in her periwinkle scrubs, a false smile plastered on her face.

"Hey, Cale," she say as her eyes fill with tears.

I don't think twice before hauling my sister into a hug. Giving her a huge squeeze, I maneuver us out of the doorway and into my apartment, kicking the door shut behind me. I usher

Heather toward the couch where she plops down with a heavy sigh.

"Tough day?" I ask as I sit beside her.

She sinks further into the couch. "Three-year-old with neuroblastoma. We knew it was in his bones and marrow, but today we found out it's metastasized to his skull."

My hands involuntarily ball into fists. It's not the same type of cancer Matty had, and though it isn't technically in his brain like Matty's was, the fact that the little boy's cancer spread to his skull was surely enough to churn up bad memories.

"I'm sorry." I pat her thigh. "That's really shitty."

Heather wipes a hand over her face. "I'm just glad my shift is over. I think I mostly needed a hug. Greg is at the office all day, but I knew you'd be good for it." She smiles over at me, and I'm relieved to find that any tears in her eyes have subsided.

When I lived in California, Heather would often call me after a hard day at work to vent, especially if she'd had a patient who hit a little too close to home. Working in an oncology ward means helping patients like Matty and families like ours. Heather always says she finds it healing, but every once in a while, it gets a little too heavy, and she knows I'm someone who will always understand that. Apparently, with my being back in Boston, those phone calls have translated to surprise pop-ins to my apartment.

"I'm always good for a hug," I say before glancing down at my watch.

One of Heather's brows arches up. "Got somewhere to be?"

"Actually..." I hesitate, unsure if I should tell her about seeing Hannah. I don't want her to get the wrong idea. Then again, maybe knowing I'm hanging out with someone of the female variety would give her some measure of satisfaction. "I'm meeting someone for lunch," I finally say.

Heather's eyes widen a fraction. "A *female* someone?"

"Yes," I reply, "but before you start making false assump-

tions, let me assure you that it's not a date. Do you remember Hannah Reilly?"

"Of course. She was such a sweetheart."

She really was. Still is. Hannah is the type of person who would give you the shirt off her back. Unfortunately, that thought leads me to imagining what Hannah looks like without a shirt. I really don't want to get a hard-on in front of my sister right now, so I quickly move on.

"Right, well, she still lives here," I explain. "I ran into her at this cool coffee shop, Waffee, and found out she works from there a lot, so I've been joining her now and then."

"I love Waffee!" Heather exclaims. "I've never been anywhere else where you can get a waffled crouton *inside* a waffled Caesar wrap." She shakes her head as if this is the greatest invention in the world. "But wait, tell me more about seeing Hannah again. How is she?"

"She seems to be doing well," I reply. On second thought, she honestly hasn't talked that much about her life. We've talked about our families and high school memories, and I've talked about the app I'm working on, but I don't know much about Hannah's current life except that she's a freelance writer with a penchant for iced caramel lattes.

"That's great." Heather eyes me skeptically. "And you're sure these little get-togethers haven't been at all date-like? You used to be kind of flirty with Hannah in high school."

I roll my eyes. "I was flirty with everyone in high school. I promise, we are *not* dating. We're just catching up, and it's nice to have a friend I already know while I'm regaining my footing here."

"Okay," Heather relents. "Hey, maybe you should ask Hannah to come to the wedding with you."

"Heather," I gently warn. "It's really nice to see you, and I feel genuinely bad that you had a shitty day, but if you're done harassing me about bringing a date to the wedding, I have lunch plans to get to."

Heather responds with a sly smile and one final hug before taking off.

🍥

I locate Hannah right away as I enter Waffee. She always seems to sit at the same table, so it's easy to find her. Her ginger hair is pulled into a ponytail, showing off her ivory skin and the sprinkling of freckles across her nose. She has a teal tank top on, and I send up a quick thank you to Mother Nature for the warming weather.

The top isn't overly revealing, but it gives just enough of a glimpse of her smooth skin to make my heart beat faster. Her full breasts fill out the tank top beautifully, and as I walk toward her, I note a couple of freckles just above her left one. My fingers twitch with the need to touch them. I squeeze my hands into fists then shake them out.

Hannah is concentrating on her laptop, almost glaring at the screen. I briefly wonder what has her so frustrated, but then she looks up and spots me. Her focused look immediately turns into a warm grin.

"Hey," she says as she shuts her laptop partway. I've noticed she always does that when approached, rather than leaving her laptop open and just pushing it to the side. I wonder if it's an innocent habit, or if she's trying to hide what she's writing. It only makes me more curious. Health and wellness is an awfully ambiguous arena. Maybe she writes articles like those ones in women's magazines...5 *Sex Positions to Spice Up Your Life*.

Shit, now I'm kind of hoping that's the type of writing she does.

"Hey." I point to the empty chair opposite her. "This seat taken?"

She opens her palms toward the chair in an inviting gesture. "All yours."

I subtly adjust myself as I sit down. Between Hannah's tank

top and thoughts of her writing sexy articles, I've gotten myself a little too excited. It's been way too long since I've had sex, and now I'm regretting not doing something to take the edge off.

"Happy Friday," I say as I slide my laptop from the bag at my feet. "Got much left to do before the weekend?"

"I have a few things to wrap up, but I'm in pretty good shape," she says. "How about you?"

"Same." I lace my fingers together and crack my knuckles. "Our app is almost ready for beta testing. Some of us have been having friends and family try it out, and we've already corrected most of the bugs they've found. Soon we'll open it up to a group of official beta testers. Once we have their feedback, we can make any necessary improvements before presenting it to potential investors."

Hannah has genuine excitement written on her features, and it makes me feel all warm and bubbly inside. Despite the fact that I'm a little embarrassed to be making a dating app, I'm really proud of the work I've done.

"Can I try it?" she asks, head tilted innocently to the side like a puppy asking for a treat.

My gaze whips to Hannah's. Her brown eyes hold nothing but sincerity. "You want to try my app?"

"Of course," she says. "It sounds so interesting. I'd love to test it out."

I blink, unsure whether to be honored that she wants to try it or terrified she'll think it's silly. "It's not that good yet. There are probably less than fifty people who have put their information into the app," I explain. "It's really only the employees and some of our networks on there. Not a huge dating pool."

"I'm not actually looking to find a date," Hannah says with a giggle. "I just want to see how the app works. You know, get the full experience."

I guess I can't really argue with that, so I agree and pull up the sandbox version of the app on my laptop. I swivel it toward her and begin explaining what she sees on the screen.

"It would look a little different on a phone, of course, but the buttons on the bottom are for your profile, which is where you take all the quizzes; your matches, which shows you all the people the algorithm thinks you might be compatible with; your inbox, which is where any messages from matches will show up; and your settings, which is where you can change things like age, distance, and gender preferences."

Hannah nods as her eyes dart over the screen. "So it chooses the matches based on your answers to the personality quizzes and birth information, and then you can message anyone who shows up as a match?"

"Exactly. The app will show you anyone with your preferred gender, age, and distance range who is a fifty percent match or higher. It will show a percentage of compatibility for each match, with the highest at the top of the list and the lowest at the bottom. That way, you can see who the algorithm believes you will get along with best, but you still have the option to pursue people who aren't necessarily perfect matches."

A smile tugs at the corner of Hannah's lips. "I kind of like that. Like, even though everything might look perfect for one match on paper, they might not actually be the best option. I like that it gives some wiggle room."

"Thanks," I reply. "You should probably allow for the maximum age and distance ranges, and be open to all genders, just to get a better feel for how the matches work. If you make it too narrow, you might not get any matches because of the small number of participants."

"Got it." She easily navigates over to the settings menu and changes her preferences. Then she clicks over to the profile tab. "Bring on the quizzes!"

I chuckle at her enthusiasm. "Take your time, and do as many as you like."

"Oh, I'm taking them all," she says. "I want to get the most accurate results."

"You might regret that," I warn. "With your preferences set

the way they are, you could wind up matching with someone's grandma or grandpa. Or both."

Hannah puts a hand over her heart. "The heart wants what it wants, Caleb."

I bark out a laugh. "Have at it, then. I have some work I can do from my phone."

I slip my cell from my pocket and start scrolling through emails. Hannah is quiet and focused as she fills out the various questionnaires. The only other people I've had try out the app are Heather and Greg, and I'm glad to see Hannah finds it as user-friendly as they did. I may not have had much to do with choosing the personality quizzes or deciding how to present the matches, but the functionality of the app is all me.

After about a half hour, she finally tears her gaze away from the screen. "Okay, I just finished the last quiz. Ready to see my matches?"

I put my phone in my pocket and angle the laptop so we both have a good view of it. "Let's do it."

I click on the matches tab and almost fall out of my chair. Because according to the app, Hannah's number one match, at ninety-six percent, is *me*.

CHAPTER 8
CALEB

Nervous laughter bubbles out of me. Sure, it wasn't unlikely that I would show up as a potential match for Hannah because of the small pool of participants, but I'm honestly shocked to be the top one. Ninety-six percent is the highest match percentage I've seen so far. Heather and Greg only got an eighty-nine, and they're happily engaged to be married.

I'm not sure what to make of our high compatibility rating. I mean, I believe in the mission of the app and all, but the personality stuff isn't really my thing. You can't put all that much stock into it, right? My dad would say it's all a bunch of hocus pocus. Luckily, we don't speak, so I don't have to listen to him criticize my work. But in this case, I don't fully disagree with him. You can't find your perfect match just by having complementary zodiac signs and Enneagram types.

Right?

"Look at that," Hannah says, pointing to the screen and snapping me back to reality. "Hey, at least my top match isn't somebody's grandpa."

I snap my mouth shut when I realize my jaw is hanging open. "Yeah." I let out an awkward chuckle that I immediately wish I could suck back into my mouth like a vacuum. I don't want Hannah to sense my discomfort when she obviously thinks this is just a funny coincidence. Little does she know how sophisticated the algorithm is and how unlikely that high of a match percentage is.

I adopt a casual charm that I hope will cover my shock. "You could do a lot worse."

She kicks her foot against mine. "Sure could."

Her compliment warms me more than it should. The fact that she thinks she could do worse than dating me shouldn't mean anything. I don't want to think about Hannah's dating life, and I don't want to think about *why* I don't want to think about it. She's just an old friend. It shouldn't affect me.

But it does.

"The app is really cool," she continues. "Thanks for letting me try it out."

"Of course." I run a hand over my beard—a nervous habit. I need to stop talking about the app. I need to stop thinking about dating. I *need* to stop thinking about how Hannah and I are ninety-six percent compatible.

"Do you want to grab some lunch?" I ask. "I'm starving."

"Sure." Hannah closes her laptop fully and stands. Her teal tank top is tucked into a denim skirt that shows off her shapely legs. God, she's gorgeous. I don't know how it escaped me back in high school. I mean, I always knew she was pretty. That was objectively obvious. But now I'm noticing more beauty in the details, like the way her hips flare out beneath her skirt, and how, when the sun hits her hair just right, some of the strands look almost golden. And those freckles above her breasts. They're just so goddamn dainty. I need to stop staring at them, lest she thinks I'm ogling what's just below.

We head to the counter and place our orders. The barista rattles off what must be Hannah's regular fare, and I choose a chicken quesadilla. When I pull out my wallet to pay for both meals, Hannah tosses me a look of confusion.

"You don't have to pay for mine. It's not like we're on a date."

Hell. Why can't the topic of me and Hannah dating just drop already?

"I know," I reply, trying to infuse my tone with a *duh* inflection so she knows for sure that *I* know we're not on a date. "But you helped me out today by adding more data to my app. Let me repay you."

Her expression softens, her lips tipping into a slight smile. "Okay. Thanks."

y waffled quesadilla crunches between my teeth as I take a huge bite. I could watch Hannah tell stories all day. She's so animated as she talks, using her hands and changing inflections to get her points across. Her brown eyes are wide and vivid as she speaks.

"So he put his arms up in the air, made himself as big as possible, and started singing 'Livin' on a Prayer' at the top of his lungs. When they say to make loud noises, I don't think that's exactly what they mean, but it worked. The bear briefly stared at him like the weirdo that he is and then turned around and walked away."

She reaches for her coffee and takes a sip, signaling the end of her story.

I lay down my quesadilla. "I can't believe your dad's gotten that close to a bear."

Hannah shrugs as if it's no big deal. "Occupational hazard. He's also come face-to-face with a moose and gotten a bit too close for comfort to a wolf pack."

"Damn," I reply. "I don't think I'd have the balls to live in Alaska—at least not the part where he does. Have you ever visited?"

"A couple times," she says. "I don't particularly love the

outdoors, and just about all recreational activities in Alaska take place in the wilderness, so it's not really my scene. My dad tries to come back to the lower forty-eight at least twice a year, though, so I see him enough. Annie, Owen, and I try to FaceTime with him once a week too."

A surge of jealousy rushes through me. How come when her parents got divorced, the family stayed relatively intact even though her dad moved to fucking Alaska, but when *my* parents got divorced and my dad moved to Illinois, he basically forgot about us altogether?

To be fair, keeping in touch is a two-way street—one I've blocked off with cones, caution tape, and concrete barricades. I can't forgive my dad for abandoning our family during the worst period of our lives. Heather has made an effort, but I can't find it in my heart to do the same.

"How about you?" Hannah asks. "Your dad moved to Chicago, right? How often do you get to see him?"

She must have heard about the divorce and my dad moving away through Owen. What she doesn't know is how much the divorce rocked our family, and that I've had very little contact with my dad since then.

I scratch at my jaw. "I don't see him much." I meet her gaze and realize that I can't lie to her. Not when she's looking at me so intently with those brown doe eyes. "To be honest, I haven't spoken to him face-to-face since he moved away."

Hannah sucks in a breath. "Oh, Caleb. I'm so sorry. I didn't realize... I shouldn't have brought it up."

"It's okay." I quickly reassure her to wipe the horror from her expression. "It's a normal question to ask. When my dad left...it wasn't on good terms. He kind of shut down after Matty died, and then one day he just sort of vanished. He obviously wasn't in a good place, but I felt betrayed that he ditched our family instead of staying and working through his problems with us. He clearly needed time and space to heal. I thought maybe after a while he would get himself together, and then we could reconcile. Imagine my surprise when a few months after he moved, he was with someone new. The divorce wasn't even official yet, and he had already moved on." I shake my head. No matter how many times I've dissected what happened, I still can't believe it.

Hannah reaches across the table, taking my hand in hers. The move seems automatic, something she would do to console anyone who was opening up to her. Her thumb rubs over the leaf tattoo on the back of my hand. It's a doodle Matty drew of one of the plants that lived in the garden window of our kitchen —plants my dad tended to because my mom has a black thumb. They all died a few months after Matty did.

"Thank you for sharing that with me," Hannah says. "That must have been so difficult to go through." She gives my hand a final squeeze before retracting hers.

"It sucked," I reply more casually than I actually feel. There are lots of colorful words I could use to describe what my dad did, but they're not appropriate to use in a public place. "I don't think about him much these days, though. Did some therapy in the beginning, but now it's more *out of sight, out of mind*, honestly." I roll my cup of iced tea between my fingers. "I'm not looking forward to seeing him at Heather's wedding."

Hannah's eyebrows shoot up. "Will that be the first time you've seen him since he left?"

"Pretty much," I reply before shoving the final bite of quesadilla in my mouth. I've been in the same room as him at family funerals and the like, but I've never approached him. If it ever seemed like he was trying to approach me, I hightailed it to a different area.

I don't want to think about what it will be like to be near my dad again. Not right now. Not while I'm with Hannah. I want to enjoy my time with her, not allow thoughts of my father to taint it.

Hannah watches as I wipe my mouth with a napkin, her eyes lingering on my lips for a moment after I'm done cleaning myself.

"You, uh..." she says. "You've got a little something caught in your beard."

Before I can raise the napkin again, she's reaching toward my face. As she plucks a morsel of food from my beard, her fingers brush against my lips. Her skin is so soft, so smooth against what I know to be slightly chapped lips. I make a mental note to find the lip balm in one of my still unpacked boxes. Her hand idles for a moment longer than necessary, and I fight the urge to pucker my lips and kiss it. What the hell has gotten into me?

She pulls her hand back and drops the crumb onto her empty plate. Pointing to mine, she asks, "All done?"

"Yeah," I reply, my lips still tingling where she touched them.

Hannah gathers our trash and heads off to the trash can. If I didn't know better, I would think she'd experienced the same surprising sensation I did by the way she rushed off. But she was so adamant earlier that this isn't a date, and that's just fine by me. I'm not looking to date right now—possibly ever—and I definitely don't want to lose one of my only friends in Boston by unleashing my cynicism about love on her.

When Hannah comes back to the table, I try to think of something to change the subject. Looking over her shoulder, I spot the bulletin board that advertises all sorts of local businesses and community events. There are ads for yoga studios, tutors, music lessons, and more. My gaze lands on a poster for a food truck festival this weekend. That sounds like fun, and I'd love to attend, but I don't want to go alone. I'd ask Hannah, but will it seem too much like a date?

Truthfully, I just want to keep hanging out with her. We've been seeing each other a lot lately, but I still feel like I know so little about her. We've talked about our families and my job, but somehow, she never seems to bring up anything about herself. I only know vague details about her job, and I have no idea what she does in her free time. Maybe hanging out somewhere other than Waffee on a non-workday would allow her to open up more.

"Hey, what are you doing this weekend?" I ask.

Hannah's gaze lifts from where she was staring at the table. "Nothing, really. Why?"

I point to the poster about the festival. "There's a food truck festival on the common, and it looks pretty fun. Want to go with me? Still not a date, of course."

Her cheeks pinken, but a smile flirts with her lips. "Sure, that does sound fun. I have a couple of things to do tomorrow, but we could plan for Sunday?"

"Sounds great. Why don't I pick you up so we only need to find parking for one car?"

"Okay," she says. After giving me her address and agreeing on a time, I stuff my laptop into its case and take off. I have a little more work to do, but I think it will be easier to do it at home, not sitting across from Hannah and thinking about our ninety-six percent compatibility rating.

CHAPTER 9
HANNAH

The key to covering up a Lupus rash is color correction. Before you go in with foundation or concealer, use a green color corrector to reduce the redness of the rash.

I wake up on Sunday morning covered by a sheen of sweat with chills wracking my body, and I know I'm in trouble. These are the telltale signs of the low-grade fever I get whenever my autoimmune diseases start to flare. Stretching my arms over my head, I let out a huge yawn. I did experience some fatigue and joint pain this week, but that's no different from any other week, so I hadn't thought to question it.

I pry myself from the bed and slowly make my way toward the bathroom, where I'm afraid of what I'll see in the mirror. My suspicions are confirmed when I catch sight of the malar rash covering my cheeks. A groan rips from my throat as I inspect the red, butterfly-shaped mark running from cheek to cheek over my nose. It's somewhat faint—not the worst it's ever been—but it's noticeable enough that I'll need to cover it with make-up. I once wrote a whole blog post about the best products to mask a malar rash, so that shouldn't be a problem.

The problem is that between the low-grade fever and blooming rash, I know my body is telling me to take it easy. It wants me to slow down so I don't enter a full-blown flare. My body is screaming at me to cancel my plans with Caleb today, but my stubborn brain stands in staunch refusal. I've really been enjoying reconnecting with him, and I want to go to the food truck festival today.

It might not be the most responsible decision I've ever made, but screw it. Why should I have to miss out on life just because I got the short end of the health stick? I might not be able to do everything I used to do, but I should still be able to have some semblance of a twenty-something's life.

My mind drifts to brunch yesterday when I caught up with Annie and Owen. I love the twins more than life itself, but that doesn't stop me from leaving our gatherings often feeling jealous of all they're able to do. Just yesterday, Owen went for a ten-mile run and prepped three different meals for the week all before brunch. Afterward, he had plans to meet up with friends for a hike then plans with different friends to go to a movie at night. A day that packed would probably kill me, or at the very least land me in the hospital.

Annie's day was a bit tamer, but she had still gone shopping before brunch and had plans to get mani/pedis with friends in the afternoon. I can usually do one major thing in a day. Brunch *or* shopping. See friends *or* do a workout and meal prep. I have to make choices other people my age don't. It doesn't bother me that much anymore, except when I get a harsh reminder of what other people my age are accomplishing.

Today, I'm making the choice to ignore my body's cues and do something social because I think it will bring me joy. It's not like I have a ton of friends. There's Rhia, of course, whose friendship has never wavered, but other than that, friends have been fleeting. After I graduated, I lost touch with most people from high school—Caleb included. When I got sick and had to leave college at the beginning of my junior year, I lost all the friends I had made there. I'd been super close with my roommate and a couple of other girls, but those friendships didn't stand the tests of distance and chronic illness.

In a way, I can't blame those girls for dropping me as a friend. Not only did I move back home, making seeing each other much harder, but I also changed as a person. Chronic illness will do that to you. I was no longer the bright, bubbly college student, eager to fill my days with plans and always up for a night out. The one and only time my friends offered to drive down to Boston to visit me, I turned them down because I could barely leave my bed, and I didn't want them to see me like that. I wasn't overly communicative during that period, often letting text messages sit unread for days because I didn't have the mental capacity to read and respond to them.

My friends made *some* effort to keep our friendships intact, but it simply wasn't enough. I was too sick to put in effort of my own, and apparently, they weren't willing to pick up the slack. There's a part of me that can't help but resent them for that. I know friendship is a two-way street, but when one friend's car breaks down, shouldn't the other meet them where they're at to help them out?

Despite the bitterness I harbor toward them, I still grieve the loss of those friendships.

A glance at the clock pulls me from my thoughts. I barely have enough time to shower and get ready before Caleb is supposed to pick me up. Scrambling off the couch, I hurry through my shower, making sure to leave enough time for the tedious makeup routine that will adequately cover my rash. Once I'm satisfied with that, I throw on a pair of jeans and a scoop-neck top, throwing a light hoodie on over it.

Realistically, it's a little warm for jeans and a hoodie, but I have to cover my skin from the sun. Both of my autoimmune diseases cause increased photosensitivity. Since the event we're going to is outside, I have to be extra careful. I slathered my usual zinc-oxide-based sunscreen on my face, but I don't have time to apply it to my whole body, so covering up with clothing it is. Plus, the hoodie is made of a light UPF fabric that has built-in sun protection.

I've just finished pulling my hair back into a ponytail when I hear the buzzer to my apartment go off. A funny tingle zings through my belly at the sound that signifies Caleb is here. He's here, at my apartment, and he's taking me to a festival. But it's *not* a date. That much he made very clear. I take a deep breath to clear the tingling from my belly before I answer the door.

"Hey," I say as I sling my pocketbook over my shoulder. I never go anywhere without that thing. I have practically a whole pharmacy of medications in there, plus extra eye drops, dry mouth lozenges, sunscreen, and anything else I might need to stay comfortable on the go.

"Hey," Caleb replies with a grin. Today he has on dark jeans and a gray t-shirt. It's a simple outfit, and yet he still looks mouthwatering. The neckline of his t-shirt flirts with some of the ink on his collarbone, and I once again wonder about the parts of his tattoo that I can't see.

"Got everything you need?" he asks, one eyebrow cocked as he takes in my oversized bag.

"Yep," I reply brightly. I know my bag's size seems a tad ridiculous. It's technically designed to be a diaper bag, which Rhia makes fun of me for constantly, but it fits everything I need. And she never balks at it when it comes time to sneaking snacks into a movie theater.

Caleb gives my bag one last skeptical look. "Let's go, then."

CHAPTER 10
HANNAH

I take in the splendor of the food truck festival as we circle the common, looking for parking. They have the whole area crammed to the gills with trucks of all sizes and colors, selling fare from all sorts of different countries. From what I've seen, they've got practically every continent represented, as well as every meal from breakfast to dessert.

I hope we don't end up doing too much walking today. The more I exert myself, the more likely I am to send myself into a full-blown flare. Everything that takes energy—from brushing my teeth to going for a walk—threatens to tip me over that invisible edge. I hadn't considered how much physical activity a festival like this could involve, only that I wanted to spend time with Caleb.

After circling the common twice to no avail, he asks, "Are you okay parking a couple blocks away?"

"Sure," I say, despite my better judgment. I don't want to sound like a wimp by saying no, and now doesn't seem like the right time to disclose my illnesses to him. I know I'll make it through this event just fine—I've gotten to know my body quite well, and I'm confident in what it can handle in the short term—but I fear the long-term consequences. It's the impending threat of a flare that makes me fidget and bounce my legs nervously the farther we drive away from the common.

"Ah!" Caleb shouts as he spots an open parking space. "There we go." He guides his car smoothly into the space, placing a hand behind my headrest as he backs up to parallel park. Why is that move so goddamn sexy? And *of course* it's his tattooed arm that stretches right along my eyeline. I catch a whiff of something woodsy, like pine or cedar—probably his deodorant, given his armpit's proximity to my face in this position—and fight the urge to turn just a little further to the left and take a big inhale.

Turning off the car, Caleb shoots me a wide grin. "Shall we?"

Shall we get out of this enclosed space that smells just like you and makes me want to do weird things like nuzzle your armpit?

"We shall," I say as I unbuckle myself and hop out the door, meeting Caleb by the front of the car. We start heading toward the festival, walking side by side down the sidewalk. I can't help but notice how he automatically falls into place on the outer edge, leaving me in the objectively safer position. Maybe some would say the move is sexist, but I've always found it chivalrous. It's one of those little things that shows an innate sense of caring and selflessness.

"What food truck are you most excited for today?" Caleb asks, shoving his hands into the pockets of his jeans as he walks.

"I saw a taco truck as we drove by that looked good. I really hope it has elotes—Mexican street corn. That's one of my favorite dishes ever."

"I'm sure *one* of these trucks will be able to satisfy your craving," Caleb says. "I have a hankering for something sweet. But I don't want to settle for your run-of-the-mill ice cream truck. I'm hoping for something with a little more pizzazz."

"Pizzazz, huh?" I tease.

"Yeah, Reilly," he says, sending an amused smile in my direction. "Everyone could use a little pizzazz in their life."

I couldn't agree more, and that's a big part of the reason I decided to come today. Yes, my health dictates a lot of my life and what I can and can't do, but within those limitations, I have choices to make. I can choose to come to a full stop every time my body shows the faintest sign of a flare to avoid any negative consequences, or I can take some chances here and there in the name of living a full life.

At a certain point while we're walking, I realize Caleb is matching his strides to mine. Not in a pronounced way that would make me feel bad about my pace—just a casual slowing to put us in sync. His legs are much longer, and I'm sure his body is much stronger and abler than mine. Yet, he's choosing to go at my pace.

"Damn." Caleb lets out a whistle as he takes in the food truck festival from its entrance. There are paths leading in five different directions, and there doesn't seem to be much rhyme or reason as to which types of trucks line each path. It seems more like it's set up for guests to meander around, exploring and discovering hidden gems amongst the chaos.

"Which way do we go first?" I ask as my gaze darts from path to path.

Caleb's eyes are doing the same. "Any idea where that taco truck you spotted was?"

I look around a bit more to get my bearings and point down path number five. "I think it was on the perimeter of the common, so maybe down there?"

He gestures toward the path with both arms. "Let's give it a try."

We drift down the path, taking in each truck as we pass by it. There's a Pho truck, a pizza truck with an actual brick oven built into it, and even a pickle truck that serves all varieties of pickles, plus treats like fried pickles and "pickle pops," which are popsicles made out of pickle juice.

Finally, we come across the taco truck about halfway down

the path. I scan the menu and pump my fist into the air when I spot what I was looking for. "Elotes. Score!"

"Sweet," Caleb says. "I've never had it before, but based on your level of excitement, I think today's the day to try it."

"It's messy but delicious," I assure him. "I'll get us two." Stepping up to the counter, I order our dishes and send Caleb a wink over my shoulder. "I'm paying for you today."

He already specified that this was not a date, and I know he did it because I made a comment about him paying for my lunch at Waffee the other day. I didn't mean to be weird about it. I'm just not used to people doing stuff like that for me. I haven't hung out one-on-one with a guy in a long time. Hopefully my comment puts him at ease, knowing that *I* know we're just here as friends.

When our orders are ready, we take them to one of the vacant picnic blankets the festival has set up all over the grassy areas of the common.

"This looks delicious." Caleb inspects his carton of corn slathered in sour cream, mayonnaise, cotija cheese, cilantro, and chili powder.

"It will be. Don't forget to add a squeeze of lime," I say, already dressing my own.

Caleb picks up the lime wedge from his carton and holds it between two long fingers and a thumb, squeezing droplets over each piece of corn. Watching his thick fingers delicately squeeze the lime is borderline erotic. It reminds me of that chef on TikTok who's always stroking orange halves and sucking on his fingers.

If Rhia was here, no doubt she would be making a sexual joke. Something along the lines of: *I bet those fingers are used to feeling sticky,* or, *where'd you learn to use such gentle pressure?*

A laugh begins to bubble up, and I try to suppress it, but a weird snort ends up escaping anyway.

Caleb sends me an amused look. "What is it?"

"Nothing, sorry." I wave my hands as if that will erase the

whole embarrassing moment like an eraser on a whiteboard. "Just thinking about something Rhia said one time."

He places his lime down. "You're still friends with Rhiannon James?"

"Still my best friend," I reply, struggling not to stare as Caleb sucks a droplet of lime juice off the pad of his finger.

"You two were thick as thieves back in high school," he says. "I remember her being over at your house almost as much as Owen was at ours."

Caleb's lips curve down just a smidge, his eyebrows drawing together ever so slightly. I know he's remembering the reason Owen was always at their place. *Matty.* I still don't know how much to ask Caleb about his brother, or how open he is to talking about what happened. He's never seemed to mind discussing the subject, but now I know his strained relationship with his father is all wrapped up in it too.

"Yeah," I reply. "She's still at my apartment a few times a week. It's good for her to get out. Sometimes she holes herself up in her writing cave for days at a time."

Caleb finishes chewing a bit of his elote. "I heard she was an author. Romance novels, right?"

I cock my head side to side as I try to think of how to answer. "That's right. Some might categorize them as erotica, but I believe they are technically romance that's higher up on the steam scale. It has to do with how much plot and character building there is, versus just sex. She could explain it better, but I would warn you off asking her, because she could go on about this stuff for hours on end."

Caleb lets out a low chuckle and swipes his fingers over his beard, brushing off any rogue corn crumbs. "I don't know. I think I might be interested enough in her answer to listen. Maybe we should invite her next time we hang out."

My heart flutters at the automatic assumption that we'll be hanging out again. Then I think about what it would be like adding Rhia to the mix and immediately shut that thought down.

"That might not be the best idea. She, uh... She tends to romanticize *everything*. If she even catches a whiff that I'm hanging out with a guy, she automatically ships us together. Her comments would be relentless."

Caleb shrugs as if this wouldn't bother him in the least. "I can handle it, but if it would make you uncomfortable, then scratch that idea." He shoves the last of his elote in his mouth, then grabs both our empty food containers and gets up to toss them in a nearby trash can. When he comes back, he puts out a hand to help me off the ground.

I go to grab my purse, but he swipes it up first. "Let me carry this for a bit. Your shoulder has got to be killing you."

I don't admit that it is, in fact, killing me, but less because of the bag and more because of this impending flare. Regardless, I don't fight him on carrying my bag. As we head back into the fray of food trucks, I come to a compelling realization.

Caleb O'Connor looks good with a brown leather diaper bag slung over his shoulder.

CHAPTER 11
CALEB

"It looks like they have freeze pops." Hannah points toward a lime-green food truck with *"The best freeze pops in town! Or is that the brain freeze talking?"* scrawled on the side of it. We're scouting out dessert, and Hannah is weirdly dedicated to finding the perfect thing to curb my raging sweet tooth.

"Eh," I mutter. "Not enough pizzazz."

She cocks a brow at me. "We could go back and try the pickle juice pops?"

I shudder. "That might be a little too much pizzazz for me."

Her answering smile is blinding. She seems to be having a blast, and she has a little skip in her step as she heads off to find another contender.

A little while ago, Hannah made a comment about how she doesn't do this sort of thing often, and I can't help but wonder why. This festival is exactly the type of thing she would have enjoyed back in high school. She was always attending town fairs and events, oftentimes even helping run parts of them. What's changed since then?

I don't have long to wonder, because Hannah is bouncing toward a truck a few yards away, her orange ponytail swishing behind her. I follow along, her giant purse feeling a little too natural hanging off my shoulder.

We approach an Indian food truck with a big sign advertising their mango lassi. I've had the creamy yogurt drink before, and it's super refreshing.

Hannah stands next to the sign with her arms crossed and one hip jutting out, the embodiment of confidence. "How's the pizzazz level?" she asks.

"Just right," I reply, like I'm fucking Goldilocks. Something about the effort she put into finding the perfect dessert is so just damn cute to me. She was nothing but patient as I shot down each option that didn't appeal to me, never taking it personally or giving up. Her satisfied grin when I approve her choice makes it all worth it.

We head to the window to order and realize who's manning the truck at the same time.

"Oh. My. Gosh. Hi!" Rupi says, her volume just a few notches too loud. Rupi was in our graduating class. She was head cheerleader, if I remember correctly, and it seems as if she hasn't lost her cheering voice in the past five years. I often used to see the cheerleaders practicing on the sidelines during our football practices. "*Project your voices, ladies!*" the coach would shout. "*Project!*" Seems like Rupi took that message and ran with it.

"Hey," Hannah says, noticeably quieter. "How are you?"

"I'm great," Rupi replies with a flip of her hair. "You're probably surprised to see me here. My parents opened an Indian restaurant when I went to college, and when I graduated, I proposed opening a food truck. I wanted to use my marketing degree while also supporting the family biz, you know? The truck makes a nice little profit of its own, but it also drives a ton of business to the restaurant." She finally stops to take a breath. "How are you?" she tacks on, as if she's just noticed she spent that last two minutes giving a monologue about herself.

Hannah takes a moment to respond, probably because her

brain needs a few seconds to catch up after that tornado of word vomit. "I'm good, thanks."

I clear my throat to smother a laugh at the difference in their answers. Rupi pretty much gave us her whole life story since the last time we saw her, while Hannah gave the most generic answer known to man.

Rupi's gaze lands on me, and I truly think she's just now noticing that I'm standing here.

"Ohmigod!" she exclaims. "Caleb!" Her eyes dart from me to Hannah and back again. "I can't believe you two ended up together. That's *so* cute."

Hannah's cheeks tinge pink, and I quickly step in so she doesn't have to deal with Rupi anymore.

"We're not together," I explain. "I mean…we're together as friends, but we're not *together* together."

Geez, way to fumble a simple question, Caleb.

"Oh," Rupi says, her tone like a deflated balloon. "That's too bad. You'd make a cute couple."

Hannah's cheeks have grown even redder, so I make to end this conversation.

"Thanks," I reply. "Can we get two mango lassis, please?"

"Sure thing." Rupi rings us up on the register, and I pay this time. She's suspiciously quiet as she makes our drinks, and I wonder if she's really that devastated that Hannah and I aren't together.

"Here you go." Rupi hands us our drinks.

"Thanks," Hannah says.

"Good luck with the food truck," I add as we turn to walk away.

We both sip on our drinks for a few paces until we reach an empty bench where we sit down.

"So, that was kind of awkward, right?" Hannah asks.

A laugh bursts from my throat. "Yeah, that was kind of awkward."

She sighs as she sinks back into the bench. "Why does it feel like the universe keeps making us defend the fact that we're not dating?"

I hadn't thought of it that way until she verbalized it, but Hannah's right. We've been dancing around the topic of us hanging out but not dating ever since we reconnected.

"Hannah..." I begin, but I'm not really sure where I'm going until the words start to spill out. "I want to be really clear that I like you, and I'm glad we're friends again. I don't want you to think you're not...attractive, or desirable, or whatever. If I *was* dating...I don't know. I think you'd probably be the type of girl I'd go for. But I'm not interested in dating. After everything with my dad...I lost faith in love, I guess." Christ, now I'm like Rupi, rambling on about myself. "Anyway, I guess I just want to make sure you know that I value this friendship, and me not wanting to date you doesn't have anything to do with you being unlikeable in any way."

I finally cut myself off because I'm not even sure I'm making any sense.

"Caleb." Hannah waits until I meet her gaze to continue. "It's okay."

Her gentle tone immediately soothes me. I guess I was worried she was going to think that I liked her enough to hang out sometimes, but not enough to date her, which is pretty silly. Men and women can be just friends. I don't know why society always thinks that's impossible.

"I value our friendship too, and I'm not looking to date either," Hannah continues. "If one of us was looking for a relationship, things might be different. But I think we're on the same page."

I let out a sigh of relief. "Good," I say. "Then let's enjoy these drinks."

s we walk back to the car, I can tell Hannah is going slower than she was earlier in the day. The pep in her step has disappeared. I'm still carrying her bag, so it's not that weighing her down. Maybe she's just tired.

I drive Hannah back to her apartment, and we part ways, agreeing that we'll see each other at Waffee this week. I'm driving toward my place when I decide I'm not quite ready to go home yet. I lived with roommates back in California, and while I'm glad to be financially stable enough to live on my own now, I miss always having people around to talk to.

Halfway to my apartment, I veer toward Heather and Greg's instead. I just saw my sister the other day when she accosted me at my apartment, but it's been a couple of weeks since I've talked to my future brother-in-law.

"Cale!" Heather says, throwing her arms around me immediately after answering the door. "I didn't know you were coming by today."

I shrug. "I assumed your drop-in the other day meant we didn't need to warn each other."

"Of course not. It's just a nice surprise." She ushers me into the kitchen, where we find Greg sticking return labels to envelopes. For wedding invitations, I presume. Or maybe they're planning ahead, and these are already for the thank-you notes.

"Hey, bro," he says when he looks up briefly from his task.

"Hey," I reply. Greg took to calling me "bro" when he and Heather got engaged, but I haven't been able to bring myself to use the nickname back yet. I know he's about to officially be my brother-in-law, but I'm not sure I'll ever be able to call him a brother. That was Matty's title, and I don't want to feel like I'm trying to replace him.

"How's the wedding planning going?" I ask as Heather and I sit down at the kitchen table.

She huffs out a sigh. "It's going. Greg is being so helpful." She shoots him a sickening, lovey-dovey look, and he responds with a tight smile, holding up a stack of envelopes. Though he's clearly not enthused by the task, he's doing it without complaint because he loves my sister. Although I still worry about her getting married and committing herself to someone, I couldn't ask for a better man than Greg.

"We still have a lot to do, but we have a plan for everything," Heather continues. "But Caleb, it doesn't even end with the wedding." She makes a big, dramatic hand gesture. "Now I'm working on my post-wedding to-do list. It's not just thank-you cards. It's also changing my last name—which means getting a new license, passport, *everything*—combining bank accounts, getting Greg added to my health insurance plan..." She shakes her head as if it's about to explode. "There's so much to do."

"I'm sure you'll get it all done just fine," I reply, knowing my type-A sister will have lists and spreadsheets galore to make sure she doesn't forget anything. Besides, I'm sure her new husband will be more than willing to help with all those logistical tasks.

"Anyway..." Heather leans forward in her chair. "I'm *so* glad you stopped by! I had a brilliant idea. My bridesmaid, Kim—you know, from college? Well, she's the only single bridesmaid in my bridal party, and you're the only groomsman not bringing a plus-one...so I think you guys should attend the wedding together! We already have you set to process down the aisle together, but this way you could sit together and stuff too. I think you'd really like her, Cale. She's a teacher, and she's really sweet, and she'll be *so fun* on the dance floor."

"Heather," I groan. My sister just can't seem to get it through her thick skull that I don't want to have a date at her wedding. "I don't want to go with Kim. Won't that mess up your seating chart, anyway?"

Heather waves her hand as if that magically erases the problem. "Kim's tiny. We can squeeze her in."

Greg shoots me a sympathetic look. By his expression, I can tell that he's already tried and failed to talk Heather out of this plan.

"Look, Heather," I say, hoping she can hear the seriousness in my tone. "I appreciate that you're trying to do a good thing here —I really do. And I'm sure Kim is awesome, but I don't want her to be my date to your wedding. I want to attend alone, as the bride's brother. Is that too much to ask?"

Heather looks up toward the ceiling as if she's really thinking hard about this, then settles her gaze back on me. "Yes, it is. It's my wedding, and I'll use it as an opportunity for my brother to find love if I want to. If you don't choose your own plus-one, I'm putting Kim next to you at our table. I'm not saying you have to do anything other than give her a chance."

I put my forehead down on the table, lightly banging it a few times.

"Heather," Greg says in a warning tone, and suddenly I feel bad that he's being dragged into this. It's typical, stubborn Heather doing what she genuinely thinks is best. Despite my differing opinion, I love her annoying ass.

"Fine." I look toward my sister. "Give me a little time, and if I can't find someone I want to bring, I'll go with Kim."

Heather's face lights up. "Yay!"

After my whole monologue about why I don't want to date Hannah today, I probably can't ask her. I'd use the app I'm working on to try and find someone to bring, but I already know it won't give me anyone with a compatibility rating higher than Hannah. Worst comes to worst, I'll go with Kim. All it will entail will be a little conversation, a little dancing, and there'll be plenty of alcohol to use as a social lubricant.

It couldn't be that bad, right?

CHAPTER 12
CALEB

I drum my fingers against the table as I sit in Waffee on Wednesday afternoon. I've barely gotten any work done because every few seconds I'm glancing at the door, hoping to find Hannah walking through. I haven't seen her at all since the weekend, despite spending an inordinate amount of time in our usual meeting place.

I thought we had a great time at the festival together, and she seemed almost relieved when we had the conversation about us not dating, so I don't know what could be keeping her away. She didn't mention anything she had going on this week that would keep her away from Waffee.

Instead of stewing any longer, I decide to shoot her a text asking what's up. I want to be caring, but casual. After a few drafts, I finally land on:

How's it going, Reilly? Haven't seen you around Waffee all week.

She doesn't respond immediately. I try to return to my work, but I'm more than a little distracted. When my phone finally buzzes, I grab it with the lightning-fast reflexes of a cat catching a mouse.

Hey, sorry. I've been sick.

My pulse immediately ratchets up. What kind of sick? Is it serious? Is she okay? Does she need anything?

I force a deep breath into my lungs before responding. Ever since Matty's illness, I know I can go a little overboard when people get sick. The first signs of his cancer were fairly innocuous things like headaches and nausea, so my brain tends to immediately overinflate common symptoms and automatically assume the worst.

After assuring myself Hannah is most likely fine, I text back a much more chill version of my questions.

U ok? Need anything?

Fine, maybe just some kind of virus.

Can I do anything? Bring you anything?

No, I wouldn't want you to catch anything from me.

I roll my eyes at the response. Of course she's thinking about my well-being instead of her own.

I would have caught it on Sunday if I was going to catch it. I'd be happy to bring you groceries or medicine if you need it.

Nah, I'm fine. Hope to see you soon.

My fingers hover over my phone as I try to decide whether to push the issue or not. My gut tells me Hannah wouldn't be honest even if she really did need something, but I don't want to annoy her by continually texting. Instead, I respond with a very cool and chill:

Back at ya.

Without the possibility of Hannah joining me, Waffee loses its luster, so I pack up to head back to my apartment to finish out my workday. I've been making tweaks based on the results we have so far from our alpha testers' feedback—things like adjusting how much information you can see about each match before clicking to view their full profile and adding a mechanism so you can see if the other person is typing in the messaging system.

I also deleted Hannah's profile from the app. I know it was probably silly, but I was worried my coworkers would see the high match percentage between us and ask me about it. They wouldn't even know that I knew Hannah or that I was the one who had her test out the app—it could have been anyone at the company—but I still didn't want to deal with any potential heckling. I get enough of that from my family.

The only evidence of Hannah's and my match profile is a screenshot I took and housed in a folder on my computer labeled "Grandma's Foot Pics." Who would ever want to open that?

At five p.m. sharp, I slam my laptop shut and stretch my arms over my head. I'm already getting hungry, but I know my fridge is practically empty. Luckily, there's a small market I can walk to down the street, so I grab my wallet and head out.

I only intended to grab a few things—a box of pasta, a jar of tomato sauce, and a loaf of bread—but when I pass the soup aisle, I come to a dead stop. Chicken noodle is on a two-for-one sale. That feels like a sign that I should pick some up for Hannah. I dump two cans into my basket and get to thinking about what else she might like.

She didn't specifically tell me any of her symptoms, but if she has a sore throat, she might appreciate some ice cream. I grab a carton of mint chocolate chip from the freezer. I personally think it's sacrilegious to mix mint flavoring with any form of dessert, but I know it's her favorite.

With my soup and ice cream, plus the items I actually came for, I check out and walk back to my car. It would be easy enough to drive to Hannah's apartment and leave the stuff outside her door. She claims she doesn't want me to catch anything from her, but she can't object if we never actually come face to face.

Should I text her to let her know I'm dropping it off? She'd probably just tell me not to. A surprise attack might be the best way.

When I arrive, I stand awkwardly outside Hannah's door. My plan to drop the bags and run seemed like a good one in theory, but now that I'm here with only a door separating me from an ambiguously sick Hannah, I can't bear to walk away without checking on her.

After the first knock, I wait a couple minutes but get no answer. Hannah could have been in the bathroom or something, so I knock again. When I still don't get an answer, I start to worry that perhaps she's asleep. Or maybe she's not actually sick, and she *is* blowing me off after we hung out last weekend.

I'm about to revert back to plan A and put the bags down when the door inches open.

"Hannah?" I ask, peering through the slight opening in the door.

"Caleb?" she croaks as she pushes the door all the way open. Any thoughts of her faking being sick vanish instantly. She's all wrapped up in a fluffy pink bathrobe, and her feet are encased in matching slippers. Her orange hair sits on the top of her head in some semblance of a bun. Sleep still crusts the corners of her eyes, and she looks a little dazed. Her cheeks are all rosy, and without thinking, I place the back of one hand on her forehead.

"You're warm," I say as I push my way into the apartment. It looks markedly different from the last time I saw it. Granted, I only caught a glimpse of it from the doorway last weekend, but I know it didn't look like this. Empty water bottles are strewn over the couch and the floor, joined by a few empty takeout containers on the coffee table. A pile of unfolded blankets sits in the corner of the living room, topped by what looks like an electric heating pad. There's a haphazard stack of books and magazines on the small table beside the couch, as well as a mishmash of small bottles.

"It's just a little fever," Hannah says around a yawn. "I'm due for more Tylenol right around now."

I place the bags of groceries on the kitchen counter, grabbing the ice cream and getting it into the freezer.

"Where do you keep the Tylenol?" I ask as Hannah slumps down onto the couch.

"Bathroom cabinet," she replies. Her eyes are already drooping. I hustle to the bathroom to make sure she gets her next dose before she falls asleep. I fill up a small cup of water and hand it to her along with two Tylenol.

"Take these," I say, joining her on the couch.

She dutifully swallows the pills. "Thank you." Confusion scrunches her brows together. "What are you doing here?"

I settle further back into the couch to let her know that not only am I here, but I'm not leaving anytime soon. "I was at the grocery store, and they were having a sale on soup. I figured if you were sick, you could use some."

"Oh." Hannah pulls the string on her bathrobe a little tighter. I can tell she's wearing clothing underneath—fabric peeks out from the neckline, and the stretch of her legs not covered by the bathrobe shows off leggings printed with kittens in various yoga poses—but she clearly doesn't want me to see her like this.

"I know you said not to come over, but..." I run my fingers through my hair, pushing it away from my face. "I guess I have a hard time ignoring it when someone I care about isn't feeling well."

Hannah's doe eyes widen a fraction before she turns away. "Sorry about the mess," she says with a grimace, her gaze scanning the living room.

I put a hand on her knee. "Don't be. No one should be expected to clean when they're sick, nor should they be expected to cook. Will you eat some soup if I heat it up?"

She nods, and I stand. I can hear the crunch of plastic water bottles behind my back as I walk to the kitchen.

"Stop cleaning and relax," I call out. The crunching stops, and I smile to myself.

The soup doesn't take long to heat up on the stove, and I pour a big serving into a bowl. I wanted Hannah to be able to stay on the couch to eat, but I'm not sure she'll be able to balance the bowl that well, so I place it on the kitchen table and peek into the living room. Hannah is still seated on the couch, now with the electric heating pad behind her neck and shoulders. Her eyes are closed as she leans back into the warmth, but I don't think she's asleep.

"Do you want to try and eat in here, or do you think you can sit at the kitchen table?"

Hannah's eyes pop open. "The kitchen is good."

I pour the leftover soup into a small bowl for me and sit across from Hannah. She ladles a small spoonful of soup and blows on it before slurping it up.

"How long have you been feeling sick?" I ask, trying to gauge how serious this illness is. Did the fever just come on today? Or has it been going on for a while now?

Hannah has another spoonful of soup before answering. "It started coming on the night after we hung out. Like I said, it might just be a virus. It'll pass."

"Have your siblings been by at all?" I think about what Heather would do if I was holed up alone in my apartment, sick as a dog. Granted, she's a nurse and therefore obligated to help the sick, but I couldn't see her leaving me on my own to suffer regardless.

Hannah swirls her spoon through the bowl of soup, drawing invisible patterns. "Owen Insta-carted me some groceries. Annie took over Mom duties and drove her to her appointment yesterday. Apparently, that was enough good deeds from them for the week."

There's an edge to her voice that I don't think I've ever heard before. Resentment.

A small grin grows on her face. "Rhia came for our usual Monday-night *Bachelor* viewing and brought me a few days' worth of takeout, which was nice."

Thank God for Rhia. At least *someone* in Hannah's life thought to tend to her needs while she was under the weather. Her mom probably would have done more to help if she wasn't laid up with a broken leg, but her siblings really should be stepping up more, if you ask me.

"You shouldn't have to be alone when you're sick."

"I'm used to it," Hannah says so softly I almost don't catch it. In the next breath, she's already moving on. "Did I see you unpacking ice cream earlier?"

"Ah, I see," I tease around my last spoonful of soup. "Even through your fever-induced haze, you couldn't miss that."

Hannah tilts her head to one side. "What flavor?"

"Maple walnut," I say with as straight a face as possible.

Disgust flashes across her face before she quickly smooths it into a polite smile. "Thank you."

I shake my head with a chuckle. "Don't think I didn't catch that face, Reilly. I got mint chocolate chip."

Her smile turns genuine. "Oh, thank God. I was hoping I wouldn't have to choke down a bowl of maple walnut just to be polite." Her lips fall into an expression of genuine concern. "But you hate mint chocolate chip. What are you going to have?"

I scratch at my beard. "I, uh... I hadn't really planned on coming in. I was just going to drop the bags for you, but then I got here and..."

"You saw how pathetic my apartment and I look?" she guesses.

I grin, glad she feels well enough for humor. "Something like that."

Hannah takes our empty bowls to the sink, piling them on top of the mountain of dirty dishes that already resides there. "I'll take care of these in the morning."

"I have a better idea," I reply. "Why don't you go sit on the couch, and I'll bring you a bowl of mint chocolate chip to enjoy while I do these dishes?"

Her eyes widen, and if I'm not mistaken, they actually start to fill with tears. "You don't have to do that," she practically whispers.

I take Hannah's shoulders and steer her over to the living room, not giving her a choice. "No, I don't. But I want to."

She sinks onto the couch like a stone, the dazed look from

earlier creeping back onto her face. "That would be...really nice. Thank you, Caleb."

By the time I return with her bowl of ice cream, Hannah has already cozied herself up on the couch, and she has a sitcom playing on the television. When she spies me, she reaches for the bowl with grabby hands.

"Here you go," I say as I hand it over. "One heaping bowl of maple walnut."

"Ha ha," Hannah deadpans, already digging into her ice cream. She spears the biggest scoop with her spoon but stops midway through obtaining her first bite. When she looks toward me, her expression is sober. "Really, Caleb, thank you for the food and for helping with the dishes. It...it means a lot."

"It's not a big deal," I reply, and truly, it isn't. I was already at the grocery store for myself, so grabbing a few extra items for Hannah was easy. And it's no chore to spend time with her. What I'm doing seems like the bare minimum, but something tells me it's a big deal to her.

"Enjoy that ice cream," I say as I head back to the kitchen to take care of the dishes. It's mostly plates and bowls with minimal residue stuck on them, so they're not all that hard to clean. It just takes me a bit since they've evidently been piling up since the weekend.

When I return to the living room about twenty minutes later, I find Hannah fast asleep on the couch, the empty ice cream bowl perched on her chest. I watch as it rises and falls with her breaths. She's completely passed out. At least she got some Tylenol in her before she fell asleep. Now, I just have to figure out how to get her into bed without waking her.

CHAPTER 13
HANNAH

Growing up, I took great pride in my reliability and consistency. I was the person that was always there for others. If we made plans, I showed up. If I made a promise, I kept it.

My best friend would say it's the Virgo in me. Others may blame it on me being an eldest sister. Either way, dependability used to be my trademark.

Then I got sick. It's hard to be reliable when your body isn't.

---

wake up to the smell of coffee, but that can't be possible. I suppose Rhia could have come over but... No. I peek over at my bedside clock, which reads 8:05 a.m. She's never up this early. She reads into the wee hours of the night then sleeps late.

Maybe I'm just having some sort of fever dream. Leave it to me to think about coffee in my sleep.

As I slowly gain consciousness, however, I realize that I do, indeed, smell coffee, which means there must be someone here. Then it dawns on me. Caleb came over last night. He brought me food and washed my dishes. And I...fell asleep on the couch. So how am I waking up in my bed?

I pry my eyes open and yawn as I shuck off the covers. I'm still in the yoga-cat leggings and white cotton tank top I've been wearing for the last couple of days. I look down at my outfit. *Shit.* This tank top is totally see-through, and I'm not wearing a bra. I'm sure Caleb didn't come over expecting a peep show. Oh well. He deserved a treat for helping me out the way he did.

As my brain fully awakens, memories from last night come flooding back. Caleb brought me soup and mint chocolate chip ice cream, remembering my favorite flavor from when we were younger. He washed my dishes. He said he cares about me. And though I don't remember it, he must have put me to bed. Caleb went out of his way to be kind to me because he knew I was sick.

And I lied to him.

Well, I didn't *really* lie. I used words like "maybe" or "might" when talking about potentially having a virus. And technically, I *could* have one, but I'm ninety-nine percent sure this is an autoimmune flare.

As I put in my morning dose of prescription eye drops, I decide I'll tell Caleb the truth. I can't, in good conscience, go out there and continue to pretend this is something it's not while he makes me coffee and continues taking care of me. Plus, if we stay friends after he learns that I lied to him, this is going to happen again. And again and again. Because chronic illnesses never go away. They just ebb and flow.

I throw a t-shirt over my tank top—though for a split second I consider leaving it off. Maybe I could use my boobs to distract Caleb and soften the blow. But no, I'm an adult, and this is a conversation I need to have.

I scurry to the bathroom to brush my teeth and do something with my hair before venturing into the kitchen, where I find Caleb standing at the counter with his back turned to me. He hasn't noticed me yet, so I take the opportunity to study him. He has on the same clothes he did last night, since he obviously didn't expect to be staying over. His jeans and white t-shirt are wrinkled—probably from sleeping on the couch—and his hair is pulled back into a small bun at the nape of his neck. I idly wonder if he used one of my hair ties or if he has his own. The muscles in his arms work as he focuses on making an espresso shot. I only have a small machine at my apartment—nothing like the impressive monster at Waffee—but it allows me to make a decent enough latte at home. Caleb is loading the portafilter into the machine when I decide to make my presence known.

"Finally coming over to the dark side?" I quip.

His head swivels. "Oh, hey. No, this is for you. I was going to bring you breakfast in bed." His brow furrows as he turns back to make sure everything is in place before turning on the machine to let it heat up.

I take a seat at the kitchen table to watch the show, which is when I notice something perched on the counter a few feet from Caleb.

"Why is my bathroom scale out here?" I wonder aloud.

"Oh." His gaze turns toward the scale, and he scratches at his beard. "I, uh… Well, I've never used an espresso machine before, so I watched a few YouTube tutorials this morning. I wanted to be able to make your latte right."

My brows lift at the thought of Caleb watching instructional videos just to be able to make me my favorite morning drink.

"I learned quite a bit." He rubs his knuckles over his jaw. "For example, I never knew that squishing the coffee grounds into the thingy is known as *tamping*. The videos recommended using twenty to thirty pounds of pressure, but I wasn't sure how to gauge that, so…" Caleb pauses long enough that I'm not sure he actually plans to finish that sentence, so I take a not-so-wild guess.

"So, you used my bathroom scale to tamp down the grounds with the correct amount of pressure to ensure it made the best shot of espresso possible?"

"Yes," he confirms, releasing a breath of relief, as if not having to admit that out loud really took a load off him. "But don't worry. I washed it and stuff before I used it in the kitchen."

I bite back a grin. "I trust you."

It's hard to tell beneath his beard, but I do believe Caleb's cheeks have turned an adorable shade of pink.

The light on the machine turns green, indicating that it's ready to dispense the espresso. Caleb focuses once more on his task, pulling me a perfect double shot. Those video tutorials must have been quite thorough.

"How are you feeling this morning?" he asks as he heads to the fridge.

"I'm alright," I answer. "The fever seems to have broken."

Caleb shoots me a wide grin. "That's great."

I chew on my thumbnail as he doctors my latte with almond milk. Now is the time to tell him the truth. I'm considering just how to do it when my gaze snags on another item on the counter: my massive pill sorter. I sit down once every four weeks and dole out the entire month's worth of pills. It's a daunting task since I take so many, but I'd rather do it once a month than every single week.

Caleb presents me my latte, wearing a proud smile. "Here you go."

"Thank you." I accept the drink but find myself fiddling with it in my hands rather than taking a sip. "Would you mind handing me that pill sorter over there?" I point to it on the counter.

"Sure." Caleb grabs it and hands it over to me. "Man, that thing is serious," he says with a chuckle.

I purse my lips, using this as the opening to my confession. "Yeah, it kind of is."

Caleb's smile slowly descends, and his brows pull together, his gaze wandering from the pill box to me. "Are you... Is this... Is this not a regular sickness?" he asks, swallowing hard. His Adam's apple dips as he takes in the number of pills I consume on a daily basis. "Are you...*sick* sick?"

"Yes," I reply, relieved he's caught on. At my answer, he pales to a worrisome shade, and I quickly realize my mistake. "It's not cancer, Caleb," I reassure him. "It's not terminal. I have two autoimmune diseases."

He grabs the back of one of the kitchen chairs as if to steady himself. Then he drops into the chair with a heavy thump. "What does that mean?"

I set my drink aside so I can give him my full attention. "They're chronic illnesses that cause my immune system to attack healthy cells in my body. The specific diseases I have are called Lupus and Sjogren's."

"Loo-piss and show-grins," he repeats back slowly. "Okay." He's staring at the table, slowly nodding his head as he processes what I'm saying. "So, basically your immune system is attacking the wrong stuff?"

"Right," I reply. "Autoimmune diseases put your immune system in overdrive. Instead of attacking invading cells like the flu or a cold, it attacks healthy cells that it mistakes for invaders. Some people describe it as your body being allergic to itself."

Caleb rakes his fingers through his beard. "Jesus."

"Autoimmune diseases can have lots of different symptoms," I forge on. "For me, they result in varying levels of fatigue and joint pain. Sjogren's specifically attacks moisture-producing glands, causing things like dry eyes and mouth, while the Lupus is more likely to affect my organs, specifically my kidneys."

Caleb is finally looking at me instead of the table, which allows me to better gauge his reaction. There's worry written on his features, but not so much that I'm afraid he can't handle what I'm telling him. With the way he lost Matty, it's only natural that he would be extra nervous about medical conditions. *I guess I have a hard time ignoring it when someone I care about isn't feeling well,* he said last night.

"What happened this week is an autoimmune flare," I explain. "All my typical symptoms are essentially exacerbated tenfold, and the fever and rash on my face appear as well."

Caleb is quiet for a beat. When he finally speaks, his voice is low. "What makes a flare happen?"

I tilt my head side to side. "Sometimes it's random. Sometimes flares are caused by stress or overexertion. A regular virus like a cold or flu can set off a flare as well. You can't always control them."

He crosses his arms over the table. "What made *this* flare happen?"

I take a sip of my latte, and my taste buds sing a *Hallelujah* chorus. "This is fantastic," I say. "Good job, Caleb."

"Hannah," he says in a stern tone that sends a shiver up my spine. "What made this flare happen?"

I drum my fingers against the side of my latte. "I just overdid it this past week. It happens sometimes. It's not a big deal."

Caleb pins me with his gaze, his espresso eyes boring into mine. "Did I cause this?"

"No," I answer immediately, registering the guilt in his expression. "*I* did. I knew I was going downhill at the end of last week, but I still chose to hang out with you."

"We could have hung out another time."

"I know," I reply. "But I wanted to go to the festival. It was my decision, and I don't regret it. Besides, if I hadn't put myself into a flare, you wouldn't have shown up here with mint chocolate chip ice cream."

Caleb rewards me with a half-smile for my attempt at humor. Then, his lips fall into a thin line. "I don't want you to be sick," he whispers.

I swallow thickly. Caleb has lost so much in his life. At only twenty-five, he's had a brother die and a father abandon him. Now, he becomes friends with me again only to find out I'm chronically ill.

"I don't want to be sick either," I say gently. "But I am, and I have to live with it for the rest of my life, which will hopefully be a long one. These diseases flare and remit and change over time, but people with autoimmune diseases typically live average lifespans."

Relief washes over Caleb's features. "Thank God." Most of

the color has returned to his face, and when he stands from his chair, he's no longer shaky. Instead, he stands tall and asks, "Can I... Can I give you a hug?"

My heart flutters at the request. "Of course," I scratch out from my dry throat.

As I stand, I'm swept into his strong embrace. Caleb's not one of those half-assed huggers. He's a full-on, both-arms-squeezing kind of hugger. My face is pressed to his t-shirt as he hangs on tight.

"I don't want to lose you," he whispers against my ear, his beard scraping my cheek.

I tighten my hold on him. "You won't."

"Good," he rumbles. "Because I just got you back."

Even though he means it platonically, the sentiment still sends a shockwave through my system. Ever since I got sick, people seem relieved when they're able to free themselves of my friendship. A relationship with me generally seems to be a burden to be carried, one that most people are desperate to put down.

Caleb is the opposite.

"You have to be honest with me about how you're feeling," he says, still not letting me go. "No more overdoing it. We can always stay in, watch movies, stuff like that. Don't do things that aren't healthy for you."

"Okay," I agree, loving the sound of a movie night in with Caleb. Now that he knows the truth, I'll feel more comfortable requesting alternative activities. He finally releases his hold on me, but he's still standing close enough that I have to tilt my neck back to look up at him.

"Thank you for taking care of me last night," I say softly.

He brushes some rogue red hair behind my ear. "Anytime," he promises. "Thank you for telling me the truth about your illnesses."

I shoot him a guilty smile. "Anytime."

His lips curve upward, a soft grin nestled amongst his beard.

We're standing so close together, our faces just inches apart. Suddenly, it strikes me just how much I'd like him to lean forward and plant his lips on mine. It's not just because he looks as handsome as ever with his long hair slightly unruly from sleeping on the couch. It's not even because he took care of me last night. I want Caleb to kiss me because he's the first person since I got sick to hear about my illnesses and want to be closer to me, not farther apart.

Realizing I've been looking up into his deep brown eyes for a moment too long, I tear my gaze away.

Caleb clears his throat. "Is there anything else I can help you with before I get going? I can come back later if you need me to, but I'm meeting Heather and Greg for brunch this morning."

"No, I'm good," I reply, clearing my own throat when my voice comes out raspy. "You've done more than enough."

"Okay." Caleb wraps me up in another much quicker goodbye hug. "You'll text me if anything comes up?"

"Sure."

He uses a finger to tip my chin until I meet his gaze. "I'm serious."

I swallow a gulp. "I will."

It's not until Caleb is out the door that I notice that takeout boxes and empty water bottles no longer litter my living room. My entire apartment has been cleaned, not just the dishes. And upon further inspection, the soil in each and every one of my many flowerpots is damp to the touch, clearly having been watered. That man must have been up half the night getting my apartment in order.

I don't think I've ever felt so thoroughly cared for in my entire life. When I took the quizzes on Caleb's app, it told me my top love language was acts of service. The glowing ember in my chest that is my heart, lit up by a mixture of comfort and gratitude, tells me it was right.

CHAPTER 14
CALEB

Relief floods me when Hannah walks into Waffee on Wednesday looking like her usual self. She texted on Monday to let me know she was going to spend a few more days resting but would be back in action soon. I just barely managed to restrain myself from going over to her apartment again. As much as I want to be there for her, I don't want to crowd or suffocate her. She clearly keeps her health issues pretty private.

There was also...a moment. After we hugged, she was looking up at me with this expression of gratitude and almost... awe? I'm not sure. We were standing super close together, and my brain was kind of boggled by the proximity. That close, I could make out every freckle on her face, every curve of her supple lips. Lips that were practically begging to be kissed.

Every fiber of my being wanted to close the gap between us, seal my lips over hers, and show her that she was safe with me. That I would take care of her in any and every way she needed. But she was vulnerable, having just disclosed her illnesses to me. I would never take advantage of that.

Now, Hannah heads straight for our usual table, wearing a bright smile and an even brighter pink sundress. The flimsy straps holding it up threaten to spill right off her shoulders. I resist the urge to jump up and tighten them somehow, not because I don't enjoy the thought of seeing more of her creamy skin but because the thought of anyone *else* getting to see it physically pains me. That's a normal friend thing, right?

"Hey," she greets me breezily, as if the other night never happened.

"Hi," I reply, happy she's feeling better but not ready to just act like things are back to normal. "How are you doing?"

Hannah drops her laptop back on the table. "I'm good. Much better. I'm gonna grab a drink. Can I get you anything?"

"I'm good." I hold up my iced tea and swirl it around a bit, making the ice clank against the side of the cup.

"Be right back."

I can't help but watch as Hannah sashays away. The dress isn't tight, but it still accentuates all the right things. It's cinched around her waist, hugging her hips before flowing down to just above her knees. With each step she takes, I catch a glimpse of the curve of her ass.

Once she reaches the counter to order, I tear my gaze away and back to my laptop. The view is much less appealing. I'm deep into the coding for Meet Your Match, making tiny little changes that require meticulous care. Realizing I probably can't give this task the attention it needs right now, I close out of my development environment.

Hannah returns to our table, placing her usual iced caramel latte down next to her laptop bag. She drops into her seat, one of her dress straps sliding all the way to the edge of her shoulder. Those goddamn flimsy spaghetti straps will be the death of me.

She pulls it back to its rightful spot and takes a sip of her drink.

I frown. "I, um..." I have to clear my throat before continuing. "I read online that caffeine can trigger autoimmune flares."

Hannah's eyebrows lift as she slowly places her drink down on the table. "You were reading about my illnesses?"

I can't tell if she's royally pissed off or just surprised to hear this. Did I cross a line here?

"Yeah," I reply carefully. "I wanted to educate myself more about them so I didn't have to ask you so many questions. I figured that might be stressful for you, so I did a little research."

A gorgeous, shy smile blooms on her lips. "That was really thoughtful, Caleb. Thank you."

"Don't thank me," I reply gruffly. "It's literally the least I could do."

A doubtful look crosses her face. "Trust me, it's more than most people do."

I want to dig deeper into that statement, but she's already speaking again.

"You can always ask me questions. I know I didn't open up right away, but I really don't mind talking about my diseases."

"Okay," I say. "So…the caffeine? It's not a problem for you?"

She shakes her head. "Coffee has never been a problem for me. I was drinking it regularly before getting sick, so I already had somewhat of a tolerance built up. Still, I never drink more than two cups a day. And actually, coffee can be anti-inflammatory, which is a good thing, since autoimmune diseases are linked with inflammation. But honestly, even if coffee wasn't necessarily the best thing for me, I'm not sure I'd stop drinking it."

Hannah must read the confusion on my face because she quickly begins explaining her stance.

"There are so many things I can't do or have because of my illnesses. I can't work a traditional full-time job, I can't go on a spontaneous trip without making sure I have all my medications and tools with me, and I can't seem to sustain friendships or relationships for the life of me. I've lost a lot to these illnesses, so when I have the chance to fight back, to say 'screw you' to autoimmune disease, even if it might not necessarily be the best thing for my body, I do it. It's why I went to the festival with you even though I knew it might send me into a flare. It's why I refuse to deprive myself of the little joys, like coffee." She takes a sip of her latte as if to punctuate that statement.

As much as I want to disagree—to say that she should be doing everything in her power to stay as healthy as possible—I actually think it's pretty badass that Hannah doesn't let her diseases stop her from doing whatever the fuck she wants.

I take a drag of my iced tea. "Well, I can't say coffee brings me any joy, but since it does for you, I'm glad you're still able to have it."

Hannah smiles, seeming pleased with my response. I wonder if other people have tried to talk her out of doing things she loves that might not necessarily be the best for her. I can see where her loved ones would, out of a misguided sense of protectiveness that doesn't consider the fact that she's the only one who knows what it's like to live in her body, with her limitations, and how frustrating it must be sometimes. How gratifying it must be to cheat every once in a while, consequences be damned.

Sometimes I think the people who love us are less worried about our suffering and more worried about how much they don't want to *see* us suffering.

"What did you mean earlier?" I ask. "When you said you haven't been able to sustain relationships since getting sick?"

Hannah fiddles with her coffee cup, running one long, slender finger around the rim. Her eyes take on a faraway look as she launches into a tale from her past.

"When I got sick, I had just started my junior year of college," she explains. "The first two years of school, I lived on campus, made friends, had a boyfriend—did all the normal college things. But when I returned for my junior year, something wasn't right. I was exhausted, getting sick all the time, popping fevers left and right. I tried to push through and keep up with everything I had been doing, but eventually, I was sleeping all the time, missing classes, and I was never hanging out with my friends.

"I got my diagnoses in mid-October that year, and I decided to leave school. At first it was just going to be for the rest of the semester, but then it turned into the rest of the year, and then I ended up never going back. My boyfriend dumped me the week I was diagnosed. I guess having a girlfriend with diseases he'd never heard of was too scary for him. My friends tried to stay in touch at first, but it tapered off pretty quickly. They didn't know how to be friends with me when we weren't living in close proximity, apparently.

"Ever since, it's been almost impossible to make *new* friends because I really don't get out much, except to here." She gestures around the interior of Waffee. "And, well, no one wants to be friends with the unreliable girl who might have to cancel plans on a dime and prefers to stay in and chat on the couch instead of going out on adventures every weekend."

She says this all so resignedly, as if she's accepted this as fact.

"Hannah…" I can't come up with a response that adequately portrays how sad and simultaneously outraged her story makes me. "I'm so sorry. Those weren't real friends because real friends can make friendship work no matter what. I hate that they made the hardest time of your life even harder for you. And that boyfriend…don't even get me started. You'd better never tell me his name, because I *will* look him up, and I *will* go punch him in the face for leaving you in that vulnerable state." I crack my knuckles as if gearing up to do just that. "And just for the record," I add, "I would chat on the couch with you anytime."

Hannah's big brown eyes are brimming with tears when I finish talking. I can't imagine she's sad at the thought of me pummeling her loser ex, so it must be the validation that her friends weren't true friends that has her getting emotional. It pisses me right the fuck off that the people who were supposed to support Hannah ended up abandoning her instead. I know just how shitty that feels because it's what my dad did to me.

Without uttering a word, Hannah gets up and skirts around the table. I'm still seated when she wraps her arms around my neck, but we fit together perfectly. I sling one arm around her waist and tug her in to sit on the corner of my chair. She's not exactly in my lap, but she's not exactly *not* in my lap. Luckily, her favorite table is tucked away in a quiet corner of the café, and it's not overly busy on this particular Wednesday, so we have some privacy.

"Thank you," she whispers as she hugs me. "You don't know how much it means that you understand."

I rub her back through the thin fabric of her dress. "I'll never understand exactly what you went through," I reply. "But I understand what it's like to have the people who are supposed to care about you walk away when things get tough. It sucks, and it's not fair, but at least it shows you their true colors."

Hannah pulls back enough for me to see her face, and my gut clenches at the twin tears sliding down her cheeks.

"I wish we hadn't lost touch in college," she says softly.

I wipe one tear away with the pad of my thumb, cupping her cheek in my palm. "Me too. I wish I had been there for you when those others weren't. I never would have left you."

She leans her face into my touch. "I know."

Once again, there's a moment. Hannah has been so open and vulnerable with me, and we're so close together, and my brain is screaming at me to comfort her with a kiss. Before my body can betray me by following through, Hannah stands, wiping another tear from her cheek.

"I'm gonna go splash some cold water on my face," she says.

Once she's gone, I take a deep breath, shaking off that visceral urge to kiss her. A little *ding* coming from her laptop catches my attention. Hannah left it open, which is uncharacteristic of her, but then again, she was a bit frazzled. It dings again, and I turn the laptop toward me, planning to look for the mute button when what's on the screen distracts me.

The noise was an email alert, and her latest email is open on the screen. It's long—multiple paragraphs long—and filled with bolded words and words written in all capital letters, like "NO

ONE BELIEVES ME" and "PLEASE HELP." At first, I legiti-
mately wonder if it's some kind of scam, like someone asking for
ransom money because their kid was kidnapped or something.
But when I look closer at the content of the message, I realize it's
a plea for Hannah's help.

The first part of the message is a dissertation on this person's
health and the symptoms they've been experiencing lately. The
second part is them begging for Hannah to guide them to a
doctor who will help them. It's pretty heavy stuff.

I'm so engrossed in the email that I don't realize Hannah has
returned until I hear her ask, "What are you doing?"

CHAPTER 15
HANNAH

'm horrified as soon as I realize what's happening. I forgot to shut my laptop when I went to the bathroom, and Caleb is looking at whatever page I left open. I wrack my brain to remember what it was. Hopefully it was just my Instagram. Or was it my email? Please tell me it wasn't the blog post I've been working on about the best brands of lubricant for vaginal dryness. I know the information is relevant and important, but I'd rather that not be his introduction to what I do for a living.

"Hey, sorry…" he trails off, turning my laptop around as if he wasn't just potentially exposed to deeply personal information. "It kept dinging, and I couldn't figure out how to turn it off…"

I snatch the laptop with a bit too much force. "There's a mute button on the top right of the keyboard." I press it and quickly scan the screen. It's open to an email that's clearly from a reader on a quest for diagnosis. Not the worst thing he could have seen, but not as harmless as something like a social media page would have been.

Caleb's lips seal into a thin line, and I realize I'm being unfair. He really didn't do anything wrong. He was just trying to stop my laptop from making noise. I know all too well how aggravating that ding of doom can be. For me personally, the irritation usually stems from the fact that it's typically announcing another message from a person desperate for help and validation. While it's part of my job to read and respond to these messages, the emotional toll it takes on me isn't insignificant. Not only is it draining to read about someone else's hard times, but it also brings up all the traumatic feelings I experienced during my own diagnosis journey.

"I'm sorry." I drop into my seat. "I shouldn't have snapped at you."

Caleb laces his fingers together on the table. "It's okay," he says. "But Hannah...that message was intense. Who was that from?"

"It was most likely from a reader," I explain, knowing it's time to lay it all on the table. "I'm not just a freelance writer. I actually make most of my money as a health and wellness blogger, specifically focused on chronic illness."

His brows furrow. "What does that mean?"

"I have a blog where I write about what it's like to live with chronic illness," I explain. "I share tips, tricks, and products to make life easier. I run ads and do paid posts, and I make a commission when people buy the products I link. My social media pages have grown popular in the chronic illness community, so that helps me make income too."

Caleb nods along. "That's really cool." He cracks a smile. "You're like a legit influencer."

I cringe, making a face like I've sucked on a sour lemon. "I hate that word, but yes, according to today's society, I could be considered an influencer. I do some paid posts on social media, but mostly it drives traffic to my blog."

He's nodding again, and I can practically see the wheels turning in his mind. "I imagine this job gives you a good amount of flexibility, and since it allows you to work from home, you can customize your days along with your energy levels."

"Exactly." I grin, relieved he seems to understand the importance of this job for me, and he doesn't seem at all put off by the whole influencer thing. He didn't immediately view my job as a joke like so many do.

"So where do emails like that fit in?" He points at my now closed laptop.

I release a sigh. "Well, the downside to becoming known as somewhat of a chronic illness expert is that people turn to you for advice. When their doctors aren't listening to them or validating them, they turn to you for help. It's an honor to be a safe space for people like that, but the long, trauma-dumping emails can be a lot to handle."

His furrowed brow is back. "I can see how it would be. You're not a doctor or a therapist, nor are you being paid as such. It's not fair of people to dump all that on you."

"I know," I say, "but I also remember what it was like to feel completely unlike myself, like my body was an enemy I had little to no understanding of. I feel for these people and what they're going through, and if no one else is there for them, how can I not be?"

Caleb shakes his head, seeming annoyed on my behalf. "It's not your job to be everyone's saving grace. No one should be held to that standard."

I shrug, not disagreeing with him, but also unable to admit that perhaps this part of my job has taken an unhealthy turn. "I'm getting better at directing those types of readers to other resources. I know I can't help everyone, but that doesn't change the fact that I want to." I slump back in my seat. "Anyway, that's not even the most stressful part of my job at the moment."

Caleb's annoyance turns to concern. "What is?"

"Well, as much as I love working for myself and having the flexibility that I do, it also means that when I turn twenty-six and can no longer get health insurance through my parents, I have to find it another way. I don't have a company backing me that can provide it."

"Ah, that sucks," Caleb says. "And it makes me feel incredibly spoiled. My company provides health insurance for free."

My eyes practically bug out of my head. "What?"

"Yeah." He nods. "A lot of start-ups with wealthier founders are doing it these days as an incentive to work for them. There are still co-pays and stuff for appointments, but there's no monthly cost for employees."

I can't help the jealousy burning in my chest that someone like Caleb, who probably doesn't even need anything beyond his annual physical—which doesn't require a co-pay, by the way—gets health insurance for free, while someone like me, who needs to see multiple specialists throughout the year, will have to pay an inordinate amount to purchase insurance through the marketplace.

Maybe I need to find myself a start-up. I've been blogging professionally for almost five years now, and I truly do love it, but with my twenty-sixth birthday looming, it's starting to seem like a change may be in order.

I've looked at prices for health insurance through the market-place, and for insurance that's decent enough for me and my co-morbid conditions, I'll either have to move into an apartment with roommates, compromising my safe space, or run way more ads on my blog, compromising my integrity.

"I can't say I'm not jealous," I admit. "I can live comfortably on my current salary, but the marketplace prices for the type of insurance I need will increase my expenses a ton. I need to figure out if I'll be able to make it work, or if I need to start looking for a job."

Caleb must read the dread on my face, because he gives me a sympathetic look. "Are there any jobs you're interested in? Maybe one of the places you've written for would want to hire you as a full-time writer."

"That's a possibility," I reply. "But no full-time job is going to give me the flexibility I have right now, even if it's remote. Right now, I set all my own deadlines, and I can usually change them if I go into a flare or something. I also love that I get to choose what I write about, and I can follow my inspiration rather than having to pitch articles that might get shot down. I haven't worked for anyone but myself, and I worry about whether or not I would like answering to a boss. I'm just so comfortable with what I'm doing."

"You also have to deal with people trying to use you as their personal advocate," Caleb challenges. "If you had a boss, you could send those types of clients to them. And although you might not get to set your own deadlines or push them when necessary, you would get dedicated sick time, which you don't have now. I know there are a lot of good things about your current situation, but not everything about a traditional job would be bad."

"I know." I shrug. "I just don't feel ready to leave this behind yet, but I don't see how I can continue at my current rate and also pay for my own insurance."

Caleb sucks out the last drops of his iced tea then swirls the leftover ice around a few times. He appears to be thinking hard about something, but I don't know what type of solution he could possibly be coming up with. Unless he can find me magically cheap health insurance or offer me a job with as much flexibility as I have now, that I also feel passionate about, I don't see another ideal option.

"Your birthday is in August, right?" he blurts out.

I narrow my eyes in suspicion. "Yeah, why?"

He nods, satisfied. "That should be plenty of time."

"Plenty of time for what?" I ask.

He meets my gaze, his eyes boring into mine as he says five words I never thought I would hear.

"For you to marry me."

CHAPTER 16
CALEB

"What the fuck are you talking about?" Hannah practically screeches. She rarely swears, so I know her reaction is a result of genuine shock. Honestly, I'm shocked myself. I had the seed of an idea, a mere inkling of a solution, and then the words just came spilling out of my mouth.

I simply couldn't deal with the worry on Hannah's face when she spoke about finding affordable health insurance or the pure dread that accompanied talk of her finding another job. After seeing Hannah in a flare and knowing more of her story—how she had to drop out of college, lost friends and a boyfriend, and still has to make sacrifices all the time for her health—the thought of her having to give up yet another thing she loves feels like too much to bear.

As I take in the mixture of confusion, horror, and—dare I say it—a little bit of *hope* on her face, I realize that I will do *anything* it takes to make Hannah happy. I will do anything to make her feel safe and comfortable. After everything she's been through, she deserves it.

"I'm talking about us getting legally married," I say. "Then you could get on my health insurance for free. Problem solved."

When Hannah mentioned needing health insurance, it set off

a lightbulb in my mind, reminding me of Heather complaining about all the post-wedding stuff she needed to do, including adding Greg to her health insurance. When people get married, they usually figure out who has the better or cheaper insurance and both get on that one. It's simply the logical choice.

"Caleb..." Hannah stands and begins pacing back and forth over the span of a few tables. I stare at my hands to keep from staring at her ass. Finally, she sits back down, resting her elbows on the table and tenting her fingers on her temples. "Problem not solved," she says with a disbelieving laugh. "We cannot get married just so I can be on your health insurance."

"Why not?" I ask, though I can already predict her answer. For most people, marriage is this sacred thing. This promise to love one another for life. But I know better. I've watched a marriage crumble and fall apart in one of those moments that it's specifically not supposed to. For better or worse, right? In sickness and in health. Yeah, *sure*. Marriage means nothing to me because I've learned that vows are broken as easily as they're made.

Hannah is staring at me like I have three heads. "Why *not*?" she whisper-shouts. "Well, for one, it's fraudulent. And two, it's just plain ridiculous." She ticks off her points on her fingers then throws her hands up in the air. "Caleb, we can't get married. We're not even *together*."

I briefly wonder whether there was a hint of regret in that last statement, but I don't have long before Hannah opens her mouth again and I need to cut her off before she continues freaking out.

"It wouldn't be a marriage for love, Hannah," I say, as if I'm explaining a very simple concept to a small child. "It would be a marriage of convenience."

She drops her head into her palms and groans. "Oh. My. God. You sound like Rhiannon right now."

"Why?" I ask, sensing that isn't a good thing in this moment.

Hannah spreads her fingers across her face and peeks at me through them. "Marriage of convenience is one of her favorite romance tropes. Well, that and fake dating." She drops her hands to the table and straightens her spine. "We can't get married, Caleb," she says for the third time so far in this conversation.

"We really can," I argue. "I never plan to get married for real. Why waste my marriage potential when it could be helping you?"

"Because it's...it's...preposterous!"

I almost chuckle at her word choice, as well as her general disbelief in my proposal. But she's so up in arms that I force myself to hold it in. Laughing right now would probably send her into a spiral. I take a breath to compose myself.

"Hannah, you're my friend," I say. "I care about you a lot. I want to help you in any way I can, and right now, this feels like a simple solution to a problem that's really stressing you out. Let me help."

"Us getting married isn't simple," she hisses.

"For me, it is," I reply.

"Okay, so say we get married," she begins. I want to fist pump in the air that she's finally entertaining my plan, but I keep my hands tucked in my lap. "What do we tell people?"

"We don't have to tell anyone," I say. "It's just a legal document that makes it possible for you to get my health insurance."

"What if one of us gets a boyfriend or a girlfriend? How would we explain it to them?" she asks.

"Well, considering we've both currently sworn off dating, I'd say that's a bridge we cross when we come to it."

Hannah sits back in her chair, crossing her arms. She's still looking at me like I have multiple heads, but also like that might not be the worst thing in the world.

"You're serious about this, aren't you?" she says, as if only just realizing this is something that could actually work.

"One hundred percent dead serious," I reply.

"Caleb..." She scrubs her hands over her face then brushes her red locks away from eyes. "I mean, the fact that you care enough to even consider this is...well...very generous. But I need you to really think about whether or not this is something you want to do. Consider all the consequences."

"I don't have to," I say. "I've made up my mind already." As soon as I thought of the idea, I knew it was the perfect solution. Hannah can have health insurance, and I can feel like I'm doing something to help her. It's a win-win.

"Okay, well, *I* need to think about it," she replies. "This is a lot to ask—too much, really—but I'm desperate enough to consider it."

"We still have a while until your birthday," I say. "Take a week. Think it over. We'll meet here next Wednesday."

As I watch Hannah depart from Waffee a few minutes later, I feel an ache begin to grow in my chest. I'm desperate for her to agree not only because I know how much this could help her stress levels, but also because I like the idea of being tied to her in some way. Obviously our marriage wouldn't be due to romantic love, but it would bind our friendship at a different level.

I told Hannah once that she's the type of girl I'd go for if I wanted to go for any girl at all. She's sweet and kind, smart, strong... If I was looking for a partner, she'd be the type I would want. But I'm *not* looking for a partner, so why wouldn't I want her as a best friend who's also legally my wife?

Hannah

As soon as Rhia enters my apartment, she can tell something's up.

"Spill," she demands as she plops onto my couch, already digging into the open bag of chips she brought with her. "Right now."

"What makes you think there's something to spill?" I ask as I join her, casually pulling a chip from the bag.

Rhia uses a finger to draw a circle in the air around her face. "You're doing something weird here. Something's up, and I want to know what it is."

I pull my knees up under me and use the few seconds it takes me to chew and swallow the chip to pull myself together. "I have to talk to you about something, but you have to promise me you won't tell anyone."

Rhia gives me a look that says *duh*.

"I'm serious, Rhia," I say. "You're the only person I'm talking to about this. I don't want anyone else to find out."

She puts down the chips and dusts the crumbs off her hands before sticking out a pinky finger. "I promise I won't say anything," she says, using our long-time tradition of pinky promises to seal the deal.

I hook pinkies with her, and we shake on it before I finally give in. "I told Caleb about my health insurance problem," I say. I've already vented to Rhia all about this, so she knows what I'm dealing with and how desperate I am to avoid the only solutions I've come up with so far. "He thinks he might have a solution."

Rhia's dark brows draw together as she crunches down on a chip. "Really? Like what?"

"Well..." I run a finger over the velvety upholstery of the couch, stalling. "He gets free healthcare through his job, so...he was thinking we could get legally married so I could get it too."

Rhia's jaw drops open, revealing a mouth full of half-chewed potato chips.

"Eww, Rhia." I reach forward and snatch the bag of chips from her hands. "Can you please finish chewing?"

She swallows hard. "I'm sorry. I must have blacked out for a second there. It sounded like you said Caleb wants to *marry* you."

I roll my eyes at her dramatics. "I did. But before your head goes to any of the places I'm assuming it will go, it's just a way to help me. Caleb never wants to get married for real, and he's looking at this as a favor to a friend. Nothing more."

"Suuure," Rhia drawls, a sphinx-like smile curling her lips. "I'm sure the big, bearded hottie doesn't want *anything* out of this arrangement except to help you out."

My eyes narrow. "What are you implying?"

"Surely he'll want to consummate the marriage," she says. "Got to make things official and all."

"Caleb's not like that," I argue. "He's not offering this for his personal gain."

"Come on, Han." Rhia gives me a pitying look, as if my naivety is pathetic. "You don't just offer to marry someone without asking for something in return."

"Caleb did," I say with a shrug, even as a kernel of doubt lodges itself firmly in my mind. The arrangement *is* awfully one-sided. Marriage is a big deal, even though Caleb doesn't seem to view it that way. It's a big favor to do for no reward.

"So, are you going to do it?" Rhia asks, her worry replaced by that sly smile once again.

I let out a long groan. "I have no idea."

Rhia reaches over to put a supportive hand on my shoulder. "You don't have to."

"I know," I reply miserably. "The problem is that I *want* to."

"What's holding you back?" she asks, giving my shoulder a little shake.

"The fact that the whole idea is ridiculous!" I say, throwing my hands up.

"Hannah." She turns her whole body to face me. "If *I* was offering to marry you to give you health insurance—which I wish I could do, trust me—would you feel differently?"

As a fellow freelancer, Rhia can't give me any better of a deal on health insurance than I can get myself. Otherwise, I'm sure she would help me in a heartbeat. I chew on her question. If Rhia was the one making the offer, I'd still feel indebted to her, but I think I'd be way more likely to say yes.

"Because, trust me," Rhia goes on. "My moms have been wishing I would get married to a woman forever. I think they're still holding out hope even though I'm hopelessly heterosexual."

I can't help but crack a smile at that. It fades as my thoughts return to her question. "I don't know, Rhia," I respond. "We've been friends forever. It's different with Caleb. We just became friends again. It's a big favor to do so soon. Plus, what if it gets... confusing?"

She scrunches up her nose. "Confusing how?"

"Well," I say, "Caleb and I are both 'hopelessly heterosexual,' as you would say, as far as I know. We've both said that we want to be just friends, but if we get married...that might change things."

"Change things how?" she asks, even though the tilt of her brow reveals she knows exactly what I mean.

"He's hot, Rhia," I say bluntly. "And he's offering me the biggest favor ever. I'm afraid if we go through with this, I might...catch feelings."

"Are you admitting that you're attracted to the big, bearded hottie?" Rhia asks, covering her open mouth with mock surprise.

I punch her lightly on the bicep. "It's hard not to be," I admit.

"You've done just fine being friends with him so far," Rhia says. "Why would this have to change anything?"

"It's *marriage*," I say.

"But it's not real marriage," she replies.

Despite understanding her point, I'm not so sure my brain will be able to process the difference.

I have some serious thinking to do.

CHAPTER 17
CALEB

"Kim is on the dating apps," Heather says emphatically as soon as we sit at our table, as if this is some Earth-shattering announcement I should care deeply about.

"Good for her?" I guess, unsure what type of response she's looking for. My mind is a million miles away, and I can't focus on anything other than what's coming a few hours from now. I shouldn't have agreed to meet my sister for breakfast on the day of my deadline for Hannah's decision on getting married. I should have known I wouldn't be able to think about anything but that.

"Not good for her!" Heather counters. "Well, maybe good for her, but *not* good for you."

I wipe a hand over my face and down my beard. "What are you talking about?"

"Kim is my back-up date for you if you can't find a date for my wedding," Heather reminds me. "If she finds someone she likes on a dating app, we lose our plan B."

Right. Kim. I sort of forgot I was supposed to be finding a wedding date amidst my plan of marrying Hannah. Shit. It's not that I *want* to go to the wedding with Kim, but if I don't, then I have to find my own date. I had toyed around with the idea of asking Hannah to go as friends, but I can't propose yet another harebrained scheme so soon after the first one.

"Don't worry about it," I tell Heather, despite my own concern. As much as I wish I could go to the wedding stag, I know Heather worries about me. She thinks me staying single will hold me back from true happiness or some shit. I need to bring a date to her wedding and seem happy about it, if only to ease her troubled mind.

She shoots me a tender smile. "I'll always worry about you, Cale," she says, tugging at my heartstrings. Heather took all the sisterly concern she held for both me and Matty combined and beamed it toward me after he died. I can't stand it sometimes. Not because I find it suffocating, but because Heather deserves a bit of peace after the hardship we faced. Isn't that the way it goes, though? The people that worry about us the most are the same ones we desperately wish to relieve of all anxiety.

"I've got it covered," I say, despite most definitely not having it covered.

Heather sighs. "If you say so," she says as she opens her menu.

can't stop my leg from bouncing up and down beneath the bistro table at Waffee. I'm vibrating with nerves as I wait for Hannah to arrive. Despite what one might assume, I'm not afraid of her saying yes. I'm afraid of her saying *no*.

If Hannah decides against marrying me, it could change things between us. I mean, I guess if she decides *to* marry me, things will change even more, but I believe then it would be for the better. If she decides *not* to, my proposal could become this weird, awkward thing that hangs between us for the rest of our lives. Either way, our friendship will be irrevocably changed, I guess.

If she says no, I'll also probably have to watch her struggle and stress out over what her next step will be, which I'm desperate to avoid. I don't think I can sit and listen to her mull over her shitty options without wanting to shake her and shout, *"You should have just married me!"* And when she inevitably chooses one of said shitty options, I'd have to watch her suffer through living with roommates—which I imagine would be quite a hardship when going through a flare—or watch her creativity wither away as she runs mindless ads on her blog.

I can't watch Hannah struggle that way. I just can't. I can't watch the light in her eyes dim. I can't watch her lose herself. I watched that happen with Matty, and there wasn't a damn thing I could do about it. I'm not about to let that happen again. This time, I can offer a solution. It's just up to her whether she accepts it or not.

I stand and smooth my jeans down my thighs when Hannah walks through the door. I don't know why I opt for this more formal greeting, but it feels right for the occasion.

"Hi," she says softly as she approaches. She's wearing another sundress—this one light blue with little white daisies on it. It's fucking adorable and simultaneously sexy as sin.

"Hey." I pull her into a fierce hug since I have no other words. If I open my mouth, I might do something foolish like shout, *"Please say yes!"*

We pull apart and sit, no more words exchanged between us. Hannah sets down a folder on the table as if this is some kind of business deal, which I guess it kind of is.

"I've thought a lot about your proposal," she begins after a few beats of silence.

I wait for her to go on, but she pauses. This is excruciating.

"I'd like to say yes," she finally continues, and my mind whirls a mile a minute. She'd *like* to? Does that mean no? Is she saying she wishes she could but she can't? Fuck.

"But I have a condition," she adds.

My mind blanks, and my worries are quickly replaced with hope. A condition? I can work with that.

"What's the condition?" I ask, my voice coming out scratchy. I'm not entirely sure I've remembered to breathe while I've been eagerly awaiting her answer.

"I need to give you something in return," she says. "If I allow you to do this for me without repaying you somehow, I'll feel forever indebted to you."

"You wouldn't be," I argue. "I don't expect anything in return."

Hannah holds up a hand. "That's not the point. "Even if you feel you don't need repayment, I need to feel like I'm earning it somehow."

I nod. "Okay. What did you have in mind?"

She fiddles with the edge of the folder. "I was hoping you would have an idea."

What is the appropriate reimbursement for a marriage to obtain an unknown number of months of free healthcare? It's not exactly something you can Google.

I look to the ceiling, then around the room, hoping it will somehow provide me an answer. I watch a small child nibbling on a waffled cookie the size of her face. Her parents are with her, chatting away with each other, blissfully ignorant to the fact that their child's face is now smeared with chocolate.

Nearby is a couple that I'm almost positive is on a first date. You can tell by the body language. His chest is puffed, trying to make himself look big and strong. Her legs are crossed, her foot shaking as she talks, probably telling him about her job, or where she went to college, or some other inane small talk. God, I hate first dates. I'm so glad I don't put myself through them anymore.

A lightbulb goes off in my brain. *A date.* Hannah needs something from me, and there's something I could really use from her. A date to Heather's wedding. Someone who would be willing to go through the charade with me and put on a convincing act for my family without giving away that I'm happily single. This is the perfect solution. I get a date to Heather's wedding, get my family off my back about finding a partner, and get Hannah to marry me so I don't have to watch her struggle to find health insurance. It's a win-win-win.

"I think I might have an idea," I say, and Hannah's face lights up with hope. I wish she didn't feel the need to repay me, but since she does, this should work out for everyone. "Heather is getting married in September, and she's been on my case about bringing a date to the wedding. She and my mom worry about my vendetta against relationships, so I figure if I bring someone to the wedding, that should get them off back for another few months at least."

Hannah's eyes narrow. "A whole marriage in exchange for one date? No way. It's not enough, Caleb."

"Trust me," I say, determined to make this plan work. "You'd be saving my butt. I know it might not sound like an even exchange to you, but this is the biggest thing I need right now. Heather has been asking me for weeks if I've found a date yet, and I keep putting her off."

"You could find a date without even trying," Hannah argues. "You could probably go out there"—she points out the window toward the street—"and ask out the first woman you see, and she would say yes."

While I'm flattered by her assessment of my eligibility, I'm not deterred by her argument. "First of all, I don't think that's true," I reply. She opens her mouth to speak, but I cut her off. "And second, I probably could find a date, but not one who would be willing to pretend we were *actual* dates while also knowing we were strictly platonic. I need someone who will help me convince my family I'm giving dating a shot, while also understanding there's no real chance between us."

Hannah lets out a long breath. I can tell she's warring with herself. She wants what I have to offer, but she's so singularly selfless that she has to feel like she's doing enough in return.

"Please, Hannah," I say, hoping a little bit of begging will do the trick. "I really need this."

She gives me a long look before opening the mysterious folder. "Fine. If you insist that being your wedding date is enough repayment, then I'm in. We can reassess the terms in six months."

I peer into the folder. There's a single sheet of paper tucked into a pocket with a bunch of words typed on it as well as some blank lines.

"Is that...a contract?" I ask.

Hannah sniffs. "An unofficial one, yes." She pulls it out of the folder pocket and writes *being my date to Heather's wedding* on a blank line following the words *I, Caleb O'Connor, will marry Hannah Reilly and add her to my health insurance plan in exchange for...*

"What are the rest of these terms?" I ask, scanning the paragraph beneath where she just wrote.

"There are clauses about reassessing the terms if I get into a relationship, if you get into a relationship, and if your company begins charging for health insurance. Finally, it states that we will reassess the terms in six months' time to determine if the deal is still mutually beneficial for both of us," she says matter-of-factly.

I comb my fingers through my hair. "Geez, you really thought of everything."

"This is a big deal," she says as she signs one of the dotted lines at the bottom of the page. She swivels the paper around and hands me her pen. "Read over the clauses and sign if you agree."

I grab the pen and sign immediately. I know she wouldn't have written anything I wouldn't agree with. She's Hannah Reilly, for God's sake. The sweet, selfless girl next door. I trust her implicitly.

"Ca—" she starts to argue, but I interrupt.

"Done," I declare, tucking the paper back into her folder. "We've got a deal, Reilly."

Her gaze shifts from me to the paper, and she blinks, as if she almost can't believe this is real. She might consider the contract unofficial, but when I sign my name to something, I mean it. There's no backing out now.

"So when are we getting hitched?" I ask.

CHAPTER 18
HANNAH

Did you know that marriage equality still does not exist in the United States? We've obviously made huge strides in terms of interracial and LGBTQ marriage rights, but there's one massive minority group that's been left out of the conversation: disabled people.

Those who are unable to work and utilize Supplemental Security Income (SSI) or Social Security Disability Insurance (SSDI) are only allowed to amass a certain amount of wealth, or they lose their benefits. And when I say "wealth," I mean the likes of a couple thousand dollars.

When a disabled person marries someone non-disabled, they are almost guaranteed to lose their benefits because their wealth becomes tied to their spouse's. If your spouse makes even a measly salary, the government will determine that they are responsible for your expenses, not Social Security.

Basically, the government has created a marriage penalty for disabled people: Get married and you lose any autonomy you may have once had by receiving disability benefits. Your healthcare can also be affected, as qualification for SSI is tied to eligibility for

Medicaid. Getting married can mean losing access to things such as in-home care, which is necessary for many.

Being disabled shouldn't mean you can't marry the one you love.

After I agreed to Caleb's proposal, things moved pretty quickly.

My birthday is coming up soon, and the wedding is just a few weeks after that, so we got right to work figuring out what steps we needed to take to make everything official. It's surprisingly simple to get married when you're not making a huge deal of it. Since we're not having a big ceremony or a reception, we just had to apply and pick a date when the Justice of the Peace was available to marry us at the courthouse.

Ever since Caleb and I signed the contract, I've felt pretty at peace with the arrangement. I freaked out after his initial proposal, but once the decision was made, I was much calmer. I like to have a plan. Now that it's the actual day, though, my nerves are setting in big time. I'm sitting in a kitchen chair in my apartment while Rhia curls my hair into delicate spirals. I believe she's planning to pin some of them back in some sort of elaborate bun. For better or worse, I gave her carte blanche over my hair and make-up for the big day.

As for my attire, we came to a compromise on that. Rhia wanted me to wear an actual wedding dress, and she even found a few options at various thrift stores, blasting my phone with photos of them over the past few weeks. I wanted to wear one of my regular old sundresses—I figured a cute yet casual look was right for a sham courthouse marriage—but Rhia absolutely insisted I wear white, and I didn't own any plain white dresses, so we went thrifting until I found a cute, comfortable, white baby-doll dress with lace accents that she deemed acceptable.

Once my hair is finished, Rhia pulls out multiple palettes of make-up and begins going to town on my face. I don't even bother asking what she's doing, because I know her answer will probably include complicated make-up terms I can't keep up with. I'll wait until the look is complete and allow myself to be surprised.

As the final step, Rhia helps me gently pull on my white dress so as not to ruin my hair or get any make-up on it. When I'm finally allowed to look in a mirror, the sight takes my breath away. My normally wavy orange hair is coiled into ethereal-looking curls with enough swept away from my face to really show off my make-up. I'm not sure if Rhia used foundation, but whatever she did doesn't cover my freckles but rather allows them to hold their rightful place on my skin. My cheeks boast a slight pink hue, and a light sheen of nude gloss coats my lips.

The real star, though, is my eyes. A delicate swipe of eyeliner and a couple coats of mascara have made my already large eyes look even bigger, and the soft bronze eyeshadow with just a hint of a sparkle on my eyelids adds a touch of whimsy. I've never thought brown eyes were anything special—more than fifty percent of the population has them—but today they look positively enchanting.

By some kind of witchcraft, Rhia has turned me into a dainty, airy, forest fairy bride. It's honestly a shame this look is being wasted on a fake marriage.

"What do you think?" she asks as she peers into the mirror over my shoulder.

"I look better than ever," I say. "Thank you, Rhia."

She places a hand on my shoulder. "That's what best friends are for." She gives me one last look in the mirror then steps away and begins cleaning up her make-up and tools. "And to be witnesses to sham marriages," she adds over her shoulder.

I can't help the snort laugh that erupts from me. "That too."

A few minutes later, I step into my nude wedges, and then we're off. Caleb and I decided to meet at the courthouse instead of going together. I'm not sure why. Maybe that old tradition of the groom not seeing the bride before the wedding is too ingrained in my brain. It may be silly, but I'm excited for Caleb to see me looking like this for the first time at the altar—er, the podium? I'm not entirely sure what the setup at the courthouse will be.

The receptionist directs us to the correct room, where the Justice of the Peace is waiting. Caleb is standing there, casually chatting away with him as if we're not about to change our lives forever. He's distracted by the conversation and doesn't see us coming at first, so I have a moment to secretly study him. He looks handsome as hell in his white dress shirt, black pants, and black tie. For a moment, I panic that I'm underdressed, but then I remember how impressed I was by my appearance in the mirror, and I relax.

His long hair is tucked behind his ears, showing off his face, and his beard is trimmed but still present, thank God. I would have been pissed if he shaved it for this.

I know the moment Caleb catches sight of me, because he freezes mid-conversation with his mouth open. His eyes widen as he drinks in my appearance. He quickly collects himself, turning to say something to the JP before approaching me. Rhia has surreptitiously stepped aside to let us have a moment.

"You look…" Caleb pauses, as if to search for the right word. "Exquisite."

"You look…very handsome," I reply because "*you look hot as hell*" seems inappropriate for the moment. "Should we do this thing?" I ask, hoping to avoid any more small talk. My nerves are sizzling through my veins, and I'm afraid I might bolt if we don't get this over with.

Caleb extends his elbow toward me, and I hook my arm through the crook of his. The connection instantly makes me feel calmer.

"Let's go," he says, leading us toward the JP. Rhia joins us, and the ceremony begins. We went with the traditional vows, and when the JP launches into them, a tingle runs up my spine. These age-old words have been spoken by so many people so many times before, and now Caleb and I are joining their ranks. It almost seems unreal.

As the JP finishes reading Caleb his vows, he replies in a strong and steady voice, "I do." He's grinning at me, not a hint of unease in sight, and his confidence bolsters my own.

The JP reads my vows next, and my response is the same. "I do." My vow comes out breathier than I intended, something about this moment stealing the air right out of my lungs. With those two simple words, I've tied myself to Caleb forever—or at least until I find a different way to get affordable health insurance.

"Who has the rings?" the JP asks once our vows are complete.

"Oh," I begin, about to tell him we won't be exchanging rings when Caleb pulls a small box out of each of his pockets.

"I do," he replies, handing one of the boxes to me. I'm flabbergasted. We briefly discussed rings and decided to save money by not bothering with them, even though Caleb felt it would make things look more authentic, should anyone question the validity of our marriage. I guess he changed his mind, because I open the box to reveal a simple sterling silver band that looks like the right size to fit Caleb's thick finger.

He opens the box in his hands and pulls out a matching sterling silver band, this one adorned with five small, oval-shaped diamonds across the top curve. It's so delicate and beautiful, and it's exactly what I would have picked out for a wedding ring.

Rhia smoothly takes the box from me and presents it to Caleb, who slides the diamond-adorned ring onto my finger. I stare at my hand for a few moments, admiring the ring as a smile curves my lips. I must be a bit too mesmerized by the shiny new piece of jewelry, because Rhia clears her throat and thrusts Caleb's wedding band right in front of my face as if it isn't the first time she's tried to present it to me.

I take the ring and Caleb's hand, sliding it onto his finger the same way he did for me. It's the only piece of jewelry I've ever seen him wear, and I have to admit, it looks sexy as sin on his finger. I briefly wonder what he plans to do with this ring, as we certainly can't wear them without people asking questions. I suppose I could wear mine on a different finger or something, but diamonds in general tend to raise questions.

My thoughts are cut off by the JP saying, "I now pronounce you husband and wife. You may kiss your bride."

Fuck, how did I forget about this part of a wedding ceremony? Caleb and I discussed attire, rings, vows, and pretty much everything else that comes along with getting married, but somehow, we never considered the kissing part. It's not that I don't want to kiss him, of course—I'm dying to know what it feels like to kiss the lips under that beard—but it feels like we'd be crossing the "just friends" line. Then again, we *are* halfway married, so maybe that ship sailed a long time ago.

I just wish I knew how Caleb was feeling right now. Is he okay with kissing me? Surely, he understands it's just part of our ruse. Hell, he's the one who bought expensive-looking rings for the sake of credibility. It's just that we didn't make a *plan* for this.

Caleb must catch the look of panic that crosses my features, because his eyes instantly soften.

"Hey," he says softly, cupping my cheeks in his big palms. "It's just me."

I know what he's trying to tell me. That a kiss is no big deal. It's just him, not some stranger I should be afraid of.

But it's not *just* Caleb. There's nothing *just* about the man. He is the single most handsome, kind, generous, thoughtful man I've ever known. He's doing me the biggest favor of my life for a reward that I don't see as comparable. I told him all my most personal details, and they didn't scare him but only seemed to make him want to be closer to me. So it's not *just* Caleb. It's motherfucking Caleb O'Connor, and it's an honor to be standing here before him.

Even if it wasn't basically required that I kiss him right now, my thoughts would have me doing it anyway.

I place my hands on his chest, and I'm grateful my wedges

make it easy for me to lift my lips up to his. I can sense his surprise at first, like maybe he thought I would need a bit more coaxing, but soon his lips mold to mine. I'm sure all we really need to seal the deal is a peck, but if this is going to be my one and only chance to kiss Caleb, I'm going to take advantage of the opportunity.

I keep my lips firmly pressed to his when he may have otherwise backed off, signaling that I'm not done, before pulling back ever so slightly to suck in a quick breath. Caleb pulls in a ragged breath of his own. Then, with his hands still on my cheeks, he tilts my head just so and seals his lips over mine once again. His beard tickles my cheeks as he kisses me, but it doesn't hurt. The hair is quite soft, and I wonder how it would feel on other parts of my body.

That thought surprises me, and I end the kiss sooner than I might have liked. My eyes flutter open to find Caleb looking down at me, eyes wide with wonder. There's a bit of lip gloss smudged on his lips, and Rhia is fanning herself behind his back. The whole scene is so ludicrous that I have to press my lips together to hold back a chuckle. Did we really just do that?

"Congratulations," the JP says, and I'm almost surprised to find that he's still present. I forgot all about him—and pretty much everything else—while Caleb and I kissed.

"Thank you," Caleb replies before taking my arm once again. "We appreciate your service." He whisks me out to his car and assures Rhia that he'll see me safely back to my apartment, which hadn't been part of our original plan but now seems like the only logical course of action. How could Caleb and I split up right now when we just got *married*? Even if it wasn't real, it seems like we need to take some time to process it together.

Caleb holds my door open as I hop into the car, then he rounds the front to get into the driver's side.

"Do you need anything while we're out?" he asks. "Or should I take you back to your place?"

"My place is fine," I reply. "Do you want to stay for dinner?"

"Sure," Caleb says as he starts up the car. "What did you have in mind?"

I shoot him a wry smile. "Takeout."

He grins back at me. "Sounds perfect."

And that, in a nutshell, is why Caleb is the absolute best. He doesn't expect me to cook some elaborate celebration dinner, and he realizes that my energy is probably waning after the excitement of the day. He just seems to understand *me* in a way that no one else—friend, family, or otherwise—ever has.

I stare at my wedding ring the whole way home. It looks damn good on my finger. It's a shame I'll never be able to show it to anyone.

CHAPTER 19
CALEB

"So," Hannah says as she drops her stuff on a table by the entryway. "I guess we're married now."

"I guess so," I reply cautiously, feeling out her mood. She seemed a bit nervous during the ceremony, but then she kissed me so enthusiastically I thought maybe I'd been misreading her. I was about to tell her we didn't have to kiss— that surely it wasn't legally required to bind us—when she reached up and stole my lips in the best goddamn kiss of my life. It was...confusing, to say the least.

Maybe it's just because I haven't been kissed in a while, but kissing Hannah was like taking a long drink of water after days in the desert. Her lips on mine brought a sense of ease I hadn't anticipated, as if I'd been waiting for that moment forever. Her kiss was a key unlocking a door I hadn't realized was closed.

Hannah shoots me a crooked smile. "I guess that means it's our wedding night. What should we do?"

I know exactly what I'd like to do. Ever since I saw her in that sweet little white dress, I've wanted to strip her down and worship her like the princess she resembles. I've wanted to discover what she looks like beneath. Is she wearing lingerie? Plain old panties and a bra? *Nothing*? I've wanted to kiss those freckles on her chest and any others I can find. I want to learn all of her.

But Hannah can't be a one-night thing or a friend with benefits, and that's all I'll allow myself. So, I wipe my mind clear of the lascivious thoughts and place the bag of Chinese takeout containers on the kitchen table. "Want to watch a movie while we crush this Chinese food?" I ask.

A grin stretches across Hannah's face. "Love it. Just let me get changed."

I want to argue. I want to tell her not to change, that she looks perfect. Or, hell, if she's not comfortable, she should just get naked, and we'll hang out like that. I wouldn't complain. But that would be creepy as hell, so I just smile and say, "Sure."

She disappears into her bedroom, and I lay out the takeout containers on the table, grabbing serving utensils for each one. By the time Hannah returns, I have a plate piled with food: fried rice, dumplings, crab rangoon, and more. It's so stuffed it's threatening to spill off the edges.

"Hey," she says with mock annoyance. "Leave some for the rest of us."

I glance over to find that she's changed into those ridiculous yoga-cat leggings and a black tank top. My gaze snags on her chest like a total perv. I don't think she's wearing a bra, and I don't know how I'm going to think straight for the rest of the night.

"I made this plate for you," I say, holding it out for her.

Hannah blinks. "Oh." She pauses as if she's not sure how to react, then she smiles. "Thank you." She takes the plate from me and heads for the couch while I make up my own.

After a bit of back and forth, we decide to watch *Say Anything*. I wanted to check out the "new releases" section on Netflix, but Hannah insisted the 80's rom-com was most appropriate for our wedding night. We get settled in beside each other on the couch, digging into our food while the movie plays. When our plates are empty and our stomachs are full, Hannah snuggles up in a blanket beside me.

I can tell she's fading, even though it's only seven o'clock. I don't blame her. It was an eventful day. All I did was throw on some nice clothes and show up, but she must have spent hours getting ready with Rhiannon before the ceremony. Chronic illness or not, anyone would be exhausted after that.

Hannah is softly snoring by the time the iconic boombox scene plays. She told me this was her favorite part of the movie, but I don't want to wake her up to watch it. She seems so peaceful in her slumber. Over the course of the movie, she's gradually leaned over toward me and is now resting her head on my shoulder. Her orange hair spills over my unbuttoned dress shirt. I think she might even be drooling a little, though I'd never tell her that.

As the final credits roll, I shut off the television and gently lift Hannah from the couch. She stirs in my arms, her eyes slowly fluttering halfway open.

"Go back to sleep," I whisper. "I'm bringing you to your bed."

A sleepy smile curves her lips. "Thanks, husband."

Her eyes close, and she's snoring again by the time I tuck her in, pressing a kiss to her forehead. I pull back, surprised at myself. One incredible kiss, and now I feel entitled to these small moments of intimacy? That's not fair. I owe it to Hannah not to blur the lines between us. I like to think I only allowed myself the treat of my lips against her soft skin because she's asleep and won't remember it, but I'm afraid if I let myself get too comfortable, I'll slip up when she's awake.

In just a few weeks' time, we'll be forced to fabricate moments like these to convince my family we're a real couple. They'll expect casual touches and kisses. Though it's been a while, they've seen what I'm like with a girlfriend. They'll be suspicious if I'm not affectionate with Hannah. I don't even want to think about how difficult those fake encounters will make it to separate fiction from reality.

For now, I need to stick to no touching of any kind. Okay, maybe that's a little over the top. Hugs should be fine, but nothing more. Kissing Hannah is simply too tempting.

Things between us feel different now, and even though that was my worst fear going into this—that our friendship would change—now it doesn't really seem like a bad thing. What I feel for Hannah is more than friendship, and I think it has been for a while now. I want to protect her from any and all harm. I want to be her shield against anything even remotely unpleasant, from chronic illness fatigue to annoyingly talkative former high school classmates.

The thought of Hannah in any kind of distress literally makes my chest ache. It feels like a weight that is my responsibility to lift. I can't quite pinpoint when her burdens became my burdens, but the weight of them feels like more than anything mere friendship could cause.

Now that Hannah is my wife, I fully intend to stick to the vows I made to her. I will absolutely support her in sickness and in health, for richer or poorer, and everything else the JP had me repeat this morning. We may not be practicing the physical side of marriage, but I damn well plan to practice the commitment side.

I just hope that when I'm forced to pretend we're more than we are, my brain doesn't start to believe it's real.

We manage to keep our marriage a secret for exactly two weeks. I should have been more careful, but Heather popped over to my apartment for a surprise visit, and I totally forgot I had left our marriage certificate out on my desk to be filed.

I emerge from my bathroom to find my sister frozen in place, the document in her hand. Her gaze slowly lifts from the paper to me. Her expression is a mixture of confusion and anger.

"Oh, shit." I tug on my beard. "You weren't supposed to see that."

"What exactly *is* this?" she asks as she slaps the paper down on my desk and crosses her arms over her chest.

I sink onto the couch, scrubbing my hands over my face. "It's not what you think."

Heather lets out a humorless laugh. "That's funny, Caleb, because I *think* it's a marriage certificate."

Crap. When Heather uses my full name, I know I'm in trouble. She's royally pissed.

"And as someone who's getting married soon," she continues, "I *think* I have some idea what a real one looks like. So would you like to explain to me what in the actual hell is going on here?"

"Heather…" I look up at her fuming form. She's still standing, arms crossed, and I feel like a little kid in time out. "Will you please sit down so I can explain?"

She lifts a brow, testing my resolve, but I just stare her down until she rolls her eyes and sits on the couch.

"I technically did get married," I begin, but I'm unable to get any more of the story out before Heather leaps off the couch and points a finger at me.

"I knew it!" she shouts. "I knew it was real. What the hell, Caleb? How could you get married without telling me? I didn't even know you were seeing someone! You're always talking about how you don't want to date. You're not interested in relationships. *Blah blah blah.* And now I find out that not only were you in a relationship, but it was serious enough for you to marry her? I can't believe this!"

After she catches her breath, Heather sinks back down onto the couch, deflating like a day-old helium balloon. Her voice lowers significantly when she says, "My baby brother got married before me, and I didn't even know it."

Shit. The sad-puppy look on Heather's face sinks my stomach. She's obviously hurt that I didn't tell her, and I hadn't even thought about the fact that me getting married first might bother her. I didn't intend to steal her thunder—I never intended for anyone to even find out I was married—but nonetheless, I understand where she's coming from.

"I'm so sorry, Heather," I say. "And I'm sorry you had to find out this way. But please, hear me out. It's not a real marriage. At least, it's not a marriage based on love. Or...not romantic love. It's a marriage in name only. I did it as a favor for Hannah."

Heather perks up a bit. "Hannah Reilly?"

Apparently, she'd been so thrown by the marriage certificate that she hadn't even bothered to look at the bride's name.

"Yeah," I reply. "I told you we were friends again, right?"

"Friends, yes," she replies. "Anything more, no."

I ignore her icy tone. "I found out that she has some autoimmune diseases."

Heather frowns. "Which ones?" she asks, her nurse mode popping its head out.

"Lupus and Sjogren's," I answer. I explain the situation about Hannah's health insurance and our fake marriage. "It's really not a huge deal, Heather," I conclude, "but I *am* sorry I had to keep it a secret from you."

Heather is silent for a moment. Then she reaches for me, pulling me into a side hug on the couch. "You have a huge heart, Caleb," she whispers in my ear. "And while I kind of want to smack you right now," she says as she pulls away, "I'm also really proud of you for helping out a friend that way. Hannah is a really nice girl, and I'm sorry to hear she struggles so much."

I release a breath, relieved she understands. My peace is immediately disrupted by the sting of pain as she slaps my chest, her engagement ring packing an extra punch.

"But we don't keep secrets from each other, Cale," Heather says. "Okay? Promise me there will be no more secrets."

I think about the other half of my deal with Hannah.

Pretending we're in a real relationship is definitely another secret, but I don't have the heart to drop it on Heather right now. Her head is already spinning, and she's one of the people I'm trying to convince with our fake-dating plan. So, I reply, "Promise."

Hopefully, our plan will work, and Heather will never find out I kept another secret. Truthfully, though, at this point I'm less worried about convincing other people we're together and more worried that I'll accidentally convince *myself* we are.

CHAPTER 20
HANNAH

I lean forward, letting the hot water from my shower pelt my sore neck. I fell asleep sitting up on the couch last night and awoke with an aching upper half. I got caught up answering DMs and emails, and I was determined to zero my inbox before going to bed. That plan obviously backfired, because now I have a pile of unread correspondence *and* an angry body.

Not for the first time, I wish I could hire an assistant to answer messages. It's my least favorite part of my job, and honestly, it's starting to suck the joy out of all aspects of it. I'll write a post I'm so passionate about then stall hitting "publish" because I'm already imagining the replies I'll get, ranging from quick questions to desperate pleas for help. It's the latter that really wears me down.

I turn off the shower and begin counting down the seconds until I can replace the relief from the hot water with that from my heating pad. I have a headache, too, so I pop a pill for that. I quickly towel dry my hair and put on a matching set of hunter-green sweat shorts and a cropped t-shirt. I'll have to change for my birthday dinner with Rhia later, but I figure I'll probably take a nap before then, so it's not worth putting on nice clothes now.

If you'd asked me as a teenager how I'd be spending my

twenty-sixth birthday, I probably would have spouted off fantasies of fancy dinners, club hopping, or some other naive vision of a glamorous adult celebration. Instead, I have plans to take a nap with my heating pad so I'll have the wherewithal to go to Hibachi with my one and only true friend.

Caleb was well on his way to becoming another one, but he's been super distant since the wedding. We've exchanged texts here and there, but nothing like the near-constant dialogue we had kept up after we first reconnected. I haven't seen him at Waffee, which he blamed on work, saying they needed him in the office because it's crunch time, getting the app ready to present to potential investors. While I know that's probably true, I get the feeling that's not the only reason he's been M.I.A.

I don't know exactly what's bugging Caleb, but I know that I miss him. We were getting so close, and then he just dropped off. Was he freaked out by the kiss at our wedding? We both knew it was just for show. And he kissed me when he put me to bed that night—which was his second time putting me to bed, I might add. Nothing happened that was unusual enough to scare him off. Maybe he felt like he'd done his good deed by marrying me, and now there was no need to keep up with the pretense of friendship with the poor, poor, chronically ill girl.

I settle myself under my heating pad on the couch, trying not to worry about whatever's going on with him. I know better than most that everyone is dealing with something they don't necessarily show to the world, so I shouldn't make any assumptions. I just wish Caleb would be as honest with me as I was with him.

Just as I get comfortable, I hear a knock on my door. I huff out a sigh of annoyance at whoever is making me get off this couch. It might be Owen or Annie dropping by with a birthday surprise, but then again, they both already sent their requisite "Happy Birthday" texts, so I don't think it's either of them. It could be Rhia, but I already have plans to see her later, so I'd expect her to be getting in her words for the day before we go out.

I take a quick peek out the peephole, and I have to stifle my surprised gasp. Caleb is standing outside my door with his hands full of coffee, balloons, and a small gift bag. Not only is he *here*, but he remembered my birthday and has come prepared. This feels like a total 180 from his near absence these past few weeks.

Stepping back, I quickly finger-comb my hair and toe off my llama slippers, shoving them beneath the couch. They were last year's birthday gift from Rhia after I kept complaining that my feet hurt when I flared, but I didn't want to wear shoes in my apartment. She figured slippers that were worn *only* in the apartment were a good compromise, and she managed to find the wackiest pair of supportive slippers out there. They're cute, but I don't necessarily want Caleb seeing them. Though, he *has* already seen my yoga-cat leggings (which were Rhia's Christmas gift to me), so I guess if he was going to judge me for my—or really, Rhia's—questionable wardrobe choices, he would have already.

As I open the door, Caleb greets me with an almost sheepish smile. "Happy Birthday, Reilly," he says as he hands me what I presume to be an iced caramel latte from Waffee with a bendy straw shaped into the words *happy birthday* sticking out of it.

I can't help but smile at his thoughtfulness. "Thanks, O'Connor," I reply, taking a sip. "Come in."

Caleb steps inside, and I close the door behind him before placing my drink on the coffee table.

It feels better than it should to see him after some time apart. He's wearing khaki shorts and a white t-shirt that offsets his dark hair and beard. A chain I've never noticed before hangs around his neck, dipping into his t-shirt, so I can't tell if it has any sort of pendant on it.

"Long time no see," I say—part accusation, part curiosity.

Caleb's shoulders tense as he places the bouquet of balloons down. "I know. Sorry about that. Work has been busy, and I guess I just got caught up."

I take another long sip of coffee. "I was beginning to wonder if you regretted marrying me."

Caleb's gaze snaps toward me. "No," he replies quickly. "Not at all."

"Good," I say. "Because as of today, I'm officially on your health insurance. You're stuck with me."

He bumps shoulders with mine. "That's not a bad place to be."

I grin. Despite our few weeks of minimal communication, in this moment, everything feels normal between us.

"Thanks for the coffee and balloons." I inspect the colorful bouquet of balloons, ranging from a glittery number twenty-six to an array of polka-dotted ones.

"You're welcome." Caleb's body shifts nervously as he holds out a small gift bag. "But this is the real gift."

I take the bag and gently tear through the tissue paper to find an oblong jewelry box. Curiosity piqued, I open the lid to reveal the most gorgeous necklace I've ever laid eyes on. Nestled in the plush box is a golden chain with a dainty disk pendant engraved with a lily—or, more accurately, what I presume to be a tiger lily.

Tears spring to my eyes at the significance of the flower. It reminds me of teenage days spent outside in the yard, trying like hell to suppress a crush on the boy next door. It reminds me of hearing about Matty's death and sending over the only thing I could think to bring a smile to Caleb's face. The symbol obviously means as much to him as it does to me.

I take the pendant between my fingers. It looks like real gold —or at least gold plated. It couldn't have been cheap, and he just dropped however much our rings cost a few weeks ago.

"Caleb, you shouldn't have."

He lets out a grunt of disapproval. "Of course I should." He bumps shoulders with me again—a chummy gesture I imagine is intended to reduce the magnitude of his next words. "You're my wife."

And that's just the problem, isn't it? This is the type of gift a husband might give his wife, but it's not *real* between me and Caleb. We're not *really* married or even in a relationship. We just can't seem to stop blurring those lines. That was one good thing about him going radio silent—there were no mixed signals. No gestures to question. Nothing that might lead me to believe we're more than just friends.

"Besides," Caleb adds. "I feel bad you can't wear the ring. I wanted to give you something you could actually use. Here, I'll help you put it on."

He removes the necklace from the box, and we move to stand before the mirror on the wall near the door. I watch as Caleb guides the necklace around my neck, sweeping my damp hair to one side. He's standing so close that his beard brushes the back of my head, and I can feel his breath on my exposed neck as he carefully clasps the necklace. Once it's secure, he arranges my hair back over each shoulder and glances in the mirror at the final product.

"Beautiful," he whispers. Then a small frown mars his brow, as if the word slipped out unintentionally.

I finger the pendant. "It is."

Caleb's frown deepens as his eyes cast down to the pendant, and I realize it wasn't the necklace he was talking about. We stay standing like that for a long moment, both staring at our reflections in the mirror. I feel Caleb's presence like a cloak surrounding me. I can feel his beard, his breath, his *eyes* on me.

The spell is only broken when Caleb's phone begins buzzing loudly with an incoming call. He drags his gaze away and glances at his phone.

I clear my throat and step away from the mirror, putting some distance between us. "Is that important? Feel free to take it."

Caleb silences the phone and shoves it back into his pocket.

"It's just Heather. Probably more wedding stuff. I'll call her back later."

"Okay," I reply.

"Speaking of...I was also hoping to go over some stuff with you today about the wedding?"

"Sure." I take a seat on the couch and pat the cushion next to me, inviting him to do the same.

"I was thinking we should go over some...ground rules," he begins. "For the week of the wedding."

I turn my gaze toward the ceiling. "No sharing secrets about stuff you did as a teenager, and don't wear white to the wedding," I joke. "Anything else?"

He gives me a look that says *be serious.*

"What kind of ground rules?" I ask, taking a slug of my latte.

"Like, what we're willing to do to sell our act. Maybe go over some hard and soft limits."

I nearly choke on my coffee. "Caleb, this isn't *Fifty Shades of Grey.*"

He gives me that look again, narrowing his eyes and pursing his lips, but this time his cheeks have turned ever so slightly pink. "I know that, but we will need to do stuff we don't normally do, and I want to make sure we're on the same page."

"What kind of stuff?" I ask in the most innocent tone I can muster. It's kind of fun to rile Caleb up. He's one of the most level-headed guys I know, so it's rare to see this side of him.

"Stop toying with me, Reilly," he growls. "Or I'll dump out that birthday latte and pop all these balloons."

I let out a dramatic gasp and clutch my cup to my chest. "You wouldn't dare."

Caleb lifts a brow. "Try me."

He begins to scoot closer, and I inch back. He's reaching for the cup in my hand, though not quickly enough to be actually trying to snatch it from me. My butt hits the armrest, and there's nowhere further to go. Before I know it, Caleb has me crowded into the corner of the couch, his woodsy scent surrounding me. It draws me in, making me want a stronger whiff. Even more than that, I want to taste him again.

"Fine!" I say a little too loudly, desperate to put a few feet between us. "I'll be serious." I wrack my brain for a good rule to set while Caleb shifts so we're sitting beside each other again. "Hard limit: no touching my ass in front of your family. It's tacky," I blurt.

A surprised chuckle falls from Caleb's lips. "That's fair. How about we keep touching to arms, legs, back, and face?"

Scenarios in which each of these touches may occur whirl through my mind. An arm around my shoulders during the ceremony. A hand on my thigh during dinner. A finger brushing a stray hair from my face. Each one sets off a little spark low in my belly.

"That sounds fine," I reply.

"How about kissing?" Caleb asks. "Head and face are kind of necessary, but how do you feel about lips? It's okay if you don't want to. We can just pretend like we're not into PDA. But it would sell it more if we kissed."

I think back to the kiss on our wedding day. How sweetly his lips coaxed mine, never rushing or forcing. How the soft hairs of his beard brushed over my skin. How I never wanted it to end.

I glance over to find Caleb peering at me with an odd look on his face, and I realize I've been silent a bit too long, lost in my own mind. "Kissing on the lips is fine," I finally say.

He nods. "Cool." He doesn't add anything more, but he begins fidgeting with his beard, and I can tell there's something else he wants to say.

"Anything else?" I prompt. I figure we've gone over the big stuff—touching and kissing are the main things we'll have to do that we aren't currently doing as friends—but maybe there's something else I haven't thought of.

"Do you think we should…uh..practice?" Caleb asks, avoiding my gaze and looking toward the balloons instead.

"Practice?" I ask, genuinely confused. The touching stuff

shouldn't be too difficult. We've hugged and touched platonically plenty of times. Plus, we've already kissed once, and I think we were pretty damn good at it.

"Yeah," he says. "You know, so we look natural in front of my family."

"Oh," I reply, understanding dawning. He doesn't want our interactions to look awkward and set off alarm bells for his family. I can understand that. He really wants them to believe he's in a relationship so they won't worry about him—a wish I can relate to. "Yeah, we can practice."

And that's how, one week later, I find myself on a date with my husband.

CHAPTER 21
CALEB

"Can you please pass the bread?" Hannah asks. She's sitting across from me in what I know—from Heather —is an LBD, or a little black dress. It hits her mid-thigh, and it's shorter and tighter than the sundresses I've seen her wear before. Her hair is down, spilling over her shoulders in waves. It's got a bit more curl to it than usual, and I wonder if she put in some extra effort since this is technically a date. The wedges on her feet make me think the same. Aside from our wedding day, I've never seen Hannah in shoes that aren't flat.

I chose La Campania for our practice date. It's a nice little Italian restaurant, and being a few towns over, it's a place where we're unlikely to run into anyone we know. I can only imagine the reactions we would get if Heather, Rhia, Annie, or Owen saw us sitting here together. Heather would try and completely fail to play it cool. I can almost guarantee that seeing us together would send her into a tailspin. Rhia would probably squeal with delight, based on what Hannah's told me about *her* wishes for our relationship. And Annie or Owen would probably *really* freak out, having only ever seen me as their brother's best friend's older sibling.

The point of this outing is to practice looking like we're

dating so it will be natural by the time we have to do it in front of my family, but so far, Hannah has seemed so nervous that I haven't even touched her. Not a hug or a hand hold, let alone anything more. She's been fidgety and quiet, and when she does speak, it's in a stilted tone I don't recognize.

"So proper," I tease as I push the bread basket toward her. "Please slather this in butter and take a disgustingly huge bite so I know you haven't been replaced by a robot or something."

Hannah rips a roll in half, places an entire pat of butter in the center, and tears off a big bite. "Happy?" she asks, her mouth still full of food.

I pin her with a glare. "I will be once you start acting normal again."

Her shoulders fall as she swallows her bite. "I haven't been on a date in a long time," she says softly.

My features soften. "Hannah. You're making this a bigger deal than it needs to be. It's just me." They're the same words I said to her on our wedding day, and they seemed to relax her then. In fact, they led to *her* kissing *me* when I thought for sure I'd have to take the lead. Maybe if I'm lucky, we'll reach the same outcome tonight.

"Caleb." She sounds exasperated. "You say that as if this whole thing is so simple."

I open my mouth to explain that it *is* so simple, but she cuts me off before I can get a word in.

"I understand this is a fake date, but that doesn't change the fact that I'm sitting across from a handsome man, in the most uncomfortable outfit I own, trying to decide if I'm smiling enough, or if I should lean forward so more of my cleavage is showing, or if I should keep my hair down or sweep it up into some sexy updo. Because, as it turns out, trying to look flirty isn't all that different from trying to *be* flirty, which has never been my strong suit. Hence me not having gone on a date in a long time," Hannah finishes with a huff.

I reach across the table for her hands. They're so much

smaller than mine. So much softer too. I give them a gentle squeeze. Those brown doe eyes meet mine, and my heart melts. I'm not sure where to start. My mind is still a little stuck on her calling me handsome. Somehow, the compliment feels far more meaningful than any time I've ever been called "hot" or "sexy." I also have a driving urge to tell her that she should show off all the cleavage she wants—I won't complain—and she most definitely shouldn't touch her hair. The orange waves remind me of a lion's mane, and I'm desperate to run my hands through it. However, my need to comfort Hannah wins out above all else.

"You don't have to try so hard," I say gently. "We don't have to do anything all that differently than we normally do. We can just hang out and talk. Maybe try to add more touching." I lift our joined hands from the table to show her we're already making progress.

Hannah smiles her first genuine smile of the night. It's small but real.

"It's that simple, huh?" she asks.

I rub my thumbs over the tops of her hands in a soothing motion. "It's that simple."

"Okay." She retracts her hands, stuffs the rest of her dinner roll into her mouth, chews, and swallows. Sitting back in her seat, she places her hands loosely in her lap. "So, how are things going with the app?"

I'm a little jarred by the absolute one-eighty in her demeanor, but mostly I'm glad she seems more comfortable.

"Really well," I reply. "We're actually planning a trip to New York just after the wedding to present it to some potential investors. If they bite, we should be able to get it up and running for the public to use."

"That's great," she says, her smile growing wider. "I can't wait to hear someone say they met their significant other on Meet Your Match and tell them I know the brains behind it."

I give a little shrug. "That's giving me more credit than I deserve, but I appreciate it."

"You don't have to be so humble," Hannah responds, her foot brushing against my lower leg.

The casual touch is so unexpected I almost jump out of my seat. It takes me a moment to recover, and I have to clear my throat before I can respond. Even still, my voice sounds like it's scratching against sandpaper as it comes out.

"It's not humility; it's the truth," I say. "I didn't come up with any of the ideas. I just did the background work. Normally, someone with my job wouldn't even go to a meeting like this, but I've gotten pretty close to the founders, and they want me there."

Hannah tilts her head to the side. "Of course they do." Her foot brushes my leg again, a longer stroke up and down the side of my calf. "You're invaluable."

Invaluable. Another compliment that rocks me to my core. Hannah is looking at me as if I hung the moon. As if I flew up and individually painted each star in the sky. I don't deserve it, but I can't deny that I love it. I *crave* it. I want her to look at me like that for the rest of my life.

The server delivers our meals, and I feel bereft at the lack of leg touches as we dig in.

"How are things going with your blog?" I ask before taking a bite of my chicken parmesan. It's not as good as my mom's, but it's damn close.

Hannah nods as she finishes chewing. "Things are going well for me too," she replies. "I just did a post in partnership with a heating pad company. They sent me three different ones for free and paid me to write about them. It was kind of hard to get a cute photo of me with a heating pad on my back, but I figured it out."

"Any photo with you in it has to be cute," I quip, pleased when a faint blush washes over her cheeks. "Any more emails like the one I saw on your computer that day?" I ask.

Hannah pushes some gnocchi around her plate with her fork.

"A few," she answers, but the small downward tilt of her lips says otherwise.

"Be honest with me, Hannah."

She tries to spear a gnocchi a little too aggressively with her fork, and it flies off the plate, landing about a foot away on the table. "I get at least one a day," she admits. "I'm at the point where I'm not sure I can deal with them anymore."

"Then don't," I reply. "Tell them you're not a doctor or a therapist, and they need to seek professional help."

"I *do*," she says. "But sometimes I feel like I've dug myself too deep into this hole. I've made my entire brand about chronic illness, and I've made myself so visible in the community that I'm often the first person people find when they start researching autoimmune diseases. It's what has allowed me to make a living out of this, but it's also slowly killing me. I want to spend my time being creative, not getting sucked into other people's problems. I want to help people, but I can't keep doing it at my own expense."

Her leg is shaking up and down beneath the table hard enough that the runaway gnocchi has inched perilously close to the edge of the table. I reach below and place a hand on her jittery leg, my fingers spreading over the length of her thigh. The dress is even shorter when she's seated, and I'm touching nothing but bare, smooth skin.

"It's not your job to help everyone," I say. "And you won't be able to help *anyone* if you keep going at this rate. You'll burn yourself out."

Hannah's leg stills beneath my touch. "I know," she says softly. "But what am I supposed to do? These people need help."

I rub my thumb in those soothing circles again. It feels vastly different doing it on her inner thigh than it did doing it on the back of her hand.

"They need help, yes, but it doesn't have to be *your* help. There's nothing wrong with referring strangers on the internet to other sources of support."

Hannah hums noncommittally and takes a sip of water before confessing, "I'm afraid if I stop replying to everyone the way I do, my business will suffer."

I meet her gaze and hope she can sense how serious I am when I say, "Then let it suffer."

Her brow crinkles, confusion clouding her expression.

"I'd rather your business suffer than *you* suffer," I explain. "And before you say it, yes, I understand that making less money could lead to you suffering, but I won't let that happen." My voice comes out lower as I say the next part. "I am your husband now, for richer or poorer, and I will not allow my wife to experience any hardship that I could possibly help."

Hannah reaches below the table and twines her hand with mine, a smile catching on her lips. "And here I thought we were on our first date."

I don't mind that she's trying to lighten the conversation— I've already made my point—so I crack a grin of my own. "You know what they say: first comes marriage, then comes the first date."

"Something about that just doesn't roll off the tongue," she jokes, and I'm relieved we're back to our usual demeanor.

Things feel lighter for the rest of the meal, though I'm sure it's not the last time we'll talk about the stress of Hannah's job. I don't see why she can't just focus on the content creation part— which still helps a ton of people by spreading information and advice—and set a precedent that she won't counsel individuals. Then again, I haven't experienced the hardship of struggling with debilitating symptoms or pursuing a diagnosis, so maybe I'll never understand the driving desire she feels to help these people.

I drive Hannah back to her apartment, my hand resting on her thigh like it did at the restaurant. I think we made a lot of progress at dinner in terms of being comfortable with one another's touch, which is a relief with the wedding coming up so soon. I insist on walking her to her door, as any good date would do, and we stop just in front of her apartment.

"Thanks for dinner," Hannah says, brushing some of her hair behind her shoulder and revealing the creamy column of her throat.

"It was my pleasure," I reply. "Thanks for being willing to practice with me."

She shifts from one foot to the other. "Do you think we should...practice a kiss?" she asks. "Just because we've only done it once, so it still might not look too natural yet," she rushes to add.

I nod as if this is the only logical train of thought. "I think we should."

Hannah nods too, but she doesn't make a move to come closer to me. I guess this time it's my turn to take the lead. Taking a step forward, I cradle her cheek in my palm and gently tilt her head back. Her eyes are half-hooded, her lips slightly parted.

I press my lips to hers, a light touch that invites more but expects nothing. She leans into the kiss, and I take it as a signal that she's open to more, darting my tongue out to taste her lips. A small moan escapes her throat, and my cock immediately hardens at the sound. I continue, my tongue tenderly coaxing Hannah's lips open. She tastes lemony from the water she was drinking at the restaurant. I want to soak up the taste, savor it since I don't know how long I'll have the pleasure of experiencing it.

How long will we continue to fake date after the wedding? How long do we have to be together for my family to stay off my back? I figure we can fake it for a few months, and then I'll be afforded a few months of post-fake-breakup melancholy before they're after me again.

I push thoughts of my meddling family aside, determined to relish every second of this kiss. Hannah's soft lips are pliant under mine. Her hands have fisted in my shirt, pulling me close

—close enough that my erection brushes against her stomach. I can tell the second she feels it, as she releases a soft gasp into my mouth. I catch it, closing my lips around hers.

There's no point in hiding how hard I am. I could pull back and laugh it off as an automatic reaction—something my lizard brain is in control of, not me—but that would be a lie. This isn't just my body reacting to a physical experience. This is my body reacting to *Hannah*. The wholesome girl next door whose brother was best friends with mine turned into the strongest, most selfless, and—I'll be totally honest—sexiest woman I know.

The slamming of a door startles me, and I break the kiss, glancing over to see Hannah's neighbor exiting their apartment.

"Sorry," the young woman mouths to me as she scurries away.

A soft chuckle rattles through my chest at her silent apology. I turn to find Hannah wide-eyed and rosy-cheeked, looking thoroughly kissed.

"I think my family would buy that," I say.

A frown ghosts across Hannah's face before her lips tighten into a smile. "Me too. Glad that's settled." Her tone is back to what it was at the beginning of our night—proper, polite, a little stiff. The kiss probably just threw her off. These interactions always make me feel a little off balance myself.

"Goodnight," I say as Hannah unlocks her door.

She throws me a small smile. "Night." She slips into her apartment, and I spend a couple of long moments staring at her closed door, secretly wishing she had invited me in. It's probably good that she didn't. My lizard brain has, in fact, come out to play, and it's bitching at me to bust through this door and get my lips back on Hannah's as fast as humanly possible. I know us parting ways for the night is the right thing to do.

So, why do I suddenly feel so lonely?

CHAPTER 22
HANNAH

Chronic illness taught me what it means to grieve for a life you could have had. Traditionally, grief seems to be reserved for loss of something concrete—loss of a loved one, of a relationship, of a job. But sometimes grief occurs for something less tangible. You might think I would have grieved my loss of good health, but honestly, the loss of the future I had imagined for myself hurt far more.

"Maine!" I call out when I catch sight of the license plate on the car merging in front of us on the highway. It's only about a two-hour ride up to Lake Winnipesaukee, where Heather's wedding will be, but the license plate game seemed like a fun way to pass the time.

"Geez, you're fast," Caleb complains. He's only been the first to spot one state—Vermont—while I've gotten Connecticut, New York, Rhode Island, and now Maine.

"Gotta keep your eyes peeled, O'Connor," I tease, though I don't think a lack of observational skills is the problem. Caleb seems distracted. He's tapping his fingers on the steering wheel but not in time to the music. Just a constant, nervous tapping that's driving me a little up the wall. I miss the loose, relaxed Caleb who drove me from La Campania all the way back to my apartment with his hand on my thigh.

"Is everything okay?" I ask. "Are you nervous about us convincing your family? Because I think we'll do just fine."

Caleb lets out a big breath, as if he's been holding it for the whole ride. "I'm not really nervous about that. I think we'll do fine too."

"What's bothering you, then?" I reach over and lightly press on one hand to still his fingers. He squeezes them around the wheel, his knuckles turning white with the force of his grip. Less annoying, perhaps, but not exactly a sign of ease.

"I haven't been to the cabin since Matty died."

"Oh," I breathe. I hadn't realized that. Caleb's family used to go up to the lake house all the time when we were in high school. I figured since Heather decided to have her wedding there, and she insisted the whole family stay at the cabin, that it was still a popular family meeting spot.

I can only imagine how many memories of Matty await Caleb at the house. It won't be easy being back in that place without him, especially with his father, who Caleb hasn't seen in almost as long. He's not arriving until tomorrow, so at least Caleb will have a bit of time to process before he enters the picture.

I tug his right hand off the wheel and into mine, resting them together on the center console.

"Tell me your favorite memory with Matty from the lake," I say, hoping the invitation will be a welcome one. I don't mean to make Caleb sad, but I think it's better to start processing what's coming now rather than waiting until we're surrounded by memories of him.

He's silent for a moment before a smile tugs at the corner of his lips. "One time, when we were probably about six and nine, we brought some French fries down to the beach. We would always get McDonald's on the ride up because it's right off the highway. We couldn't wait to get to the beach when we arrived, so we just brought our food with us."

Caleb's hand noticeably relaxes into mine as he begins the story. His smile grows, and I find myself smiling along with him as I anticipate what might come next.

"There was this family of ducks that liked to hang out at the beach. Matty was always kind of afraid of them even though they usually left us alone. I thought they were fun to watch while they swam around or ate from the wild blueberry bushes. But this day, they would *not* stay away from us. They must have smelled the fries. They were walking around, just inches away, poking their beaks into our laps. Matty was petrified, so he threw a bunch of fries as far as he could to get them to go away."

A chuckle slips from Caleb's lips. "It worked for a minute, until the fries were all gone, and then the ducks *swarmed* us." He breaks into a full-on laugh, unable to finish the story as he remembers the scene.

"Then what happened?"

Caleb finally settles enough to speak. "Matty stood up, threw the entire container of fries toward the lake, and *sprinted* all the way back to our house." He shakes his head as the smile that's been lighting up his face slowly falls. "I miss him."

I squeeze Caleb's hand. "Me too." I suppose it's inevitable that every happy memory with Matty will be followed by the sadness that there won't be another opportunity to create more. "Why don't we stop at McDonald's on our way to the cabin?" I suggest.

Caleb glances over at me, his espresso eyes filled with grief. "Yeah?"

I give his hand another squeeze. "Yeah."

An hour-and-a-half later, we're throwing away the trash from our ten-piece chicken McNuggets and two large fries—we each needed our own, obviously. We didn't talk any more about Matty. Instead, I tried the tactic of total distraction by discussing pop-culture gossip. Even still, back in the car, Caleb's anxiety is higher than ever. His fingers are tapping a mile a minute, and tension is vibrating off him in waves.

As we approach the cabin, the knot of tension in my own gut pulls taut. *It's showtime.*

The cabin is adorable—a two-story, rustic thing with siding that looks like real logs. There's a covered deck in the front, dotted with whimsical charms. A hammered metal sun sits above the front door, and various wind chimes hang from the rafters. It looks like a happy, lived-in family home, and it breaks my heart that Caleb hasn't been able to bring himself back here.

We get out of the car and head around to the trunk, where all our bags are. I'll be the first to admit I'm an overpacker, but having a chronic illness makes that a bit of a necessity. You never know exactly what symptoms are going to pop up, so you have to plan for them all. In addition to a week's worth of outfits, including my fancy rehearsal dinner and wedding clothes, I've got all my medications and usual products, which include dry mouth wash and lozenges, eye drops, and a microwavable heated eye mask, plus a couple different heating pads, compression socks, sleeves, and knee braces. I managed to cram everything into a duffel bag, wheeled suitcase, and backpack, but it was a tight fit.

Caleb pops the trunk, but before we dive in to grab our stuff, I catch his wrist. "You doing okay?"

He sighs, sagging against the car. "Yeah. I just feel like today's already been three days, and we haven't even entered the cabin yet."

"Stress will do that." I pull him into an impromptu hug,

hoping to instill some amount of comfort. "Don't forget, I'm here for you," I whisper next to his ear.

He returns my embrace, wrapping his arms around my waist. I could swear he nuzzles slightly into the crook behind my ear, but that could just be him getting close enough to whisper back, "I know."

"Caleb?" comes Heather's voice. "Hannah?"

I hear flip-flops slapping against stairs as I pull away from Caleb.

"Hey, sis," he says as Heather bounds over to give him a hug of her own.

"I'm so glad you're here!" she squeals. "You too," she adds as she pulls me into a tight embrace.

Heather hasn't changed much at all—same tall, willowy body, wavy auburn hair, and a huge enthusiasm for life. It's nice to see she didn't lose that when she lost Matty.

"Hi, Heather," I say with a grin I can't help. Her joy is contagious. "Thank you for having me. It's beautiful up here." We look around the property together, from the flower garden in the front yard, bursting with late-summer flowers like goldenrod and aster, to the shimmering lake in the distance.

"It really is," she agrees. "I couldn't imagine getting married anywhere else."

"Are you ready for the wedding?"

Heather lets out a dramatic sigh. "I'm ready to be married, but I don't know if I'll ever feel fully ready for the wedding. You guys were smart to go the courthouse route."

Caleb swats her arm lightly. "Be quiet," he hisses. "No one else can know about that."

Heather mimes zipping her lips, then smiles fondly as she glances between the two of us. "I'm just glad you're giving things a real go, even if the marriage isn't real."

I sidle up to Caleb like the happy girlfriend I'm pretending to be and twine our hands together. "Me too."

"Do you need help bringing in your bags?" she asks.

"Oh, you don't have to—" Caleb begins, but his over-exuberant sister cuts him off.

"Don't worry, I wasn't offering. Greg!" she calls, and a tall brunet in a polo shirt and cargo shorts comes dashing outside. The dutiful fiancé, I presume.

"Hey, guys," he greets us, giving Caleb a hug and introducing himself to me with a handshake.

"Honey, do you mind helping with their bags?" Heather asks him sweetly.

"No problem," he replies, grabbing two of mine. Caleb grabs the other one plus his own bags before I even have a chance to pick one up.

"I can help," I offer.

"No need," Heather says with a flip of her hair. "Our guys have it." She links an arm with mine and begins leading me up the stairs to the cabin behind *our guys*.

The inside of the house is as charming as the outside, with flannel touches and wildlife artwork throughout. It's clearly an all-season cabin, with a large wood stove taking up one corner of the living room and a pair of vintage skis mounted on the wall, juxtaposed with a row of coat hooks teeming with beach towels. A carved wooden owl perched on the mantel watches us with beady eyes as we head for the staircase.

"We have you set up in one of the guest rooms," Heather explains as we climb the stairs. "Greg and I will be staying in another until after the wedding, when we'll move to a hotel. Dad and Marcie will take the master when they get here, and Taryn and Taylor will be on a blow-up mattress in their room. Mom has graciously agreed to take the third guest room."

Caleb snorts. "Yeah, I'll bet she was *real* gracious about it." He pauses on the stairs and throws a look at me over his shoulder. "Mom got the cabin in the divorce."

"At least she's not on a blow-up mattress like the girls," Heather retorts as we continue our ascent.

"They're two and three," Caleb says dryly. "I don't think a blow-up mattress is that much of a slap in the face to them."

"Mom is happy to do whatever it takes to make this wedding week a success," Heather says as we stop in front of an open doorway. "And I know you are too." She gets up on her toes to kiss Caleb's cheek then ushers us into the room.

Greg places our bags on the floor. "Let us know if you guys need anything. Both bathrooms are stocked with the basics, and there are extra pillows in the closet."

"Thanks," I say as Caleb drops the rest of the bags on the ground.

"We'll let you get settled," Heather says. "But be ready for dinner at six. Greg is grilling steaks!"

They leave the room, and Caleb shuts the door while I hop onto the queen-sized bed. The *single* queen-sized bed.

Somehow, in all the plotting and planning we did for this trip, the thought of our sleeping arrangement never occurred to me. Obviously, they would put us together in a bed—they think we're a real couple. But now that means I have to sleep beside Caleb for five nights without accidentally cuddling him.

"So...this bed," I say, falling back into the pillows. "Think it's big enough for both of us?"

Running his fingers over his beard, Caleb chuckles. "Considering I'm about twice the size of you, I'm probably the one who should be worrying about that. They said there were extra pillows in the closet, right?" he asks, opening the door and pulling out three pillows. He places them in a line down the middle of the bed. "Hopefully this will keep me from rolling over and squishing you in my sleep."

A tug of something that feels like disappointment pulls at my chest. He's created a barricade. He wants us to stay separated so badly that he's created a physical barrier to keep us apart. I'm not sure why that bothers me so much when I was the one who brought up my worries about the bed situation in the first place, but it does.

"Good idea," I say with zero passion.

"What would you like to do until dinner?" Caleb asks, unaware of my discontent. "Do you need to rest? Or do you want to go down and see the lake?"

My heart warms at his consideration. The fact that he realized I might want to rest dulls some of the ache. "I'd like to see the lake," I reply.

CHAPTER 23
CALEB

The scents of lemon and sunscreen fill my nostrils as I slowly awaken. I can tell it's morning without even opening my eyes. The coos of the mourning doves leak in through the cracked window, and sunlight brightens the backs of my eyelids.

I'm so comfortable in this bed. The chill of the morning air is tempered by the fluffy comforter thrown over me, creating my ideal sleeping temperature. The pillows I'm resting on have molded perfectly to my head overnight. But it's something else too. Something warm and solid beside me. *Hannah.*

I register a small, soft hand on my chest. After a moment of confusion—because I *know* I wore a shirt to bed—I realize Hannah's hand has snuck *under* my t-shirt, as if seeking out my warmth in the middle of the night. I blink my eyes open to find that she's still on her side of the pillow barricade. Her left arm is the only thing crossing it, but somehow that's enough to completely throw me off.

The skin-to-skin contact is not helping relieve my morning wood, which usually goes away after a few minutes. I hesitate to move, because if I wake Hannah, not only will she likely be embarrassed that she has cuddled up to me in her sleep—she was the one who was worried about the bed's size, after all—but she might also catch sight of my erection.

Instead, I decide to close my eyes and wait to see if she'll wake up first. Besides, I don't hate the feeling of her hand on my chest. It's not a chore to hang out here like this for a bit. My mind wanders back to dinner the night before with Hannah, Mom, Heather, and Greg. Mom and Heather peppered us with questions about our relationship: how we reconnected, who made the first move, did we have feelings for each other back in high school, blah, blah, blah. Hannah did wonderfully. She never seemed nervous, never hesitated when answering their barrage of questions.

We had previously discussed some key points of our fake backstory to make sure we were on the same page: we reconnected at Waffee (the truth), I made the first move (pretty much the truth, considering I'm the one who proposed the fake marriage), and no, we didn't have feelings toward each other in high school (the truth...or at least that's what I've always told myself).

Hannah really sold the act with lots of affectionate glances toward me, touches on my shoulders and thighs, and a sweet kiss on the cheek that made the others audibly gush. If I hadn't known it was all fake, I might have believed it myself.

I have to admit, the affection felt...nice. It's been a long time since being with a woman involved more than just a quest for release. Even if none of this is real, it makes me wonder what it would be like if it *was*. This type of affection and support... Would it be worth it to give a relationship a shot? Could taking that chance possibly pay off? Or would it inevitably lead to heartbreak?

A light knock on the door startles me, and my eyes pop open.

Hannah awakens beside me, her eyes lazily blinking open. They grow wide as they take me in, and I can tell the moment she realizes her hand is tucked beneath my shirt, because she lets out a gasp, her fingers involuntarily retracting before she yanks them out.

"You guys awake?" comes Heather's hushed voice.

I glance at the clock on the bedside table. It reads nine-twenty-seven. *Shit.* I hadn't realized it was so late.

Hannah throws me a panicked look. "Heather?" she mouths.

I nod. "Just a second," I call out.

Hannah watches with horror as I toss the pillows separating us into the corner of the room.

"We have to look like we just slept together all night," I whisper. "Cuddle up to me."

She quickly complies, sidling up to me and resting her head on my shoulder. I swing her legs over my lap, realizing too late that she'll feel my goddamn morning wood after all.

I clear my throat before saying, "Come in," toward the door.

Heather cracks it open and peeks in as if to make sure we're decent before coming all the way inside the room.

"What, did you guys have a pillow fight last night?" she jokes with a glance toward the small mountain of pillows I created.

"Something like that," I mutter.

"Greg picked up pastries for everyone from our favorite place," Heather announces. "Dad and Marcie will be here in a couple hours, so we figured you'd want to get ready and eat before then."

Right. Dad and his shiny new family are arriving today. The rehearsal dinner is tonight, and Dad claimed he couldn't get out of work to arrive any earlier. I wonder if that's true, or if he was just trying to minimize the amount of time spent around me and Mom. I'm sure the only reason he agreed to come to the cabin at all is for Heather, who's the only family member he's still on good terms with.

Hannah must sense my unease, because she places a hand on my knee beneath the blanket where Heather can't even see it. This touch isn't for show. It's just for me.

I shoot her a quick, grateful glance. "Thanks, Heather," I say. "We'll be down soon."

Heather retreats, and Hannah and I untangle ourselves.

"Do you want the bathroom first?" I ask.

"Sure," she replies, but she remains sitting on the bed next to me. "How are you feeling about seeing your dad today?"

I shrug. "Heather suggested we go for a boat ride so at least there's something for us to do other than sit around staring at each other."

"That's a great idea," Hannah says with an encouraging smile that slides into a smirk. "And that way if things get awkward, you can just jump into the lake."

I playfully whack her knee, though that's not a bad idea.

"Who's going?" Hannah asks as she slips out of the bed.

"Dad, his wife, Marcie, their girls, Taryn and Taylor, Heather, Greg, and…I hoped you'd come with us," I reply. "I can make sure we're back in time for you to rest before the rehearsal dinner."

Hannah pauses gathering her clothes and toiletries and turns to me, her face softening. "Of course I'll come. And thank you."

Relief floods my veins. It's not just about convincing my family we're together. I want Hannah close to me. I can only imagine how it will feel being around Dad again, seeing him interact with his new family. His new wife. His new *kids*. I have a feeling it will take strength I haven't needed in a long while. The kind of strength only being beside Hannah can give me.

"Good," I say with a wink. "I hope you brought a bathing suit in case we end up needing to jump ship."

I can't get over the fact that my dad looks exactly the same. A few more grays and wrinkles maybe, but overall, he still looks like the man who raised me. The man who taught me how to ride a bike, how to multiply fractions, and how to talk to girls. The man who held Matty's hand as he transitioned from this world to the next and then held me while I sobbed uncontrollably.

Whatever changes took place inside him that allowed my dad to abandon our family are not apparent on the outside, but that only makes me more skeptical of him. He looks the same, but I know he's not.

Our initial reunion was awkward to say the least, with Dad leaning in to give me a hug and me curbing it for a handshake. He took it in stride, but I didn't miss the sorrow that ghosted over his face. Too bad. He made his bed. Now he can lie in it.

Taryn and Taylor, at two and three respectively, are adorable little girls with their mother's blonde hair and blue eyes. I've never met them in person, only having seen them in pictures on social media and Christmas cards. They couldn't look more different from Heather and me if they tried, with our dark eyes and hair in varying shades of brown. The fact gives me solace, creating a degree of separation between us.

I have nothing against my half-sisters. I'm mature enough to realize they aren't responsible for anything my dad did, but seeing or hearing about them has always left a sour taste in my mouth. It's a reminder that my dad moved on and replaced us as soon as shit got tough. They are living, breathing reminders of his betrayal.

All that aside, I have to admit they're adorable. When we were first introduced, the girls were shy, clinging to Marcie's legs and giving me only the smallest of smiles. I managed to make them giggle by asking their ages then telling them they must be twelve and thirteen. Such a cliché joke, but it always gets the job done. Tears sprung to my eyes when Taylor's nose scrunched the way Matty's always did when he laughed. In that moment, I made it one of my goals for this week to get to know them better.

Zooming around Lake Winnipesaukee on my family's boat, I'm finally beginning to loosen up. The girls are gawking at the other boats, jet-skiers, and tubers that share the water with us.

Dad and Marcie have mostly been enveloped in talking to Heather and Greg about the wedding, so Hannah and I have been able to relax on the bench at the back of the boat. She's never been to this area before, so I point out different sights as we cruise around. She looks adorable in her sunhat and sunglasses, orange hair whipping in the breeze so hard at times that she has to hold the hat down so it doesn't go flying.

I'm *this* close to actually being relaxed when my dad breaks away from the group and heads our way, taking a seat just across from us. Hannah must feel me tense up, because she grabs my hand and laces our fingers together.

"Beautiful day to be out on the water," Dad says.

"It is," I agree, giving him nothing to keep the conversation going. Maybe he'll get the hint and leave us alone.

No such luck. After an awkward pause, he starts again. "I have to say, it's really nice to see the two of you together." Dad turns toward Hannah. "How are you and your family doing?"

"We're doing well, thanks," she replies politely. "Annie and Owen graduated college this past spring, and they're both great. Annie's an associate at Ernst & Young, and she plans to follow that path all the way to making partner. Owen is helping coach football at the high school. I think he'd like to move up to the collegiate level eventually, but this is a good starting gig."

"That's great," Dad says. "Owen was a hell of a player back in the day. I'm sure he makes a great coach. And what do you do, Hannah?"

"I'm a freelance writer," she replies simply, with none of the zeal she gave Annie's or Owen's job descriptions.

"She's written for a lot of really big health and wellness publications," I add, despite my earlier plan to starve this conversation with silence. I can't let Hannah sell herself short. Even if she doesn't want to talk about her blog or the fact that she's created a vibrant virtual community that literally pays her bills, she deserves some recognition for the important work she does.

"Oh, that's great!" Dad says. "I remember reading your articles in the school newspaper."

Hannah's cheeks pinken. "I like to think my writing chops have improved a bit since then."

Dad goes on to talk about some article she wrote about the championship football game my junior year. How can I reconcile this man who used to read my school's newspaper with the one who chose to leave our family just years later? It's like he's two completely different people. The doting father turned deserter.

Hannah gives my hand a squeeze, and I realize Dad has asked me a question.

"Heather told me you're at a new startup?" he asks again when I meet his gaze.

"Yeah," I reply.

Dad's hopeful grin falls an inch. I know he's looking for more —conversation at the least, reconciliation at most—but right now civility is about all I can handle.

"I love the beard," he says, trying again. When will he get the hint that I don't feel like chatting? "How long have you had it?" he asks.

I stroke my beard. "A couple years now."

He nods. "It suits you."

It doesn't hit me until this very moment that my beard might be a way of setting myself apart from him. Growing up, people always said I looked like my dad. Same smile, same ears that stick out just a little more than I'd like. Now I've grown a beard around that smile and hair to conceal those ears.

Taryn saves me from having to engage in any more stilted conversation. "Hi, Daddy!" she shouts as she flings herself into my father's lap.

My heart stutters at the greeting. It's the first time I've heard either of the girls address my dad. Hearing that little voice reminds me so much of Matty. He called Dad "Daddy" long after Heather and I graduated to simply "Dad." In fact, he called him that until some kids at school heard him say it at drop-off and made fun of him for it. They stopped after I threatened to beat them all to a pulp, but Matty never called Dad that again.

They always had a special relationship, while I was a mama's boy through and through. Heather didn't play sides. Always the judicious one, she kept her affinities for Mom and Dad equal. But Matty...he was Dad's little sidekick. Maybe losing him was just too much, but I've always had this horrible notion that perhaps, without his favorite child, this family just wasn't worth keeping.

And even though I'm a grown man with a good life, that rejection still fucking hurts.

CHAPTER 24
CALEB

I had been joking about the bathing suit thing, but when it turned out to be an unseasonably warm September day, Hannah and I donned our swimsuits under our clothes in case we wanted to go for a dip. After a full lap around the lake, we decide to do just that, finding a shallow area to stop.

Hannah pulls a tube of sunscreen out of her bag and begins applying it to her exposed skin. I have to tear my gaze away when she props one foot up at a time on the seat and rubs the white lotion over her long, silky legs. I *cannot* get a hard-on right now. I begin applying some sunscreen of my own to distract myself.

Out of the corner of my eye, I notice Hannah removing her shorts and top, but it's not until I turn fully toward her that I realize she's wearing a bikini. *Fuck.* The navy-blue two-piece swimsuit sharply contrasts her pale skin and seems to accentuate every curve of her body. We bump over an errant wave from another boat's wake, and her perfect tits bounce a few times. I attempt to look away, but they demand my attention. Two beautiful, round mounds, and those goddamn freckles above her left one. They're practically begging for my mouth, or my—

"Babe?" Hannah asks sweetly, and my gaze snaps to hers. In

that moment, I realize two things: I was totally staring at her boobs, and my dad is totally staring at us.

"Hmm?" I mumble, playing off innocence.

"Could you help me get my back, please?" She holds out the tube of sunscreen.

I take it, and Hannah turns around so I can reach her back. *Damnit. God-fucking-damnit.* I think this view is even worse for my rapidly hardening cock. Her ass looks amazing nestled in the navy fabric. What I would give for us to be alone right now, and for everything we've been faking to be real.

I squeeze sunscreen onto my hands and begin rubbing it into her shoulder blades, mesmerized by the sight of my hands on her skin. I swear Hannah's shoulders relax beneath my touch, so I dig my thumbs in a little deeper, rubbing in circles as I go. I make sure to give any freckles I find an affectionate swipe.

I'm careful to cover every inch of her flawless skin. I'd never be able to forgive myself if she got burned. I slide my fingers beneath the strap around her back just in case her swimsuit gets jostled and the sun touches skin it shouldn't. It would be so easy to just flick the clip of the strap open and uncover the paradise waiting to be explored beneath her top, but instead, I keep moving my hands down, protecting her lower back with sunscreen.

"You guys all set?" my dad asks as I finish rubbing it all in. Taryn and Taylor are all prepared with their floaties on their arms, their faces streaked with sunscreen they wouldn't sit still long enough to get fully rubbed in.

"Yep," I reply hoarsely, capping the sunscreen and tossing it into Hannah's bag. She doesn't meet my eyes as she tucks her discarded clothes into her bag, and I wonder if she was equally affected by the sensation of my hands on her body.

"Let's go swimmin', guys!" Taylor shouts as she snaps a pair of shark goggles over her eyes.

"Tay, you'll be with me, and Taryn will stay by Mama," Dad instructs. They each help their individual charges into the water, and I take Hannah's hand to guide her to the edge of the boat. She slips on a slick patch, and my hand darts to her hip to steady her. My fingers dig dangerously low into her flesh, spanning the strap of her bikini bottoms with my pinkie beneath it and my pointer finger above.

Hannah sways into me as she catches her balance. "Thanks," she whispers before stepping into the water.

"No problem, *babe*," I say with a wink as I follow her in.

The water is on the cooler side this late in the summer, but that doesn't stop the girls from splashing around like they're in warm bathwater. Hannah laughs when Taryn leaps from Marcie's arms with a shriek, her floaties keeping her head above the water.

"Caleb, watch this!" Taylor hollers. My heart expands as I dutifully watch the enthusiastic three-year-old jump up before diving into a belly flop, her floaties keeping her from submerging completely. When she rights herself, I clap and whistle as if she's just done a perfect ten of a gymnastics routine.

The little girl beams, and I once again notice her resemblance to Matty. It almost makes me regret missing the first few years of her life. Maybe if I'd made an effort to meet the girls sooner, to know them better, it would have helped me to see Matty live on in them. I'm almost sorry I've avoided their existence.

Almost. Because while it's fun to see hints of Matty in them, they're still a tangible reminder of what my dad did.

After a half hour in the water, Taryn begins to fuss, and Marcie announces that she needs a nap. Dad suggests we all get back in the boat and head home so Taryn can sleep. Heather and Greg agree that heading home is a good idea. However, Taylor absolutely *refuses* to get out of the water, angrily stomping and splashing at the idea.

Marcie offers to stay with her while Dad takes Taryn home, since Marcie doesn't know how to drive the boat, but this sets Taryn off. Apparently, she is displeased by the idea of going with her dad instead of her mom. In the midst of both girls' tantrums, Hannah pipes up with an idea.

"Why don't Caleb and I watch Taylor while you all take Taryn home, then someone can come back and pick us up?"

Dad's brow wrinkles. "Are you sure?" He gives me a pointed look. "You don't mind?"

"That's fine," I reply, telling myself it's because it looks good to back up my girlfriend's idea, but also because I'm secretly craving more time with Taylor. The kid's a hoot, and it feels like I have a little piece of Matty with me.

Dad, Marcie, Heather, and Greg take off with Taryn, and Taylor flops onto her back, floating around under our watchful gazes.

"My daddy tells us about you and Matty all the time," the little girl says, her gaze toward the sky, as if she's telling a casual story and didn't just electrocute my brain circuits.

I drag my fingers over the surface of the water, watching the ripples it creates. "What does he tell you about us?"

"He talks about what you were like as kids, when you were as old as me and Taryn," Taylor states matter-of-factly. She kicks her feet to propel herself farther through the water. "And he says that he misses both of you."

The simple statement stops me in my tracks, and I freeze, my hand hovering over the water. I've always felt as if I lost my father right after losing Matty, as if my family was torn down the middle in one fell swoop. I never really considered that my dad might feel the same. Obviously, he lost Matty like the rest of us, but Heather stayed in contact when he left. I could have chosen to as well. Instead, Dad must have felt as if he lost both of his sons.

I can't decide if this makes me feel sad or vindictively thrilled.

Hannah sidles up to me and winds an arm around mine, taking my hand in hers. I know this touch is purely for comfort. She's not trying to convince the three-year-old we're together.

She's just showing that same silent support she has been since we arrived at the cabin.

"I miss him too," I finally say.

"You should come visit us in Illinois," Taylor suggests as she rights herself in the water, her floaties holding her up where she's not quite tall enough to reach the bottom.

"Maybe," I hedge, not wanting to break the kid's heart with a hard no.

"Heather has. It was really fun. She took us to the movies and bowling."

"That does sound fun," I reply, unwinding myself from Hannah and taking a big step through the water toward Taylor. "But I'm pretty sure swimming and doing cannonballs is even *more* fun."

I scoop the little girl up and toss her in the air, catching her lightly as she crashes down into the water. Her head submerges for a split second—just long enough to completely soak her. She sputters for a moment as she spits out the lake water that filled her mouth before shrieking with delight.

"Again!" she demands.

I comply, tossing her a couple more times. When I see my family's boat in the distance, I warn Taylor that we only have another minute or two to swim. She frowns, but it quickly flips into the cutest little smile as she gazes up at me through her shark goggles.

"I love you, Caleb," she says as she wraps her arms around my waist. They're nowhere near long enough to reach all the way around, and that simple fact reminds me just how small she is. How innocent. She hasn't had her heart broken yet. Hasn't experienced the type of loss that changes a person. The world hasn't had a chance to harden her. I make a wish that it never does.

I pat her little head. "I love you too, kid."

CHAPTER 25
HANNAH

Caffeine and alcohol can actually play a protective role for those with autoimmune diseases, but they can also be detrimental, especially if used to excess. I might afford myself the luxury of coffee, but I avoid alcohol due to potential medication interactions. Luckily, my best friend doesn't drink much, so it didn't affect our relationship, but living a sober lifestyle can be a big loss for many young people who enjoy drinking as a social activity.

Whether or not to drink alcohol with an autoimmune disease is a very individualized decision based on your body's reactions to it and the medications you're on. Always consult your doctor with questions regarding alcohol intake.

"It's ten-thirty," Caleb announces, rolling to his side to look over at me. He never reconstructed the pillow barrier in our bed, so we slept without it last night. I'm not sure if he was just too lazy, or if he no longer felt the need for it. Just in case it was the former, I hugged a pillow and slept facing away from him all night so there would be no more accidental chest touching.

"Okay," I say with a sigh, prying myself up from the pillows. We've been taking it easy this morning, lazing in bed and playing on our phones, but it's time to get ready for the ceremony. It will be held outdoors on a nearby property with an indoor/outdoor reception to follow.

We had the rehearsal dinner last night at the cabin—a big lobster boil for the nine of us staying here plus the maid of honor, best man, four bridesmaids, and three groomsmen. Everything seemed to go smoothly at the dinner. They seated Caleb and me as far from his dad and Marcie as humanly possible, which I think helped. Caleb has been nothing but cordial with his father, but I can tell it takes a lot out of him. He's always so tense when they talk, even if it's about the most mundane subjects. Sometimes when I watch them interact, it feels a bit like Caleb is a ticking time bomb. I'm afraid if his dad says or does the wrong thing, he could explode.

The saddest part of it all is the pure love shining on Caleb's dad's face whenever he looks at his son. You can tell he misses him deeply, which begs the question of why he alienated him in the first place. I remember Mr. O'Connor being a super-nice guy in high school. I can't picture him leaving his family, but who am I to know what the grief of losing a child will do to someone?

I would stand by Caleb whether we were pretending to be together or not. Even still, I can't help but feel a little bad for his father, and I can't help but wonder if there's more to the story.

Grabbing my bag of toiletries, I take the first shower so I can do my hair and makeup while Caleb takes his. The dress I'm wearing has a deep V-cut down the front, so I'm wearing my hair down to temper it. I choose fairly neutral makeup, in part because it's a lakeside wedding, and in part because I'm no makeup expert, and trying to look good in front of Caleb's entire family is *not* the time to try out a new look.

Once we're both ready, Caleb drives us the few minutes it takes to get to the venue. It's a big, beautiful, old ballroom with massive gothic arched windows overlooking the lake. Behind the building is a large grassy area framed by flowers, and from the passenger side window, I can see rows of chairs set up for the guests. I know from what Heather has said that there's also a wooden wedding arch.

We park, and Caleb goes off to join the other groomsmen in whatever pre-wedding preparation they have to do. I wander around the venue, psyching myself up for a day of playing my part. If I thought Caleb in a swimsuit yesterday was hot, then Caleb in a tux today is *scorching*. The better he looks, the more it scrambles my brain, making it difficult to parse out what's real between us and what's not. All that matters tonight, though, is that his family sees him happy and seemingly in love. I can deal with my own feelings later.

While circling the ballroom for the fourth time, I peek into one of the small adjoining rooms to find a worker putting together bouquets for the tables. I watch for a moment as she slides stem after stem into a vase, arranging the different colors and greens in an artfully balanced design. The wedding colors are blush and sage, so the bulk of the bouquets are peonies and eucalyptus.

The woman looks up and catches my stare. "Can I help you?" she asks.

I put my hands up in a *sorry I bothered you* kind of way. "My boyfriend's a groomsman," I explain. "I'm just killing time before the ceremony."

"Ah." She wipes a rogue petal from her hands. "It looks like it will be a beautiful one."

"The bouquets are gorgeous," I reply. "This might be a weird request but...could I join you in putting them together?" I've always found any form of gardening relaxing, and this seems like the perfect distraction for me until I need to transform into girlfriend mode.

She shrugs. "Sure, if you want to. I'm running a little behind anyway. The arch took me longer than I expected." She points through one of the windows toward the wedding arch, which I now see is decked out in the same peony-and-eucalyptus motif.

"It's stunning," I breathe. To be completely honest, I'm one of those women who has thought a lot about what I want my wedding to look like. Yes, I have a Pinterest board full of inspiration photos. Yes, I have ideas about color schemes, flowers, and a dress. I had ideas about what I wanted in a ring too, and somehow Caleb picked out one that might as well have been on my inspiration board. That's just a coincidence, though. I would never reveal to him just how much thought I've put into engagement and wedding stuff. I'm sure he'd see it as silly at best and sad at worst.

The woman shows me how to put together a balanced bouquet, and soon I get lost in flower arranging. Between the repetitive motion of placing the flowers and the creative process of choosing how much of each color and texture to have, it's a therapeutic experience. I forget all my worries about being convincing for Caleb's family, and hiding the fact that I'm actually becoming more attracted to him each day, and the fact that we're legally married, which still kind of makes my brain feel like it's exploding.

I lose track of time, and at some point, Caleb appears in the doorway, stopping short and sagging against the doorframe.

"There you are," he says, relief evident in his tone. "What are you doing in here?" he asks with a perplexed smile as he notices I'm elbow deep in a bucket of peonies.

"I was helping put the bouquets together," I reply. "It's relaxing."

Caleb steps into the room, his gaze scanning the sea of vases in various states of fullness. "I'm glad," he replies, "They look great, but the ceremony will be starting soon. You should probably get out there."

"Oh." I retract my hand and pat around for my cell phone before remembering I left it at the cabin. Seriously, all dresses should come with pockets. "How close are we?"

"We're set to start in ten minutes," he says, reaching out a hand that I take.

"Thanks for letting me help," I say to the woman.

"Thank you *for* your help," she says with a warm grin before we hurry from the building, making our way outside. Almost everyone is already in their seats, and suddenly I'm nervous about where *I'll* sit. Caleb will be standing up for Greg, so I could wind up all alone in the back row, looking like a misplaced loser.

I should know better by now, though, that Caleb wouldn't let something like that happen to me. Hand in hand, he marches me all the way up the aisle to where his family sits. I notice empty seats next to both his mother and Marcie, and I quickly realize two things: he saved a seat for me next to his mom, and his dad must be walking Heather down the aisle. The former makes little carbonation bubbles fizzle in my chest. The latter pops those bubbles as I wonder if Caleb will view that as some sort of betrayal.

I take my seat, and his mom pats me on the arm with a smile. Her eyes already swim with tears, which instantly makes the backs of my own eyes burn. Weddings always make me cry.

"I'll see you at the reception," Caleb says in a low voice before placing the sweetest kiss on my lips. I'm struck by how natural it feels to have his mouth against mine. His touch is no longer foreign, his kiss no longer anxiety-inducing. Butterflies still swarm my stomach each and every time we touch, but they're not nervous ones anymore. I don't know exactly when the change happened, only that it most certainly did.

When Caleb walks away, I'm left with lips tingling from his kiss, eyes burning with unshed tears over a mother preparing to watch her daughter wed, and a chest full of the lingering bubbles that even my worst worries couldn't pop.

The ceremony is wonderful. Heather has fantastic taste, which I should have guessed by the flowers, but the music, readings, and mix of traditional wedding vows and unique vows written by her and Greg themselves is simply sensational. I cry three separate times. Each time, I catch Caleb watching me with a funny look on his face, and I make an effort to pull it together.

Afterward, there's an outdoor cocktail hour while the bridal party takes photos. Once again, I'm left to my own devices without Caleb, and I end up sticking close to his mom's side. Of course, most of the people in attendance want to talk to her, so I spend a lot of the hour being introduced to new people as Caleb's girlfriend.

When it's finally time to go inside for the reception, I'm itching to be reunited with him. I miss his solid, soothing presence by my side. I know I'll have to wait a while longer, because the bridal party is going to be announced and come in one by one, but I'm already anticipating the night ahead of us. What began as nerves before the wedding has blossomed into excitement. Or maybe it always was.

Rhia once shared something with me that her therapist taught her: we often mistake excitement for anxiety because the sensations they cause in our bodies are so similar. Since they're both forms of arousal, they can make our hearts beat faster, make us sweat, and make our stomachs flutter. Maybe I haven't been nervous about pretending to be Caleb's girlfriend at all. Maybe I've been excited by the prospect.

"Hey, baby, you doing alright?" Caleb asks as he comes up beside me.

My body jolts like I've just stuck my finger in an electrical socket, surprised partly by his presence and partly by the endearment. I *am* walking beside his mom, though, so I know it's part of the act.

"I thought you had to walk in with the bridal party?" I ask.

"I wanted to check on you first," he says as he hands me a glass of lemon water, my drink of choice. Not only is it a refreshing alternative to alcohol, but the lemon can also help stimulate saliva production and help with my dry mouth. He must have remembered my order from the restaurant on our date. My heart squeezes at the thought.

Caleb places a hand on my arm, just above my elbow, as he leads me into the ballroom.

"I'm good," I reply, then I let out a gasp as I take in the fully transformed ballroom. The bouquets I helped put together sit elegantly at the center of each table, amidst white and gold plates and flatware. Tasteful, blush-pink bows adorn each chair, and matching swaths of chiffon drape across the ceiling. Candles flicker from every flat surface that won't be used for eating.

My eyes widen as I look around, amazed by all the work that's been done in the couple of hours since I last stood inside these walls.

Caleb gives me that same funny look he was giving me during the ceremony—an ever-so-slight frown and almost wistful eyes. "You really want all this someday, huh?" he asks.

"Yeah," I grudgingly admit, because I know he wants nothing to do with real marriage or anything that comes along with it—elaborate wedding included. "But we both know I'm a long way off from it."

Caleb doesn't respond, just leads me to a seat with a place card that has my name written in flawless calligraphy. "Here's our table," he says as he pulls out my chair. "I'll join you as soon as I can."

"Okay," I reply, settling as his mom takes the chair next to the one assigned to him. They have her seated between Caleb and Heather, who will obviously sit beside Greg. Next to him is Caleb's dad, then Marcie, Taryn, and Taylor, who have all taken their seats. Well, Taryn is currently standing on her seat and scanning the room, but they're all at the table.

Caleb subtly glances around the table, giving a quick, satisfied nod. He gives me another one of those familiar-feeling kisses before he's off again. I make small talk with his mom until it's time for the bridal party to file in, followed by the bride and groom. The maid of honor and best man lead the way, followed by Caleb and bridesmaid Kim. She's almost as tall as him in her heels, her honey-blonde hair wound into a breezy updo. She looks exquisite in her sage-green dress. It hugs her slim figure, framing her perfectly perky boobs with its scoop neck. Who has ever looked that good in a bridesmaid dress? They're supposed to be hideous—unflattering cuts or taffeta monstrosities.

An ember of white-hot jealousy burns in my belly as I watch Kim dance into the ballroom, her arm hooked in Caleb's. They make a gorgeous duo. Her blush-pink-tipped fingers clutch my husband's arm a little too tightly for my liking, and the ember burns brighter. Is Kim the kind of girl he'd usually be interested in? Blonde and big-boobed? I wouldn't blame him. She's very good looking and probably a lot of fun, based on the twerking interlude she took as they passed the DJ. But she's nothing like me.

They finally finish their entrance, and Caleb takes off toward our table while Kim heads for the table beside us, where the rest of the bridal party will sit. She's *definitely* staring at his ass as he walks a bit ahead of her. His tuxedo pants hug it quite nicely, as I recall from studying him earlier myself.

Upon his return to the table, Caleb leans down to give me another kiss. He's really showing off for his family this evening. I'm not sure if Kim is still watching, but in case she is, I decide to do a bit of grandstanding myself. I have no idea if she's actually interested in him, but just in case, I decide to stake my claim.

When Caleb goes to pull back, I grab his tie and deepen the kiss. There's been no tongue involved in any of our kisses since our practice kiss outside my apartment after our first date. Tonight, there's tongue.

After kissing a few moments longer than is probably appropriate, I release Caleb's tie, and he pulls back slightly, his eyes blazing. He doesn't look like he wants to stop, but we realize at the same time that the DJ is announcing Heather and Greg's entrance, so Caleb takes his seat beside me.

We might no longer be kissing, but he does keep a hand planted firmly on my thigh, as if to say *hold that thought*.

CHAPTER 26
CALEB

Dinner is awkward. My mom, Hannah, and I tend to branch into our own conversations while Dad, Marcie, and the girls talk amongst themselves. Heather desperately tries to bring the conversations together and unite the table. We humor her by trying to find topics we can all chat about, but the truth is we have nothing in common. Dad's gone back in time to the toddler years, while Mom is empty-nesting, her millennial children having forged their own paths in life.

The toasts are sweet and a welcome break from the forced socialization. The best man and maid of honor go the humorous route with their speeches, while Mom goes sentimental. I'm glad Heather had Mom make a toast instead of Dad, who would traditionally get the opportunity as father of the bride. He got to walk her down the aisle, *and* he gets the father-daughter dance, neither of which he deserves, in my opinion. Mom makes a comment in her speech about wishing Matty could be here but knowing he's watching from wherever he is. There's not a dry eye in the room.

Dad and Heather have their dance first, and I spend most of it focused on touching Hannah—holding her hand, playing with her fingers, anything to distract me from the main event. Afterward, Greg and his mom perform a choreographed routine to a show tune from their favorite Broadway musical. It's a little chaotic but very cute. Dad and Heather wouldn't have been able to pull something like that off—he lives too far away for them to put it all together in advance.

As soon as the DJ begins his setlist and announces it's time for the dancing to begin, I grab Hannah's hand and haul her to the dance floor, as far away from my father as possible.

"Hey," I say once we're camouflaged in a sea of dancing bodies. "Sorry to drag you over here without asking. Do you feel like dancing?"

Hannah grins up at me and gives a little shimmy. "Let's do it."

We get down to a mix of the current chart-toppers and early 2000's pop classics. Dancing with Hannah, I feel at ease for the first time today. She's smiling through every song, loose and free as she moves her body to the music. She doesn't hesitate to shimmy and shake as I cycle through my collection of silly dance moves. From the robot to the sprinkler, they get increasingly ridiculous as I see how hard they make her laugh. I don't know if there's a better sound or sight than Hannah laughing.

Her smile fades when a slow song comes on. She looks a little unsure of herself, those doe eyes widening. We've just spent the last twenty minutes making fools of ourselves, but she chooses now to get self-conscious. I won't have it.

"Dance with me," I say, reaching a hand toward her in invitation.

Hannah's lips flicker upward as she takes it. I settle a hand on her hip, and she places hers on my chest as we start swaying to the music.

"How are you doing?" she asks, tipping her chin up and lifting her gaze to meet mine.

"I'm good," I assure her. But it's Hannah, so I can be completely honest. "Happy the hard parts are over."

She smooths her hand over my lapel. "I'm sorry there had to be any hard parts for you."

"It's okay," I reply. "Just sucks to see my dad get such a spotlight on Heather's special day. And sucks not to have Matty here."

"I know." She gives me a sad smile. Then she leans in so her cheek is against my chest, a form of a hug without halting our dance. My lips are right next to her ear, and I can't help but drop a kiss behind it. We stay like this for a long moment, though I think I'd be happy to stay here forever.

Eventually, Hannah lifts her head, sucking in a gasp when I immediately lead her into a spin. A giggle spills from her lips as she regains her bearings, twirling before returning to her rightful spot in my arms. For a final flourish, I dip her low, her hair fanning out behind her as she throws her head back. When she's upright again, gripping my shoulder to steady herself, it feels as if the air has changed. Electrified. Like there's a livewire running from my body to hers through our connected hands.

I drop my forehead to hers, wondering if she feels the change too. The song fades away, but I don't want it to be over. Or maybe I just don't want my connection with Hannah to be severed.

"Want to go outside for a bit?" I ask. We've been dancing for a while. We could probably use the break. And I can't bring myself to go back to the foolish dance moves after the moment we just shared.

Hannah nods. "Sure," she says breathlessly.

I keep hold of her hand and lead her out the door, back toward where the ceremony was held. A few others loiter by the chairs and the wedding arch, but we walk past them all down to a little wooden gazebo at the edge of the lake.

Hannah gazes out over the water, currently bathed in the soft light of golden hour.

"It's stunning," she whispers.

I keep my gaze on her, taking in her rosy cheeks and hair slightly disheveled from dancing. "Yes, it is."

Her gaze turns to mine. There's a question in her eyes, but I can't quite tell what it is.

I lift a hand to her face, running my thumb over her pink cheek. "Are you feeling alright?" I ask.

"It's not a Lupus rash," Hannah says, reading my mind. "Just the curse of having fair skin and exerting myself more than usual." She smiles wryly. "Besides, you're not supposed to be worried about *me* when I'm here to support *you*."

I still my thumb and cup her cheek with my palm. "I'll always worry about you, Hannah."

Her lips part slightly. How could she be surprised by this revelation? I've told her before—more than once—how seriously I take my commitment to her. Even if we'd never signed legal documents, it wouldn't change a thing. I realize our relationship has been a bit transactional, but what I feel for her is the realest thing I've ever experienced.

"Thank you, by the way," I add.

Her tongue darts out to wet her lips. "For what?"

"Everything," I say before leaning down to kiss her.

"Caleb," Hannah whispers, gaze darting side to side. "No one's looking at us."

I take her other cheek in my hand. "I don't care." This kiss isn't for show. It's for me.

My lips descend, catching hers as I hold her face in my hands, tilting her head to the exact angle I want. Despite her hesitation, Hannah seems ready for the kiss, her lips parted and pliant. She certainly doesn't seem hesitant anymore as her hands find my shoulders, fists bunching in my shirt and tugging me closer.

A low moan fills the space around us, and it takes me a moment to realize it's coming from me. It might have been enough to embarrass me if Hannah didn't immediately follow up with a hungry groan of her own, as if hearing proof of my pleasure was enough to loosen her own inhibitions.

I drop my hands to circle her waist, enjoying the feel of the slippery, smooth fabric of her dress beneath my fingers. The delicate curves below it feel even better. Hannah is so, *so* soft. What I really want is my hands on her skin, but since we're in a semipublic place, the logical part of my brain that's still working at about ten percent capacity reminds me that I can't rip this dress off to get at what's underneath.

Hannah's arms wind around my neck as if she can't get close enough. We're chest to chest now, the kiss turning feverish. Her eager participation gives me the courage to drop a hand, resting it low on her back. When she doesn't seem to mind that, I glide it even lower.

In the millisecond of space between frantic kisses, I hear the ghost of a whimper emerge from Hannah's lips, and it has me squeezing a handful of her ass. Another moan that I have no control over spills from my throat. We're all hands and lips and throaty sounds, and I don't have a single thought of my complicated relationship with my father, or Hannah's and my deal, or whether anyone's watching us or not. I'm just here in this moment with her, and it's perfect.

A boat horn blares, startling us. Hannah lurches backward, wrenching her mouth off mine. She lifts a hand to her lips, touching them lightly. "What are we doing?" she asks softly.

I'm still loose and lax from our kiss, so I mistakenly go with a brash answer. "I think most people would call that kissing."

Hannah crosses her arms, turning to look out at the lake. The boat that forced us apart is chugging along, creating a small wake behind it. She doesn't look back at me when she speaks. "We're pretending to date, we're legally married, and now we're *actually* kissing? Caleb, this is…confusing."

"Hannah." I tap her elbow in an attempt to gain her full attention. "I want you. Is that clear enough?"

Her wide-eyed gaze turns to me. "What?"

"I want you." My voice comes out gravelly with need, something that once again might be embarrassing if I wasn't so fucking far gone for this girl.

"I don't understand," she sputters, genuinely baffled.

"We're pretending to date, we're legally married, and neither of those things has any bearing on the fact that *I. Want. You*," I explain slowly. "And unless I'm way off base, I think you want me too."

Hannah rubs her hands up and down her arms, making me notice the goosebumps that have erupted there. "Caleb, I... Of course I do," she says with a laugh that sounds anything but humorous. "It just feels..."

"Complicated?" I supply. "Scary? Yeah, I feel those things too. But fuck it... I still want you."

She finally drops her arms, that protective stance shattered. "So what are we going to do?" she asks.

"Let's go back to the cabin," I suggest.

"Caleb, you can't just leave your sister's wedding."

"Why not?" I ask. "All the important stuff's over."

"They haven't cut the cake yet," she points out.

I let out a frustrated groan that sounds lightyears different from the sounds I was making just moments ago. "Fine," I say. "We make one more appearance, eat our cake, and then we're out of there."

Hannah's lips pull up into a coy grin. "Deal."

Even after we return inside, the goosebumps remain on Hannah's skin, so I drape my tuxedo jacket over her shoulders in case she's cold. The sight of her drowning in my jacket only has me more eager to get her back to the cabin—some primal instinct, probably.

Somehow, in the fairly short amount of time we were gone, Kim's gotten absolutely plastered. She's currently on the floor, most likely attempting to do the worm, but she looks more like a fish out of water, flopping around on her belly. I'm so glad I brought Hannah instead of agreeing to be Kim's date.

Heather and Greg cut their cake, a gorgeous three-tiered chocolate ganache cake with vanilla buttercream frosting. Thank Christ our table is served first. I wolf down my slice while Hannah takes her time, sucking every inch of frosting off her fork and moaning with pleasure every few bites. I can't tell if she's teasing me or not, but either way, I'm getting harder by the second.

Once she's finally done and the dance floor is open again, sufficiently distracting everyone, I grab Hannah's hand and make a break for it. On our way out, I see Taryn and Taylor passed out in two of the velvet chairs in the lobby area, with Marcie watching over them. *Fuck. Yes.* That means we'll have the cabin all to ourselves for a while.

I give Marcie a quick wave before dashing out the door with Hannah in tow, bringing her to my car and ultimately back to the cabin, where I hope to bring her pleasure until she begs me to stop.

CHAPTER 27
HANNAH

The drive back to the cabin is excruciating. Caleb and I are like a couple of horny teenagers trying to sneak in a tryst in one of their parents' houses while they're not around. He's driving well over the speed limit, and he's had to adjust himself twice since sitting down in the driver's seat. The fact that all this urgency is for *me* is, well, really freaking exciting.

When we finally arrive, the car jolts to a stop before Caleb flings his door open, jogging around the car for mine. He pulls me from the car, and I stumble for a moment, making us both chuckle at how ridiculous we're being. Those carbonation bubbles in my chest are back, and I feel effervescent, like I'm walking on clouds as we approach the cabin. I'm downright giddy.

As soon as the front door slams shut, Caleb's mouth is on mine. He slides his jacket from my shoulders, tossing it over the back of the couch in the living room. I grab his slightly loosened tie and yank at the knot until it comes undone, then pull it off and cast it aside with the jacket.

"Let's get upstairs before we wind up leaving an entire

clothing trail," Caleb suggests, grabbing my hand once again to haul me to our room.

Somehow the sight of the bed—*our* bed—strikes me as soon as I lay eyes on it. This is real. Me and Caleb. We've been sharing this bed for days now, but this is the first time we're *sharing* the bed. I should be nervous. I haven't slept with anyone since my college boyfriend. It's been five years with no intimacy, and I should be worried about performing. But I'm not. All I feel is excitement and heady anticipation. I've never trusted a man as much as I trust Caleb. He's gone above and beyond to prove that he cares about me, and I have no doubt that care will translate into the bedroom.

Caleb tugs his shirt out of his pants and goes for the buttons, but his fingers are shaking. I wonder if it's nerves or excitement. I wonder which one it *really* is, and which one he's experiencing it as. I don't want him to be nervous, but if he is, I'll do my best to care for him the way I know he would for me.

I take his hands off the buttons and replace them with my own, carefully undoing them one by one. If I'd left him to his own devices, he'd probably have ended up ripping the damn thing down the front to get it open. I don't know if the shirt is rented or not, but I don't want him ruining a perfectly nice dress shirt.

Caleb's espresso eyes track my movements as I undo the last button and gently drag each arm out of its sleeve until the shirt falls to the floor. I've slowed the pace down, but he doesn't seem to mind. He's watching me intently, as if memorizing my every move.

With his shirt out of the way, my gaze snags on his necklace. I vaguely recall noticing a chain tucked into his shirt, but I never thought much about it. The chain isn't what captures my attention now, though. It's what hangs from it.

Caleb's sterling-silver wedding band is suspended mid-chest. He's wearing his wedding ring. As I quickly scroll through my memories, I realize he's been wearing it ever since we got married. He's been *wearing his wedding ring.* Maybe not on his finger in the traditional sense, but he's had it on his body, nonetheless.

"You…you wear this all the time?" I ask, taking it between my fingers then letting it fall back against his chest.

Caleb takes the ring in his fist and holds it there. "I wanted to keep it close to my heart," he says.

My stomach bottoms out, dropping low to make room for my rapidly expanding heart. Pushing up on my tiptoes, I give Caleb a quick kiss then wrap my arms around him, pressing my face into his neck. The hug turns our passionate encounter tender for the moment, and I love that we can flip from hot to sweet and back again in the space of a heartbeat. It's something I've never experienced with another man, and something I think is only possible when you've known someone for so long. When you've created a level of comfort that allows for layers of affection.

When I pull back, I take my time studying Caleb. I saw him shirtless on the boat yesterday, finally saw the entirety of his tattoo collection, but now I have full access to them for the first time. I'm not sure where to start. Clasping his shoulder, I rub my thumb over the large, holey leaf inked at the very top of his bicep. I recognize it as coming from a monstera plant, as I have one of those in my own collection.

There's something scrawled just above it, at the very top of his tattoo sleeve. I lean in a little closer for a better look and realize it's Matty's signature. All the other tattoos, the many doodles and sketches that dance down Caleb's arm, seem to flow from Matty's name. It's such an unbelievably beautiful tribute to his brother, and despite the heat of the moment, I find myself getting a little choked up.

I lean forward and press a kiss on Caleb's bicep, right on the signature tattoo.

He shivers and grabs me by the waist, yanking me forward and crashing his lips to mine, promptly ending my brief tattoo tour. I wish I'd had more time to explore—not just the tattoos, but also his body—and I promise myself there'll be time later. Caleb is burly, with the type of body you can tell is muscular, but not honed or cut. Like, his stomach isn't flat, but you can see his biceps without him flexing. I want to touch every inch of him, discovering where hard muscle meets soft flesh.

The downy brown hair on his chest tickles against the exposed skin on mine as we kiss. His hands tangle in my hair, gently pulling my head where he wants it. I run my palms over his bare back, relishing the warmth of his skin.

Caleb's fingers find the top of the zipper on the back of my dress. "Can we take this off?" he breathes, winded from our kiss.

"Yes," I whisper.

His hands aren't shaking anymore as he slides the zipper down and helps me out of the dress. It falls down my body, pooling on the floor and leaving me in just the thin, black lace bra and panties I wore to reduce any lines beneath my dress.

Caleb's eyes are all over me. He saw me in a bathing suit yesterday too, but my lingerie leaves a lot less to the imagination. My excited nipples strain against the lace of my bra, begging for his attention. My panties sit low on my hip bones, only covering the essentials.

He hauls me in for another kiss, his hands roaming my body as his lips devour mine. They find my ass like they did in the gazebo, but this time, it's skin-on-skin contact, and I lose all control. I arch into him, hitching my leg up and hooking it around his waist as if trying to climb him like a tree. He grabs my other cheek and lifts, encouraging me to do the same with my other leg. Soon, I'm lifted completely off the ground, my legs circling his waist as he carries me toward the bed. He sets me down gently, lowering my back to the mattress as he hovers over me, gaze pinned on my breasts.

"Caleb," I whine when his looking isn't immediately followed by touching.

I'm rewarded with his devilish smile. "Did you need something?" he teases. He's suspended above me, his wedding ring dangling down right into my field of vision. I grab it to tug him closer.

"Kiss me," I insist. "Touch me."

He grins and kisses a spot on my chest, right above my left breast. I think I have a couple of freckles there. "Kiss you where?" he asks, skimming his fingers up my side. "Touch you where?"

"Here," I beg, cupping my breasts and practically shoving them toward his face.

"Here?" he asks, pressing his lips between them, where the two cups of my bra connect and very obviously *not* where I'm dying for him to kiss me.

"No," I complain, skimming my fingers over my nipples for a taste of relief.

"Here?" he asks, kissing the side of a breast.

"Warmer," I reply.

"Here?" he asks, only having moved his lips an inch closer to where I want them.

"Caleb, *please*."

"Oh," he says, as if understanding just dawned. "*Here*," he says before sucking my nipple between his lips, instantly soaking the lace of my bra. *Bullseye.*

My hips shoot off the bed, searching for friction. "Yes," I hiss as he sucks and licks one nipple and then the other, working me up without even getting me fully naked.

Caleb pulls back, looking down at his handiwork. "Hannah," he growls, pinning me with a disapproving glare. "Your bra is all wet. We'd better get that off you."

I sit up shakily, living for a teasing Caleb. "I could use some help, if you wouldn't mind," I say.

"If you insist," he says as he reaches for the clasp, undoing my bra and tossing it toward where my dress lays on the floor before diving back in, head dipping to lavish my bare breasts with more kisses.

I thread my fingers into his hair, playing with it as he works me over. I give some of the strands a light tug, and Caleb lets out a moan like the one in the gazebo. I had never heard him make a sound like that, and it only made me want to hear it again. It has now become my personal mission to hear him make that sound as often as possible. I tug a little harder, and I'm well on my way toward accomplishing that mission when Caleb's lips slip from my nipple with a pop.

"You're driving me nuts," he says against my breast.

"You're driving *me* nuts," I reply as I writhe beneath his mouth.

He looks up, piercing me with his gaze. "Is this a bad time to make a joke about nuts?"

My chest shakes with laughter, and the movement catches Caleb's eyes again.

"Fuck," he mutters. "Do that again."

"What?" I ask. "Laugh? You'll have to make me."

His eyes darken as he shifts so we're face to face. "I'd rather make you come."

I think my lips drop open at his carnal words, but I'm not even sure because Caleb immediately catches them in a kiss. It feels like his hands are everywhere—my breasts, my hair, my hips. One of them trails down my stomach, his fingers pushing just under the elastic of my panties.

"Caleb," I grab his wrist, halting his progress. "Hold on."

He retracts his hand, pulling back so he can see my face. "What's wrong?"

The tender care in his expression slays me. This man. This sweet, sweet man, who also just told me he wants to make me orgasm, would so clearly do anything I asked him to right now.

"Shit…" I mutter. "I don't mean to ruin the moment. I just…"

I try to think of the best way to explain this without completely throwing our night off the tracks.

"Talk to me, Hannah," Caleb says, stroking my cheek. "You can tell me anything." He shifts so he's on his side, head resting on his fist.

"So, you know how my Sjogren's is called 'the dryness disease'?" I ask, and he nods in confirmation. "Well, it causes more than dry eyes and mouth. Another common symptom is vaginal dryness. I'm lucky I only get it mildly, but it does affect me...sexually. I *do* get wet, just not wet enough."

I don't bother mentioning that I only know this from intimate exploration on my own, not with another human, since my college boyfriend dropped me like a hot potato as soon as he heard the words *chronic illness*. At home, I keep my bedside drawer stocked with lube for any time I need to take care of myself, but I never expected I would need it on this trip, so I didn't bring any.

"What does that mean for us?" Caleb asks.

I swallow hard. "It means I can't have sex without lube, and I don't have any with me."

He seems to be thinking for a moment before he nods. "I don't have condoms here anyway."

The way he says this, as if it's no big deal, worries me at first. I think he's about to call this whole thing off—chalk it up to a horny, heat-of-the-moment mistake that we'll eventually laugh off. But when he grabs a hair tie from his pocket, smoothing his overlong tresses back into a stubby ponytail, then shucks off his tuxedo pants, I realize he has a different plan in mind.

CHAPTER 28
HANNAH

Caleb crawls over me again, and I want to complain that I didn't have enough time to admire his tree-trunk thighs and the prominent bulge protruding from his boxers, but I can't find my voice. You know that cliché about guys getting turned on by women putting their hair up in ponytails before giving them head? I understand it now.

"Can I use my mouth on you?" he asks as he fingers the edge of my panties.

I nod, my voice still hiding somewhere deep within the recesses of my body. I feel like I could spontaneously combust at any moment.

"Will that be...uncomfortable for you?" he asks, and I shake my head vigorously, struggling to wait now that I know what's coming.

Caleb's mouth spreads into a lazy smile. "Good," he says before dragging my panties down my legs and flinging them away. The hungry stare he focuses at the apex of my thighs heats me to a boiling point.

Despite the complete lack of control I have over my mind as thoughts of his mouth on me spiral around in dizzying circles, some latent part of my brain has the wherewithal to realize that

Caleb barely even reacted to my problem. He didn't seem disappointed for even a second when he realized my medical issues might mess up our night. As if my disease is no hurdle, no obstacle to overcome, but rather simply something to work around.

All coherent thoughts flutter away as Caleb settles himself over me, dipping his head to lick up one inner thigh and then the other before heading dead center. His tongue explores for a bit, lapping at my slit and teasing my opening. Then he pulls back slightly and does something I didn't necessarily see coming, but I definitely don't dislike.

He. Spits. On. My. Pussy.

A feral groan leaves my throat. Caleb really said: *No lube? No problem.*

He uses one thick thumb to spread his saliva around on my clit, slow clockwise circles that have me bucking into his touch.

"So pretty," he murmurs as he watches his finger work. His gaze lifts to mine, which is also entranced by the sight. "Does that feel good?"

"Yes," I sigh, eyelids drifting shut as he lowers his head again. His beard scrapes the skin on my inner thighs as he feasts. It's a heady combination of sensations—the coarseness of his beard mixed with the softness of his lips and languid strokes of his thumb. The mustache hair that lightly tickles my clit when he draws his thumb away feels like a tease.

I'm mourning the loss of that finger when he eases a different one inside me, curling it until he elicits a whimper. I open my eyes to find he's watching his handiwork again, gaze pinned on where his middle finger pushes in and out of me. He looks completely fascinated by what he's doing.

"Is that okay?" Caleb asks when he notices me looking at him.

"It's great," I reply with a wide smile I can't control.

He grins back at me before concern clouds his expression. "And what I did earlier…that was okay too?"

I reach for his face, taking his cheek in my palm to reassure him. "Everything you do is perfect, Caleb."

He twists his head to place a kiss on the center of my palm. "Good."

Pulling his finger from me, Caleb takes my ankles and slides me down the bed until my ass is perched on the bottom edge.

"What are you doing?" I squeal as he arranges me, kneeling to the floor and placing the soles of my feet on his shoulders.

"We might not be able to have sex tonight," he answers, "but that doesn't mean we both can't enjoy this."

I don't understand what he means until I catch movement below the edge of the bed. I realize he's lowered his boxers, and when only one hand comes back up above the edge of the bed, I know the other is wrapped around his cock.

Looking me in the eye, peering straight into my soul, Caleb spits again, and then his middle finger is back inside me, his tongue laving my clit. From the limited motion I can see of his other arm, I can tell he's timed the thrusts of his fingers with the strokes of his own cock.

"So soft," he murmurs against my skin. "Tastes so good."

I toss my head back on the mattress, fully surrendering to this wild, erotic moment. If you had told me twenty-four hours ago that Caleb O'Connor would be jerking himself while eating me out, I would have called you ridiculous.

Yet, here we are.

He guides a second finger inside me, his mouth still pampering my clit, and I push my feet into his shoulders in an effort to get closer. I'm climbing higher, soaring toward orgasm, when Caleb curls his fingers to hit a spot that tips me over the edge. Then, I'm pulsating around his digits, crying out as pleasure overtakes me. My thighs tremble as they push against his ears, and I'm unsure if they're trying to trap him there or close together to avoid overstimulation.

It's veering toward too much when Caleb expertly slows the strokes of tongue, continuing with long, slow pulls that draw out every ounce of my pleasure. He doesn't stop until I've worked through every last aftershock. My body has melted into a puddle on the bed, totally sated.

"Fuck," Caleb mutters, gently removing my feet from his shoulders.

My legs splay out wide, my body limp and my brain too muddled for modesty. I lazily blink my eyes open to find Caleb standing, and I catch my first sight of his cock—long, and hard, and so clearly seeking release that I can't believe he hasn't blown already.

All that excitement from touching *me*. Tasting *me*. I hadn't even seen his cock until a moment ago, let alone touched it, and he's about to come just from pleasuring *me*.

Caleb steps to the edge of the bed, at the perfect position to push inside of me if only we had condoms and lube. He cups his heavy balls in one hand, stroking himself with the other with quick tugs. It doesn't take many before he comes with a low groan, aiming himself at my belly and painting it with his pleasure. The absolute ferocity in his eyes, the way his teeth bite into his bottom lip, the fact that his beard is damp from what he did to me...it's all so sexy I'm already ready to do what we just did all over again.

"Shit," Caleb says, wiping a hand down his beard once he finishes. "I'm sorry. I didn't ask if I could..." He gestures toward his cum on my belly.

"Caleb." I scramble to sit up and kneel on the bed, putting us around eye level, and grab his shoulders. "Stop second-guessing yourself. Everything you did was...so *hot*."

"You liked that?" he asks with a satisfied smile.

"I loved it," I correct.

He treats me to a sweet, slow kiss before pressing his forehead to mine. "I don't want to do anything that makes you uncomfortable. We made so many rules for ourselves, but not for this."

"We don't need rules for this." I pull back to catch his gaze. "This is just us."

Caleb's eyes soften, and he kisses my forehead. "I'll get us cleaned up." He pulls up his boxers and heads for the bathroom across the hall. I hear water running before he returns with a wet cloth, using it to wipe his cum from my skin. I'm honestly a little sad to see it go. Without a physical reminder of what we just shared, I'm liable to think it was all a dream.

He discards the cloth and grabs a couple of his t-shirts—one for himself and one for me. I pull it on, and I'm immediately enveloped in his woodsy scent. Maybe it's something in his laundry detergent? I never want to take this shirt off...unless maybe it is Caleb taking it off me.

A yawn escapes my mouth. It's been a long day between getting ready for the wedding, attending it, and then everything the night turned into. I haven't done this much activity in one day in a very long time.

"Let's go to bed," Caleb suggests, pulling back the covers. It's not even that late yet, but the thought of drifting off in Caleb's arms, surrounded by his scent, is too tempting to pass up. I climb in, pleased when he scoots in beside me and bands an arm around my waist, holding me close.

There's *definitely* no pillow barricade tonight.

CHAPTER 29
CALEB

C arefully placing the cardboard tray of iced coffees on the passenger seat, I set off toward the cabin. Leaving Hannah in bed asleep in just one of my t-shirts was downright grueling, but this errand run had to be done. I left her a note on my pillow in case she wakes up. The last thing I want is for her to wake up alone and think I took off as though last night was a mistake or something. When she sees what I got for her while I was out, she'll know that's not the case.

Back at the cabin, I find my mom already awake and cooking breakfast in the kitchen. The mouthwatering scent of sizzling bacon wafts toward me as the front door cracks open, quickly followed by a hint of cinnamon.

Mom glances over her shoulder at me. "Hi, sweetheart."

"Hey, Mom," I reply, setting one of the coffees on the counter next to her and noting the French toast she's flipping in its pan.

"You're up early," she notes.

"Mmm," I reply noncommittally, taking a sip of my own coffee.

"And you took off early last night," she adds.

I scratch at the back of my neck, which is suddenly warm. "Right...sorry about that."

Mom turns and places a hand on my cheek. "It's okay, sweetie. I don't think Heather even noticed. And I'm just so glad you're happy with Hannah."

You have no idea how happy, I want to say. But all I say out loud is, "Me too."

"This should all be ready in about twenty minutes." She gestures to the various pans on the stove. "Your dad, Marcie, and the girls will be joining. I hope you and Hannah will too. Heather and Greg are sleeping in, but they'll come in a couple hours so we can all go on that hike."

I let out a groan. "She seriously still wants to do that?" I ask. Only Heather would want to go on a family hike the day after her wedding and the biggest party of her life. I know she's taking advantage of the fact that we're all here together in one place for the first time in years, but honestly...shouldn't she want to stay holed up in that hotel room with her new husband all day?

"Yes," Mom says sternly. "And she doesn't want to hear any complaints."

"I'll have to see if Hannah's up to it," I say, which is partly true and partly just an excuse to hopefully get us out of the hike. I have a much better idea for how to spend our day.

Mom's features soften. She knows about Hannah's illnesses, and I think she also loves the fact that I'm looking out for her.

"I'm sure Heather will understand if she's not. I know she's grateful Hannah was able to make it to yesterday's events."

I grab Hannah's and my coffees from the tray. "I'll let you know." I point to the remaining two coffees. "Dad and Marcie can have those."

Mom raises a brow. "They can have them, or you got them for them?"

I shrug. "Does it matter?"

"Caleb," Mom says on a sigh. "Not everything with your father has to be a fight."

"I haven't fought with him this whole time," I point out.

"You haven't exactly been warm and welcoming either."

"Why would I be warm and welcoming to the man who ditched us during the hardest time of our lives?"

Mom looks down at her pan, head hanging in defeat. She never speaks ill of my father, and I think that only fuels my own hostility even more. If she and Heather won't voice their contempt, I'll do it enough for all three of us.

Suddenly, the sight of Mom cooking for her ex-husband and his new family while she lectures me on forgiveness makes my skin crawl. "We'll be down for breakfast," I say, scooting up the stairs to our bedroom. When I swing the door open, I'm disappointed to find that not only is Hannah not waiting for me naked in bed, but she's not in the room at all. The note I left her has been moved from the pillow to the nightstand, so she must have seen it.

I place my spoils on the bedside table and take a seat on the bed, pulling out my phone to make sure I didn't miss any texts from Hannah. I've just pulled up our text thread when she breezes into the room, stopping short in the doorway when she spots me.

"Hi," she breathes, frozen in space. She's freshly showered, her hair damp and hanging around her shoulders. She's still wearing my t-shirt, though it's now stylishly tucked into a pair of denim cutoff shorts.

"Hi," I reply, slowly standing, as if any sudden movements might have her darting off like a scared animal. Any trace of the uninhibited woman I slept with last night has vanished, leaving a shy, timid one in its wake.

I grab one of the iced coffees and hold it out to her. "They didn't have iced caramel lattes at the general store," I say, grabbing one of the plastic bags of items I got. "So I got these too."

Hannah shuts the door and takes a few steps toward me. She accepts the coffee and peeks into the bag, which contains a small carton of almond milk and a bottle of caramel syrup, like you'd put on an ice cream sundae. I have no idea if she can make a decent latte-like drink with these, but the adorable grin on her face when she sees them is worth it even if not.

"Thank you." She puts the bag on the bed. "That was really thoughtful."

"I got you some other things too," I add, handing her the other plastic bag. She opens it and looks inside, her eyes lighting up like the sun peeking over the horizon at sunrise, brightening her whole face.

"What did you do?" Hannah asks with a giggle.

"I prepared," I reply as she continues gawking at the contents of the bag. Inside, there's a box of condoms and one tube of every type of lube the general store sold. There have to be at least ten kinds. Warming, cooling, tingling, flavored... I figured we could do a "choose your own adventure" type of thing.

"What are you, some kind of lewd Boy Scout?" she asks as she dumps the collection out on the bed.

I hold up three fingers in the scout salute. "At your service."

Hannah shakes her head, laughing. "When are we going to use all this? Aren't we hiking with your family today?

"I thought you might not feel up to it," I say.

Her brows shoot up. "You thought I might not be up for hiking, but I'd be up for the type of physical exertion that requires ten different types of lube?"

"I *mean*," I say, "I thought you *might not be up to it*." I use air quotes as I say the last part.

"Caleb," she grumbles. "We can't skip this after we left the reception early."

"I promise, we can," I reply. "We're having breakfast with both my parents, Marcie, and the girls, and then we're having dinner with all of them *plus* Heather and Greg. I think that's plenty of family time for today. I'm going to need a break in between and something to keep my mind off the drama." I place my hands on her waist and pull her into me.

"What did you have in mind?" Hannah asks, cocking her head and giving me *fuck-me* eyes.

"Well, I'd like to test out some of this lube," I say, kneading her hips and appreciating her lovely curves. "Maybe put that caramel syrup to better use than just adding it to coffee."

Her eyes flare with excitement. "Thinking creatively today, I see."

"Got that right," I say, dipping my head to give her a kiss. "I'm going for my innovation badge today."

CHAPTER 30
HANNAH

Let's talk about sex, baby! Autoimmune diseases can impact intimacy in a wide variety of ways. Fatigue can lead to lower libido, as can hormonal changes. These may be especially significant in autoimmune thyroid diseases like Hashimoto's and Graves'. Inflammatory Bowel Diseases like Crohn's or Ulcerative Colitis often lead to discomfort or body-image issues, such as embarrassment due to an ostomy, that affect one's sex life. Vaginal dryness from a disease such as Sjogren's or Multiple Sclerosis can certainly be an obstacle to intimacy too.

These are just a few examples of how autoimmune diseases can impact intimacy, but have no fear! It is possible to have a rockin' sex life with an autoimmune disease.

The front door swings shut after Taylor, who's trailing the group going hiking today. She was disappointed to hear Caleb wasn't coming, but he promised to play Go Fish with her after dinner, which went a long way toward brightening her demeanor. The little girl so obviously worships him, and I think she might just be the perfect bridge between Caleb and his father.

"So…" Caleb says, leaning against the front door and crossing his arms. "We have condoms. We have lube. We have the house to ourselves for hours. Whatever will we do?"

"I was thinking we could play some cards," I suggest as I approach him. "Get you ready for some grueling Go Fish tonight."

"Only if it's strip poker," he says, opening his arms to welcome me into them. I wind my arms around him, resting my head against his chest. He's so big, and warm, and *safe*.

"I don't know how to play poker," I reply. "I'd rather just fuck."

Caleb sputters out a laugh, his chest shaking beneath my cheek. "Okay, I have to admit, I wasn't expecting you to be that blunt about it," he says once he catches his breath from laughing. "But obviously, I feel the same way."

I pull back to meet his gaze. "Let's get to it, then."

He smiles, and his lips find mine, soft at first, feeling me out. I'm the one who deepens the kiss, leaning into him and sliding my tongue between his lips. As far as I'm concerned, last night was foreplay. Today, I'm ready for the real deal.

Caleb takes the hint, grabbing my ass to haul me as close as possible, our pelvises rubbing together as he devours me. The feeling of him rapidly hardening against me stokes the fire building in my belly.

"Fuck," Caleb mutters when he pulls back to drag in a shaky breath. "There's nothing I want more than to pin you to this door and fuck you right here," he says in a low voice. "But our supplies are upstairs."

I run my fingers down his beard and give it a tug. "First one up gets first crack at the caramel syrup," I whisper, hoping it will take him a second to process what I said as I take off, sprinting toward the stairs. We race up them, Caleb hot on my heels before he ultimately pulls ahead, passing me in the hallway just outside the bedroom. He dives onto the bed, throwing his arms up in victory.

"Damn it," I pant, out of breath.

"Don't worry," Caleb drawls. "I think my win is your win too."

I consider that. Obviously, whatever he wants to do to me with the caramel syrup will be for my benefit, but I won't let us jump straight to having all the attention on me again, even if Caleb did seem to enjoy it last night.

"Only if I get five uninterrupted minutes with your body before the syrup comes out," I say.

His eyebrows lift. "Only five?"

My lips widen into a smirk. "I'd ask for more, but I don't feel like pushing my luck."

Caleb scoots to the edge of the bed, widening his legs to make a home for me between them. "You can ask for whatever you want, sweetheart, and I'll do everything in my power to give it to you."

I settle between his knees, playing with the hem of his shirt. "I want your clothes off."

Caleb reaches behind him with one hand, pulling his t-shirt off in one swift tug. "Done."

I give his chest a gentle shove, lowering him down onto the bed. "I mean all of them," I say as I begin sliding his sweatpants off his legs, followed by his boxers.

Caleb watches me intently as I undress him. "You've gotten me naked," he says when I'm done, his voice gravelly, bordering on hoarse. "Now what are you gonna do with me?"

I climb onto the bed, positioning myself atop him and straddling his hips. "I'm going to get to know you the way you did me," I answer, leaning in to sprinkle kisses down his jaw, pausing at his lips for a long moment before pulling back to admire him. I start at his chest, running my fingers through the light layer of hair there before trailing them down over the curve of his stomach.

Caleb sucks in a breath as I gently scrape my nails over his hips, his hard cock bobbing toward me in invitation. I can't suppress my amused grin at the eager little guy, but instead of giving it the attention it craves, I decide to tease a little longer.

Lowering myself again, I allow my mouth to follow the same path my fingers just did, lips and tongue skating over Caleb's stocky torso. His hands are all over me, squeezing and kneading different areas as I work him over. When I finally reach his erection, it's straining toward me, pleading for my mouth. I take the tip in for a quick suck, lapping up his precum before drawing him deeper. I don't have the saliva to do this for long, but I want to give him what I can.

Caleb lets out a garbled groan when I take him the deepest I have yet. One of his hands lands on my head, fingers threading into my hair. He holds me there for a few more sucks before grasping a handful of hair by the roots and lifting me off his cock.

"I think it's been five minutes," he growls, scooting out from under me and reaching for my t-shirt, tugging it over my head. "Oh yeah," he murmurs once I'm bare from the waist up. He buries his face between my breasts, nuzzling in. A giggle escapes my throat when he licks up the column between them.

"Caleb!" I cry when he turns his attention to my nipples, tugging at them with his teeth.

He glances up at me with a sly smirk. "Had enough?"

I run my thumb down his jaw. "Never."

His eyes blaze. "Take your shorts off, and I'll grab the syrup," he instructs, hopping off the bed and grabbing the bottle of caramel syrup, a bottle of lube, and a condom. Boy scout level: 1,000.

I shuck my shorts off and lie on the bed, awaiting my prize. I may have lost our race, but I feel like the true winner here.

Caleb climbs over me, opening the bottle of syrup. "Stay still," he instructs as he begins squeezing a trail of syrup around one breast and then the other before heading down the midline of my body, just past my belly button. It feels thick and sticky and like it'll be a bitch to clean off, but if it's Caleb's tongue doing the work, I'm not going to complain.

He snaps the cap on the bottle shut and places it on the bedside table, grabbing a hair tie while he's there. The muscles in his arms flex as he ties his hair back—an act I'm learning indicates Caleb means business. He settles himself on the bed, clearly eager to dive in. Unsurprisingly, he begins at my breasts, licking up the pathway of syrup that runs between them.

I squirm beneath him as his mouth moves across my breasts, licking and lapping. My fingers tangle in his hair, urging him lower. His tongue follows the trail down to my belly, wiping all the syrup from my skin. Once it's mostly gone, he dips his head to give my clit a few loving kisses before working his way back up my body, removing any rogue traces of syrup.

"How does it taste?" I ask huskily when he reaches my breasts again.

Caleb's eyes gleam up at me. "Delicious." He holds the bottle of syrup by my mouth. "You want to try?"

I nod, opening my mouth. He squeezes a dollop into it, watching as the syrup drips down, some of it landing on my lips. I dart my tongue out to lap up what I can.

"Swallow it," he says, not taking his eyes off me.

I swallow, the sticky, sweet syrup sliding down my throat. It's so thick it's hard to get down.

"You missed some," Caleb says with a mischievous glint in his eyes before kissing me hard. We both taste of caramel, rich and sweet, our tongues gliding together.

"The caramel's good, but you taste better," I say as I grab his cock and give it a firm stroke.

A hungry growl leaves Caleb's lips. His fingers find my pussy, dipping in then raising to his mouth so he can suck them. "The same goes for you," he says.

I grab the bottle of lube he got out for us—a plain, generic lubricating gel. Nothing fancy, but it should get the job done.

"I figured we'd go simple for the first round," Caleb says, taking the bottle from me. He squeezes some into his hand then cups between my legs, spreading it all around.

"There's that word again. Simple," I say with a teasing smile. "You always say everything is so *simple* when it's anything but."

"You're right," Caleb says as he mounts me. "There's nothing simple about us. We're complicated," he says as he notches himself at my entrance. "And confusing." He slides the tip inside. "And messy." He pushes farther. "And perfect." He bottoms out with a grunt.

I moan as my body stretches to accommodate him. It's a tight fit, but the way he fills me up feels heavenly. He pulls almost all the way out before slowly pushing back in, giving me time to acclimate.

"Caleb," I cry as he does another leisurely slide in and out. His slow and steady pace is the sweetest torture—for both of us, if the way he's biting into his bottom lip hard enough to leave a mark is any indication.

"This feel okay for you?" he asks as his eyes search my face.

It registers that my expression of tortured pleasure is probably indistinguishable from that of being in pain. "Y-yes," I stammer as he pauses, balls deep inside of me. "Just…faster, please."

A slow smile spreads over Caleb's mouth. "You got it," he says, capturing my lips in a kiss as he begins pumping faster. I sigh into his mouth when he finally hits the pace I crave.

"You're taking me so well," he praises. "If we need more lube, just say the word."

I nod silently, unable to form the words to thank him for his thoughtfulness amidst the swarm of sensations that envelop me. The weight of him between my thighs, the scrape of his beard against my skin when he kisses me, the wedding band hanging from his neck, swinging between us as he pounds into me. It's all almost too much, and yet just not quite enough. There's something missing...something I need...but I can't quite remember what it is through the haze of pleasure.

I can't quite put my finger on what I'm craving...until Caleb does. He presses a thumb to my clit, delivering the sweetest friction. My hips jump, thanking him for knowing my body better than I do at this moment.

"Are you close?" he asks, nose tucked into my neck, dropping sloppy kisses wherever his lips can reach.

"Yes," I hiss as his thumb flicks my clit.

"Good," Caleb says, "because I can't hold out much longer."

I reach for his hair, working the elastic out and threading my fingers into his loose locks, giving them a gentle tug. "I don't want you holding out at all," I reply. "I want you to give me everything, Caleb."

His only response is a low moan. His hips work faster, plunging into me as his thumb plays my clit like a guitar, producing the sweetest music I can imagine. It reaches a crescendo when he husks, "I want everything too, Hannah. Give it to me."

My body responds to his whispered command, everything clenching and tightening in an attempt to catch hold of the pure bliss rocketing through my veins. Caleb roars as I contract around him, plunging into me one last time before he hits his own high point with a rugged grunt.

We lie there for long moments, fitted together like two puzzle pieces, suspended in time as my body unwinds like a broken cassette tape. I'm all loose limbs and complete carnal satisfaction. I'm wearing a dreamy smile that probably borders on goofy, but I can't be bothered to wipe it from my face.

Caleb slowly lifts his body off me, though the weight really didn't bother me. It felt less like a burden and more like an anchor, keeping me tethered to this moment instead of drifting off in my head to worries and fears about the status of our relationship.

With a swift kiss on my lips, Caleb lifts himself up. "Be right back." He slides from the bed and heads for the bathroom to take care of the condom. When he returns, he pauses at the edge of the bed, gazing at me laid out in it. He looks my body up, and down, and up again. "You're breathtaking," he says.

My hair must be a wild mess, and I'm sticky with sweat and syrup, but Caleb is looking at me as if I'm the most stunning woman he's ever laid eyes on. He joins me on the bed, gathering me into his arms and tangling his legs with mine.

"That was..." I say, but I can't come up with a word to adequately describe how life-changing that sex was. The thought and care with which Caleb approaches me has always blown me away, but seeing that play out in bed was better than I could have imagined.

He nuzzles between my breasts again, heaving out a sigh as if this is his happy place. "For me too," he mumbles.

I trace the tattoos up and down his arm, winding my fingers around doodles of dragons, spaceships, and mushrooms. The moment is pure peace, our sated bodies intertwined as only the sound of our breathing fills the room. I don't know how long we stay like that, enjoying the peace that comes with both the silence and safety of being in the arms of someone you trust implicitly.

Eventually, the driving urge to clean myself up works its way into my consciousness. I nudge Caleb's cheek with my nose. "I need to shower. Join me?"

His head pops up to reveal a mischievous grin. "I have a better idea." He untangles himself from me and snags his boxers from the floor. "Race you to the lake!" he shouts as he speeds toward the doorway, pulling his boxers up as he goes.

I have absolutely no idea how he went from loose-limbed and snuggling between my boobs to ready to run in the space of a second, but I race to catch up.

"Not fair!" I call out as I frantically search for something to cover my body. I don't have time to look for my swimsuit, so I just grab Caleb's big t-shirt and pull it over my head. Hopefully it's late enough in the season that none of his neighbors will be around, because with one gust of wind, I'll be showing off a lot more than my legs.

"First one there chooses the next type of lube we try!" I hear before the front door slams shut behind Caleb. And I slow down, because I'm honestly dying to know his plans for some of the bottles he bought.

CHAPTER 31
HANNAH

After not one but two outdoor showers—since the first one ended up devolving into activities that just left us messy again—Caleb and I are cuddled up on our bed, fully clothed this time. We're expecting his family to return at any moment, and I, for one, am strongly resisting the urge to rub up against him like a cat in heat until he strips off my clothes and fucks me into tomorrow.

Now that I've had him, it feels like I'll never get enough. I don't know what's going to happen when we return home. Is this a *what-happens-in-New-Hampshire-stays-in-New-Hampshire* type of situation, or is Caleb open to some sort of relationship now? It's been a while since we talked about it, and I know at least my feelings have changed. Where I was once afraid to open my heart for fear of being found inferior again, Caleb showed me that it's possible for someone to love all parts of me—even the ones I have trouble loving myself.

"What are you thinking about?" Caleb asks, stroking his thumb over my jaw.

I roll onto my side until I can meet his gaze. His eyes are soft, accepting, lulling me into honesty. "You," I say as I play with his beard. "Me. Us."

He runs his fingers over my shoulder, down my collarbone, toward his favorite place. "What about us?"

I'm about to launch into a monologue of questions and fears when the front door opens downstairs, inviting in a raucous cacophony of voices. I pick out Taylor's exuberant lilt, recalling moments from their hiking adventure, followed closely by Taryn's high-pitched whine. She's probably overdue for a nap. The adults' voices take off in all directions as they disperse. Caleb's mom's voice is getting closer to us.

"Kids?" she calls from the hallway.

Caleb heaves out a sigh and rolls off the bed to open our door.

"Hey, Mom," he greets her with a peck on her cheek. "How was the hike?"

"It was nice," she replies. "We took lots of breaks because of the girls, so it was just about my speed." She peeks around Caleb's big body to find me lounging on the bed. "How are you feeling, honey?"

Heat floods my cheeks as I recount how I spent what was supposed to be restful time. It may not have included much rest, but it definitely left me rejuvenated. "Much better, thanks," I say. I feel a little bad about lying to get us out of the hike, but honestly, it was worth it.

"Good. So, you'll both be joining us for dinner, then?" she asks.

Caleb rakes his fingers roughly through his hair. "I guess so."

"Caleb," his mom chides.

"Yes, Mom, we'll be joining you for dinner," he forces out.

"Good," she says. "Your dad is grilling, and I'm going to boil some corn and make a salad while the girls rest."

"I'll help you," I pipe up, peeling myself off the bed. Helping prepare dinner will help alleviate some of the guilt I feel for skipping the hike.

"Thank you, Hannah," his mom says with a warm smile.

"I'll help too," Caleb says in a tone that implies he'd rather do anything but.

His mom gives him a firm pat on the shoulder. "That would be lovely."

I slide out the doorway around Caleb to follow his mom down the stairs. He trails close behind me.

"Just lovely," he whispers for my ears only as he palms my backside through my thin athletic shorts. I stealthily slide one pant leg up and to the side to show him there's nothing beneath them.

His groan reverberates the rest of the way down the staircase.

"Great burgers, honey," Marcie says to her husband as she squirts ketchup onto Taryn's plate. Apparently, the little girl likes to dip her potato chips in it.

"Thanks," Caleb's dad replies. "The sides are excellent too." He nods toward me, Caleb, and Caleb's mom. Heather and Greg went back to their hotel-room-slash-love-nest to clean up before dinner and arrived just as we were sitting down to eat. The eight of us are gathered around the large outdoor picnic table with a gorgeous view of the lake while we chow down on the homemade meal.

"Where are you going on your honey sun again, Heather?" Taylor asks. She's taken three nibbles of a hot dog, and now she's squirming in her seat like she's ready for a new activity, even though she should be exhausted from hiking for half the day.

Heather's brows draw together. "My what?"

"I think she means your honeymoon," Caleb's dad says with a grin. "She's always mixing up words like that."

"Ah, I see," Heather says with a chuckle. "We're leaving for St. Thomas at the end of the week. It's an island in the Caribbean."

"Oh." Taylor looks unimpressed. "Will there be ducks you can feed like there are here?"

"Probably not," Heather answers. "But there will be lizards called iguanas and lots of cool fish we can see when we go snorkeling."

An apathetic, "Hmm," is Taylor's only reply. Apparently, the run-of-the-mill ruddy and wood ducks around here are more appealing to the three-year-old than the more exotic creatures of St. Thomas.

"That mix-up reminds me of Matty," Caleb's mom says with a soft smile. "He also confused words like that."

Caleb's entire body stiffens beside me at the mention of his baby brother. The topic somehow hasn't come up in any of the family conversations I've been a part of so far. I imagine everyone's been carefully tiptoeing around the obviously missing member of the family.

"Remember when he came home from his first day of kindergarten and announced there was a boy named *Man* in his class?" his dad asks, grinning as he recalls the memory. "We had to dig out a copy of the class list to check." He turns toward Caleb, whose stiff posture reminds me of an animal that senses danger. "You were the one who noticed there was a little boy named *Guy* in the class and realized that was who Matty was thinking of. Do you remember that?"

Caleb sniffs. "Yep," he replies before taking a huge bite of his burger, clearly not in the mood to reminisce.

"I remember that too," Heather chips in when it becomes obvious Caleb doesn't plan to add any more to his statement. "Matty was *so* embarrassed. I'm pretty sure he avoided the kid for weeks so he wouldn't accidentally call him the wrong name."

All the adults except Caleb chuckle. He stares at his plate, his expression halfway between annoyance and agony. He places his half-eaten burger down with more force than necessary.

I swallow the bite I've been chewing and place a hand on his thigh, unsure whether I'm offering comfort or trying to keep him from standing up and starting a fistfight with his father. His muscles relax slightly under my touch.

"After your honeymoon, will you and Greg come visit us in Illinois?" Taylor asks, clearly not sensing the tension that's covered the table like a veil.

Heather smiles at her half-sister. "I'm not sure when I'll be able to get more time off work, but I'd love to visit soon, yes."

Taylor beams at her. "Awesome! I can't wait to show you my room. I have *thirty-six* stuffed animals. Maybe I'll have even more by the time you come!"

Heather wiggles her eyebrows up and down. "Maybe I'll have to bring you one when I visit."

Taylor's eyes widen comically. "That would be so cool!" The tension from earlier seems to have been diffused until she opens her mouth again. "Will you come too, Caleb?" she asks.

All eyes at the table turn to Caleb.

"No, I don't think I will, kiddo," he replies.

"Why not?" Taylor asks with a pout.

Caleb gives her a sad smile. "It's complicated," he says. "But maybe you'll come visit Heather in Boston some time, and I can take you and Taryn bowling or something." It's hard to miss the way he singles out only visiting with the girls.

Caleb's father takes a sip of water and clears his throat. "You know you're welcome to visit us any time," he says. "Our door is always open."

Caleb nods but offers no further comment.

"It would be really nice for you to see where your father lives," Marcie adds. "It's been three years, Caleb."

I know immediately that this is the straw that's going to break the camel's back. Caleb's muscles coil even tighter than they were before. He's rigid as a board, his hands clenched into fists in his lap.

"I know exactly how many years it's been," he says icily. "Because it's the same number of years since Dad abandoned our family."

"Caleb," his mom warns, which only seems to piss him off more.

"No, Mom, I'm not going to let us sit here and pretend like we're some big happy family," Caleb snarls, "reminiscing and making plans for future visits. We can parade around like everything's okay and have Dad walk Heather down the aisle, but that doesn't make what he did okay. It wasn't okay then, and it's not okay now."

Heather's face has paled to the color of the wedding dress she wore yesterday. I'm glad this torrent of grief and blame held off until today, but it would have been ideal if it could have waited even longer. This week is supposed to be about her, and Caleb has made a valiant effort to keep it together, but this outburst was a long time coming.

Marcie already has Taryn and Taylor out of their seats. "Girls, I think it's time to head in for bed," she says as she herds the girls away from the table and inside the cabin.

"Caleb." His mom shakes her head. "This is not the time or place."

Caleb throws his hands in the air. "What would be, Mom? What's the right time and place to confront Dad about throwing away his wife and two remaining kids just because his favorite one died?"

Shit. There's a lot to unpack there.

"Caleb," Heather tries to cut in, but he's on a roll.

"I can't stand that he got such a spotlight in your wedding," Caleb rants. "And, Mom, I don't understand why you're all accommodating of him and his new family—letting them stay at the cabin, cooking them meals... These are the people he replaced us with!"

"Caleb," Heather tries again, and part of me wishes he would shut up and listen to what his sister has to say, but another part of me realizes he needs this outpouring of emotions—and probably some individual and family therapy, but that's a problem for another day.

"I'm not going to lie to Taylor and tell her, 'Sure, I'll come visit you in Illinois.' I'll come see Dad's perfect new home with his perfect new family. I'll pretend like he didn't just up and leave when times got tough for *our* family."

"Caleb!" Heather shouts, hands outstretched toward him as if she's ready to strangle him. Actually, she just might be. "Dad didn't abandon us because Matty was his favorite or because losing him was hard. He left because Mom had an affair."

The silence that follows is unlike anything I've ever experienced. No one speaks. It seems as if even the birds have stopped chirping. Heather's words stay suspended in the air, creating tension thick enough to cut with a knife.

"What did you say?" Caleb finally asks.

Heather's eyes are huge—she definitely didn't mean to spill that secret—and she looks toward her mom, who nods, giving her permission to speak.

"When Matty died, things obviously got rocky between Mom and Dad. A few months later, Mom had an affair with another man. *That's* the real reason Dad left."

Caleb deflates, practically collapsing into himself. I wrap an arm around his waist as if I could ever be strong enough to hold him up.

"I shut down after Matty died," his dad admits after Caleb has a moment to process. "I isolated myself when I should have leaned on you all and been there for you to lean on too. I wasn't able to offer emotional support to any of you, but most of all, your mother."

"It's not your fault, Dad," Heather says quietly, reaching out for his hand.

"Your dad and I grieved in different ways," his mom offers. "He blocked everything and everyone out when all I wanted was connection. When I couldn't get it from him, I sought it elsewhere. It was wrong and short-lived, but it's what happened."

Heather squeezes her mom's arm in a silent show of support. It's clear by the mature way they're approaching the subject that there have been countless conversations about it—ones Caleb was not privy to.

I drop my arm, curling it into my side. After feeling so welcome this week, I suddenly feel like an imposter in this conversation. This is heavy stuff that should be kept in the family. I want to excuse myself, but I can't seem to manage it while Caleb looks so bereft.

"I...don't get it," he says, shaking his head in disbelief. He looks toward his father. "How could you let me believe all these years that you were some kind of monster who didn't care about his family when Mom's mistake was the reason you left?"

His dad hangs his head at that description of how Caleb's been viewing him. When he looks up again, his eyes are glassy. "We had just lost Matty. You needed your mother. You two have always been so close. If we had told you what happened back then, you would have pinned *her* as the monster. I didn't see how you could grieve for your brother without her, so we made the decision not to tell you. *I* made the decision not to tell you." He runs his hands over his face. "I had hoped after a while you would come around, but it's clear to me that I hurt you enough to potentially ruin our relationship forever."

Caleb looks between his mother and father, then at Heather. His gaze zeroes in on her. "You knew. How did you know?"

Heather presses her lips together guiltily.

"She's the one who first found out," his mother supplies. "She caught me on the phone, talking to my...friend...and confronted me about it. Told me to tell your dad or she would."

And the pieces come together. I always questioned why Heather had a much better relationship with her father than Caleb did.

"How could you keep a secret like that from me?" Caleb asks. He sounds pissed, but I know he's really just hurt and confused.

Heather crosses her arms. "I felt it was up to Mom and Dad to tell you. They never thought it was the right time, so I kept quiet."

"Siblings aren't supposed to keep things like that from each other."

Heather's nostrils flare. As someone who's slightly removed from the situation, I can see that Caleb is just looking for someone to place blame on when, in reality, everyone played their part in this mess. But Heather isn't playing the martyr today.

"I'm not the only one keeping secrets in this family," she says.

My stomach drops because I know exactly what's coming. There are less than a handful of people in this world who know our secret, and she's one of them.

"Mom, Dad, did you know that Caleb and Hannah are married?" Heather asks in a sugary-sweet tone.

CHAPTER 32
HANNAH

h. Shit.

As if this conversation couldn't get any worse.

"Heather!" Caleb cries.

His sister shoots daggers at him with her eyes. "Just making sure there are no more *secrets* in this family."

Shit. This is bad. Like really, really bad. If his parents find out our marriage is fake, it's a slippery slope to finding out our relationship is too. My mind is whirling, and while I am now a factor in this equation, I still think this is a conversation that would be better had among family only. I stand, dusting some crumbs from my shirt.

Caleb's mother looks stricken. "What?" she asks, looking between me and Caleb.

I look down at him. "I'm going to let you talk to your family," I say quietly. He can decide which lies he wants to keep up and which ones he wants to dispel. I can't handle any more hard truths tonight.

"Hannah." Caleb reaches for my hand.

I take it for a quick squeeze then drop it. "I'll be upstairs."

I turn and walk away before the desperation coating Caleb's features can convince me to stay. I've stood by and supported him all week, and while I have no regrets about that, it's left me drained. I have nothing left to give.

Tears sting my eyes as I enter the cabin, and they're falling by the time I'm climbing the stairs. Caleb's family's faces flash through my mind. Heather's seething anger over the family's secrets, fed by years of having to watch her brother hate their father because he didn't have the full story, while she did. The sadness in his dad's eyes as he watched his son learn the truth and realize he spent three years villainizing a victim. His mom's wounded expression when she found out the child she's closest to is married and she didn't know it. And finally, Caleb's look of anguish as I walked away. The image is tattooed on my mind, and I know it will haunt me for years to come.

Fuck. We really messed that one up. Of course, Heather chose a shitty moment to drop the bomb, letting it fuel a fire that was already burning white hot, but our secret hurt people. *We* hurt people. And while that was absolutely *never* our intention, it was the impact we had, and we have to live with that.

Before I even realize it, I have my bags open on the bed, and I'm shoving clothing in various states of disarray into them. I only pause to shoot out an S.O.S. text to Rhiannon, and then I dart to the bathroom to grab my toiletries and cram them in wherever they'll fit. I slow down as I pack my medications to make sure I don't miss any, and then I'm at full speed again, snatching up anything I see in the room that's mine—phone charger, flip-flops, a rogue scrunchie…

I hear footsteps coming up the stairs, and then Caleb is there, shoulders hunched and expression defeated. "Hannah, I—what are you doing?" he asks, freezing in the doorway.

"I'm going home," I reply as I pull the zipper on my duffel bag shut.

"Why?" he asks, still not moving.

I huff out a humorless laugh. "Did you not see what just happened down there?"

Caleb's fingers rake through his beard. "I'm...so sorry about that. That was...messy."

I set aside my own feelings for a moment, tucking them just behind the compassion I feel for him. "Are you okay?"

His enormous sigh holds years' worth of pain. "I'm...I don't know. I'm not thrilled with anyone in my family right now, and I don't think they're too happy with me either. There's a lot of healing to be done."

I nod as I shove a few more things into my wheeled suitcase.

"Please don't leave."

I can't even look at Caleb as I push balled-up wads of clothing down into the corners of my bag to make them fit. "I have to. I can't do this anymore."

"Do what?" he asks.

I straighten and gesture back and forth between us. "This. This marriage was supposed to be a favor between friends, but it's turned into a lie that hurt your entire family. I can't stay here and pretend to be your girlfriend, which, let me remind you, is just another lie for your family to uncover. Not to mention that we've gone and blurred the lines of our agreement, and I don't know *what* to make of that." I shake my head. "The last couple days were a huge mistake."

Caleb's eyes burn into mine. "No, they weren't. We could never be a mistake."

"Then what do you call us?" I demand. "What are we?" I know the answer I'm desperately hoping for, and I also know it's not one I'm likely to get.

"Friends," Caleb says, as if it's that fucking simple.

I roll my eyes and yank the zipper on my bag to close it.

"*Best* friends," he quickly corrects.

"Bullshit," I spit out, done playing the part of the sweet, compassionate girlfriend. I need to look out for myself right now, and I'm afraid my feelings have already gotten too deep to climb out from gracefully. "I already have a best friend, and we don't sleep together."

"Hannah..." Caleb sits on the edge of the bed and drops his head into his hands. "I don't know what to tell you. My head's a little fucked right now."

I sigh because, despite just calling him out on his bullshit, we *are*, first and foremost, friends—even if we've turned into something else entirely. We have shit to figure out, but it's small fish to fry in light of what he just found out about his parents.

"I don't want you to worry about us right now," I say, sitting beside him and leaving a healthy distance between us. "You need to focus on your family stuff. Stay here. Talk to your family. To your dad. We can work things out when you get back. You need to be here right now, but I can't be."

"How will you get home?" he asks. "There are no Ubers around here. I'd lend you my car, but I don't want you driving upset."

The fact that he has the wherewithal to think about my safety amidst the drama swirling around this cabin like a tornado tears my heart in half. Caleb has done nothing but look out for me, and here I am, feeding him to the wolves while I run away like a frightened deer. I can only hope I'm making the right decision, and some time alone with his family will begin mending what's been broken.

"Rhia's on her way up now," I tell him. "She's going to take me home. She'll be here in about an hour." There's a distinct lack of emotion in my voice as I relay this information. It's like the human side of me has shut down, and I've turned into a robot. My capacity for big emotions is shot after the rollercoaster of the past few days.

"Can I..." Caleb looks me over with sad eyes. "Can I hold you until she gets here?"

I wipe away the tears staining my face as new ones fill my eyes. I guess I'm not a robot after all. "Sure," I say as I climb into his lap, allowing myself this one last luxury since I have no idea what awaits us once this storm dies down.

Caleb shifts us back onto the bed and wraps me in his arms,

fitting my head under his chin. There's nothing sexual about this encounter. No one tries to make a move. We're both too depleted to do anything but lie there together, stewing in the secrets that have been exposed today.

⌒

"Did you at least get to bang him before all hell broke loose?" Rhia asks after I've relayed the whole story to her.

"Rhiannon James," I chide, but her crude question brings a very welcome smile to my face.

"What?" She glances away from the road for a moment to look at me. When she sees my amused expression, she goes on. "I just want to know if Caleb's cock is as big as I imagine it to be. He has some real Big Dick Energy, that one."

"I'll say this…you were right about his beard being a real pussy tickler."

Rhia's maniacal screeching fills the car, and I can't help the laugh that pops out of me. Only this girl could have me giggling right after getting my heart broken.

"I knew it!" she cries, gently punching me in the shoulder. "You go, girl."

"Yeah, well…" I turn my gaze out the window, watching the headlights fly by on the other side of the highway. "I'm not sure there's any more where that came from. Caleb's a commitment-phobe."

"Well, considering you just told me he thought his dad had abandoned their family, I can't really say I'm surprised," Rhia points out. "His main example of love was his parents, and he saw his dad flee their marriage, and now he finds out the reason why is that his mom cheated on him. He hasn't exactly had sterling models of what commitment looks like."

I sink into the seat with a sigh. "I know. And I know that now is *not* the time to push him to admit we're more than just friends.

But I can't be the only one feeling this way. The way he looks at me, Rhia…"

"Yeah?" she asks with a hopeful smile aimed my way.

"Yeah," I reply. Caleb has feelings for me. It's plain as day, but with all that's transpired, it might take him some time to come around to them. I'm going to need a lot of distraction while he does, because if he tries to come at me with some "best friends" bullshit again, I'm liable to say something that could ruin us forever.

"We need space," I decide out loud. "He needs to work stuff out with his family, and I need to figure out how I'm going to get affordable health insurance. Because I can't stay married to Caleb."

CHAPTER 33
CALEB

t's been almost twenty-four hours since the truth came out. I didn't sleep a wink last night, and I'm feeling it today. Exhaustion has seeped into my bones, and I vaguely wonder if this is the type of fatigue that Hannah feels on a regular basis.

Hannah. Boy, did I fuck that one up. Her face when I called us best friends? Fucking *devastating.* But how was I supposed to sort through my real feelings when I had just found out that everything I thought I knew was a lie? It wasn't fair to drop the *what are we* question on me after that debacle of a family dinner.

We all retreated to our own corners after the meal, but Mom and I ended up staying up late, talking. She explained her side and how she regrets what she did and how she hurt my dad. She also said she regrets that they waited so long to tell me the truth, but honestly, I can see why they did it. I was a wreck when Matty died, and I don't know what I would have done if I'd known it was my mom who drove the family apart. Would I have vilified her the way I did my dad? Then whose shoulder would I have cried on all those long nights when all I could think about was a future without my little brother?

Heather and I talked this morning. She looked as beat as I

feel, her eyes rimmed with dark circles. I don't think any of us have had a moment's rest since *the conversation*. I told her it wasn't her fault that Mom and Dad burdened her with a secret that wasn't hers to keep. She reminded me that our parents are humans too, and we all made mistakes in this scenario. We hugged it out.

I haven't felt ready to face my dad yet, but as the sun falls lower in the sky, I know it's time. I can't let this day pass without confronting him. I've been holed up in the house most of the day, and I haven't seen him, so I assume he's laying low outside. I pull on a light sweatshirt and begin searching the grounds. Dad's not in his old favorite Adirondack chair out on the porch or in the hammock where he used to sneak in naps while Mom thought he was landscaping.

I spot his hair, the same color as mine but just a little grayer, peeking over a bush as I make my way down to the lake. I find him sitting on a rock, staring out over the water. In about an hour, we'd normally be treated to a gorgeous view of the sunset, but tonight, angry gray clouds dot the sky, likely ruining our visibility.

"Hey, Dad." I take a seat on a rock beside him, planting my feet in the sand.

"Hey, son," he says, tearing his gaze away from the lake and giving me a wan smile. "How you holding up?"

I huff out a breath. "Been better." Scratching at the back of my neck, I bark out a humorless laugh. "Fuck, I don't even know what to say to you. Sorry for hating you all these years? Sorry I've ignored you and cut you out of my life? Sorry Mom broke your heart?" I can think of a million more apologies I could make, but none seem to come close to making up for the rift I've created between us.

"You have nothing to be sorry for, Caleb," my dad says. "How were you supposed to react to your dad leaving so soon after losing your brother? You had every right to be pissed." He stretches out his legs in front of him, windshield-wipering his feet through the sand. "And as for your mom breaking my heart...I was numb at that point. I couldn't feel much of anything. I needed some serious help. I moved back to be closer to my parents, and I got a therapist. I started attending a child loss support group. That's where I met Marcie. Did you know she lost a son too?" he asks.

I shake my head. I don't know much about Marcie. Never asked many questions. And now I feel like shit that I haven't made an effort to get to know my stepmother. I didn't even attend their wedding. Granted, it was a small civil ceremony, but I know Heather was there. From what I've seen of Marcie this week, she's a sweet woman and a fantastic wife and mom. When she made the comment about it having been three years, she was just trying to encourage me to let my dad back into my life. She's been dealing with his side of this grief for almost as long as I've been dealing with mine.

"He was two months old," Dad explains. "SIDS. We have totally different stories of loss, but we still connected instantly. We started arriving early to every meeting so we could chat beforehand. We talked about memories of our kids and shared pictures of them. We wondered what their futures would have looked like. Eventually, we started moving our conversations elsewhere—the park across the street, a coffee shop—and that turned into dinner dates. We could talk for hours—about our kids, but everything else too. She listened to me. And when I didn't want to talk, she sat with me in silence."

"She helped you grieve," I say, realizing Marcie helped my dad the same way my mom helped me, with long conversations and sometimes just holding presence. And unless things had gone the way they did, neither of us would have had that opportunity.

"Your mom and I...we had a wonderful life," my dad continues. "And we created a beautiful family together. But I can say the same about Marcie and me too. I can't help but feel like I was meant to find her. I have no regrets, and I hold no resentment toward your mother. We've moved on. We talked this morning, and we're good. We've *been* good. We just want you to be happy, Caleb. Are you happy?"

I give him a look that says, *really?* because we're sitting here, hashing out my parents' breakup and the resulting fallout. It's not exactly a joy-inducing subject. But then my mind flashes back to the past few days with Hannah. Her smile, her laugh, her moans of pleasure as her body moved beneath mine... This time with her has been heaven.

"Not right now, necessarily, but in life? Yeah, I'm pretty happy."

"Good," Dad says, grinning at me with a disbelieving shake of his head. "I can't believe you're married. I'm so glad you found someone to spend your life with."

I hang my head, staring at the sand. I'd rather count every individual grain on this beach than admit there are yet more secrets between us, but at this point, it feels best to get it all out.

"I have to tell you something. Heather already knows, and I told Mom this morning. Hannah and I *are* legally married but only so she could get on my health insurance plan."

"Huh?" Dad asks.

"Hannah is sick," I explain. "Lupus and Sjogren's—they're autoimmune diseases. She needed affordable health insurance, and mine is free through my company. It seemed like a simple solution to her problem to legally tie her to me so she could be on my insurance. I mean, marriage is just a piece of paper, right? And we can end it anytime."

Dad takes a deep breath in through his nose as if he needs to calm himself before responding. "Caleb..." he begins. "Marriage is so much more than a piece of paper. In fact, the piece of paper is just the beginning. Marriage is a promise to love someone, to fight for them, and to do whatever best serves the relationship at any given point. For your mom and I, that ultimately meant separating, but there were lots of hard moments when we chose to fight for our marriage. You don't raise three kids and see one of them through a brutal battle with cancer without a few bumps in the road. Marriage isn't something to take lightly." He sends me a questioning look. "Didn't it complicate your relationship to get married without it being real?"

"We weren't together when we got married. We were just friends. In fact..." I hesitate because this next secret is one I haven't even confessed to Heather or Mom yet. "We're still just friends. Or maybe we're more now? I don't really know."

Dad puts his hands in the air. "Okay. Back up. What are you talking about?"

I sigh, letting my shoulders fall beneath the relief of finally getting it all out. Every dirty detail. "Hannah and I reconnected when I got back to town and became friends again. *Just* friends. I agreed to marry her as a favor, but she felt she needed to repay me somehow. So, she agreed to be my wedding date and to pretend to be my girlfriend for this week. Mom and Heather are always on my back about finding someone, and I thought if they could see me in a relationship, they would finally leave me alone."

Dad nods slowly, processing. "So, all of this has been fake? You and Hannah?"

"Well, it started out that way. But then...this week...things started to get real."

"Real how?" he asks.

I flash my eyes at him in a *please* look.

Dad chuckles. "Never mind. I don't think I want to know. What I *do* want to know is why you didn't just ask her to be your date for real? You two seem great together, and it seems like it would have made things a lot easier."

I stretch my neck to both sides, stalling for time. Looking back, it probably would have been a lot easier to ask Hannah out for real. But I wasn't ready to put myself out there then, and to be honest, I'm not entirely sure I'm ready now.

"Hannah and I had just reconnected," I explain. "It was so nice to have her back in my life, and I didn't want to fuck it up by trying to make things romantic. It felt safer to stay just friends."

Dad's gaze fastens on mine. "Playing it safe is fine. It's comfortable. But it will almost never push your life forward, Caleb. If you want something more, you're going to have to take some chances. They might not always pan out, but when they do...it makes it all worth it."

My eyes well up at the piece of fatherly advice—the first I've received in years. I haven't always played it safe—not when I played football in high school, or when I moved away for college, or for my first job. But ever since losing Matty and estranging myself from my dad, safety has become more of a priority. Feeling settled in my life and relationships has guided every decision I've made. It's why I decided to take a job closer to home. I've been cocooning myself.

Is that what I did with Hannah too? Cocooned myself in a fake scenario so it didn't feel so scary? Was I just hiding my true feelings beneath the cover of our pretend relationship?

"Look at that," Dad says, and I follow his gaze out over the water, where the clouds have parted to reveal a sliver of a gorgeous sunset. Pinks, purples, and a bold burnt orange paint the horizon. The striking colors draw my eyes, and I can't look away. We enjoy the view in silence for a solid minute before the fast-moving clouds cover the sun's canvas again. We're left staring at a dark-gray sky, reminiscing about the show Mother Nature just put on. And I realize that even if we only got the pleasure of seeing it for a fleeting moment, it was worth it to get to experience it at all.

CHAPTER 34
HANNAH

No New Posts

"A little to the left," Mom says, and I nudge the vase of decorative leaves to the left for the fourth, and hopefully final, time.

Even though Mom is out of her cast now, she still needs to be careful about bearing weight on her leg, as well as engaging in any potentially dangerous activities. That's how I find myself up on a small ladder in her kitchen, helping her swap out the summer decorations she displays on top of the cabinets for the fall ones. Ever since I brought her to get her cast removed, she's been trying to do all her usual busybody activities. I continually have to remind her to take it easy.

"Perfect!" Mom declares with a clap.

I release a sigh of relief. "What next?"

Even though decorating my mom's kitchen on a questionably stable ladder isn't my idea of a perfect Sunday morning, it does prove to be a decent distraction. Since leaving Caleb in New Hampshire last week, I've thrown myself into tasks like this to get my mind off the shitshow that went down there.

I haven't written a word for my blog, nor have I braved any

of my inboxes. I just can't deal with anyone else's problems right now. Instead, I've focused on more mundane tasks, like cleaning out my closet, vacuuming my car, and doing whatever my mom needs help with around her apartment.

It's been good to get some space from Caleb and our situation, but he doesn't exactly make it easy. He texts at least once a day to check on me, and since I can't bear to ignore him, I always send the shortest responses possible.

How are you?

Fine.

Do you need anything?

No.

When can we talk?

Soon.

A few days ago, Caleb texted me that he was home from New Hampshire. I'm glad he spent more time up there with his family, hopefully mending some fences. Then, he texted to let me know he wasn't leaving for his big business trip in New York until Monday. He asked if we could talk before then, but I just didn't feel ready yet. So, I sent him my wordiest response yet: *You should stay focused on your work before the big trip. We can talk when you get back.*

His response was his shortest reply yet: *Okay.*

It's the uncertainty of how our conversation will go that holds me back from having it. I have no idea where Caleb's head is at. Will he have decided that we made a huge, silly mistake we should laugh off and put behind us? Or will he think I'm more drama than I'm worth and say we should cut off our friendship entirely? Or—and I still hold a kernel of hope for this deep in my heart—will he possibly decide he wants to make our relationship the real deal?

Every single one of those possibilities elicits some level of anxiety in me.

Once Mom is fully satisfied with her decor, I return to my apartment to do my daily half hour of job searches. No matter what Caleb decides, I know I can't stay married to him. I can't stand to have anything phony between us anymore. I started putting things in motion to dissolve our marriage the morning after Rhia drove me home from the cabin. And without my marriage to Caleb, I'm going to need a job with benefits.

I find a couple of promising leads that I bookmark before my body is totally spent. Going up and down that damn ladder today did more of a number on me than I realized, so I hunker down on the couch with my heating pad for the evening before another night of shitty sleep.

On Monday, I awake with a familiar heat in my cheeks. I'm not surprised I've thrown myself into a flare with the amount of activity I've been doing to keep myself busy. My head is killing me, which is a newer symptom I've been experiencing the past few times my diseases have flared up. When the headache hasn't abated by Tuesday, I call my doctor for an emergency appointment. Rhia offers to drive me into Boston for it.

After a slew of tests, the doctor diagnoses me with high blood pressure resulting from kidney damage from my Lupus. It's the first time I've heard words like "kidney failure" and "transplant" thrown around in regards to my disease progression, and while those potential complications are years off—if they even happen at all—it's discouraging that I've made so many changes to my life to accommodate this disease, yet it still continues to worsen.

The doctor prescribes me a blood pressure medication to begin taking immediately, and then Rhia drives me home. Apparently, I look as shitty as I feel, because she refuses to leave me alone in my apartment, instead opting to sleep over. We watch an 80's rom-com, and I fall asleep on my couch, just like I did the night Caleb took care of me during a flare. Only, Rhia doesn't carry me to my room and kiss me on the forehead like he did. She just passes out beside me on the couch.

By morning, she's hogging the entire blanket, and I wake up chilly but without a headache, which is good enough for me. It's already ten o'clock, which is late for me, but I know Rhia usually sleeps in. I take a couple minutes to stretch before heading to the kitchen to grab a granola bar and my pills. I return to the couch and take a few bites before swallowing my medications, including the new blood pressure pill. I must be noisy enough that I wake Rhia, and she sits up with a huge yawn.

Turing wide eyes on me, she blurts out, "Shit! Sorry. This is so embarrassing. What's your name again? I don't usually do one-night stands, but..."

I whack her with a dinosaur-chicken-nugget-shaped throw pillow—ironically, a gift from her. "You are so strange," I say, but I'm wearing a fond smile.

She reaches forward to ruffle my already messy hair. "How ya feelin', kid?"

I puff out a breath through pursed lips. "Fine, I guess. My headache is gone."

"That's good," she says encouragingly. "Why don't I make you something more substantial?" she asks, pointing to the crumpled granola bar wrapper I tossed on the coffee table.

"Okay," I reply. "The fridge is fully stocked."

I almost never have groceries in the house, but going to the store was one of my distraction errands a few days ago.

Rhia heads for the kitchen, and a few minutes later, the scent of my favorite maple breakfast sausages wafts into the room. Nausea creeps up my throat, which is odd because I usually love the smell of them. I decide to head out to the kitchen to tell her I might not be so hungry after all, but I only make it a couple steps before lightheadedness overtakes me. I probably stood up too fast.

My vision grows spotty, and I reach for the back of a chair to steady myself, but my hand never quite makes it. The edges of my vision begin closing like I'm heading down a tunnel that's getting smaller and smaller as I approach the exit. I can feel myself falling, but I'm powerless to do anything to stop it.

And then everything goes black.

awaken on a stretcher, confused and looking into the face of a very handsome paramedic.

"What happened?" I croak out.

"You passed out," he tells me. "Your friend here called 9-1-1. She told us you have Lupus?"

"And Sjogren's," I add weakly.

"Right," he says as they carry me out of my apartment building and begin loading me into an ambulance. "We're going to get you to the hospital so they can check you out."

"I'm coming too," Rhia says, trotting alongside the paramedic, her already pale face whiter than I've ever seen it. The fact that she didn't crack a joke about the paramedic "checking me out" tells me just how scared she is. I reach for her hand to give it a reassuring squeeze as she takes a seat beside me in the ambulance.

The paramedic explains everything he's doing as he hooks me up to an oxygen monitor and a blood pressure cuff. It squeezes my upper arm to an uncomfortably tight degree before finally releasing and giving me sweet relief.

"Your blood pressure is really low," the paramedic says with a frown. "Are you on any medications?"

If I wasn't so disoriented, I'd laugh. "Just a few," I say.

"I grabbed your phone," Rhia says, handing it to me and reminding me just how much I adore her. I keep a note in my phone with all my medication names, dosages, and prescribers. I open the note and hand it to the paramedic.

He scans it with skillful eyes. "When did you start taking the last one?" he asks, indicating my new blood pressure medication. *Duh.* Suddenly, it all makes sense.

I close my eyes in defeat. "Yesterday."

"And did you take it this morning?

I nod, eyes still closed.

"That's probably why you fainted," the paramedic says.

"Your dosage may be too high, and your blood pressure dropped when you took it. The doctors at the ER will do other testing to find out for sure."

"Okay, thanks," I say. While it's annoying to be heading back to the hospital for the second day in a row, I'm honestly relieved it's not for a worse problem.

Rhia stays with me in the ER, entertaining me with funny memes she's saved on her phone and stocking me up with junk food from the vending machine. The doctors run their tests and determine the paramedic was correct about the cause of my fainting. They want to keep me overnight to monitor my blood pressure and give me IV fluids, since I'm also mildly dehydrated. With my comorbidities, they don't want to take any chances.

Annie drives my mom in to visit since she's still not cleared to drive yet, and they bring me some basic toiletries and a change of clothes. The two of them hang out until I'm brought to the room I'll stay in overnight. A kind nurse brings me a mediocre hospital dinner of grilled chicken, mashed potatoes, and a vegetable medley of peas, corn, and carrots. Once my visitors have all gone, I settle into my hospital bed, adjusting it to a comfortable angle, and start scrolling through the meager channels for something palatable to watch.

My eyes are just starting to drift shut when the door to my room flies open, alarming me. Did one of the many machines I'm hooked up to report something was off in my body? Did my blood pressure tank again?

But it's not a nurse or a doctor who enters my room. It's a tall, bearded brunet who smells like cedar and pine and makes my heart skip a beat. Like, literally, my heart monitor blips.

"Hannah." Caleb rushes into the room. "Thank God you're okay."

"What are you doing here?" I ask, blinking and glancing at the clock. It's just after nine p.m.

"Rhia texted me that you were in the hospital," he says as he pulls a chair to my bedside. "I was in the investment meeting when she sent the text, so I didn't see it for hours, and then it took hours to drive here..." He plunks down in the chair and tugs at his beard. "*Are* you okay?"

"I'm fine," I reply. "Just a blood pressure issue. Not a huge deal."

Caleb's big body relaxes into the chair. Part of me feels bad that he's been so stressed in his rush to get to me, and part of me resents that he can obviously care so much and yet still not admit to his true feelings. I don't have the energy to sort out my own feelings at the moment, conflicting as they are, but I know for certain that something's got to give.

"How did you get in here?" I ask, glancing at the clock again. "Visiting hours ended over an hour ago."

Caleb leans forward, resting his elbows on his knees. "I told them I'm your husband, and that I was just getting into town. They let me right in."

I flop my head back on the pillows behind me and groan.

"What's wrong?" he asks, immediately on high alert.

"Caleb." I sigh. "You can't use your status as my husband to your advantage just when it suits you."

His eyes narrow, making his deep brown irises look even darker. "I *am* your husband," he rumbles.

"In name only," I shoot back.

"Hannah, when I married you, I told you I would uphold my vows, and that's exactly what I'm doing," he snaps. "In sickness and health. I know you aren't ready to talk yet, but I *am* your husband, and I *will* stand by you like I promised."

"You insist on calling yourself my husband, yet a couple of weeks ago, when I asked you what we were, the answer was '*best friends,*'" I hiss.

I peek over at my heartrate monitor as it beeps faster and faster. I need to cool it before a nurse really does come in here to see what's wrong.

Caleb drops his head into his hands and scrubs them over his face. "I'm sorry," he says quietly when he finally resurfaces. "I guess you were right when you said this wasn't going to be simple," he adds with a sad chuckle.

I press my lips together as I feel the backs of my eyes start to sting. I really don't want to cry right now, but seeing Caleb sitting there exhausted and heartbroken physically pains me. So, with a deep breath, I spit out the words I've been working up the courage to say for weeks.

"I want a divorce."

CHAPTER 35
CALEB

Hannah's words spiral through my mind an inordinate number of times before they finally register. She wants a divorce. She's done. Done with me. Done with *us*.

"Hannah," I begin, but my voice cracks, so I don't say anything more.

"Our deal isn't working," she says, her gaze glued to the wall. She looks so tired, lying in her hospital bed. So fragile. "I don't want to fake anything anymore."

I rub my eyes, the weight of the past few weeks crashing down on me like a tidal wave. My family's secret. Mine and Hannah's. All the pain the truths caused. I don't want to fake anything anymore either.

My dad's words float through my mind: *Marriage is a promise to love someone, fight for them, and do whatever best serves the relationship at any given point.* I might not like the idea of a divorce, but if being married to me is bringing Hannah pain, I'll end it right now.

"I'll do whatever you need," I say. "You know that."

Tears leak from Hannah's eyes, and she still won't look at me. "Good." She nods. "I'll get the papers to you as soon as I have them."

She's already thought this through. This isn't a spur-of-the-moment decision. In our time apart, while I was making peace with my family, she's been plotting to divorce me. And at this point, I can't really say I blame her. I coerced her into marrying me because I was so desperate not to see her suffer. I told her I wasn't interested in dating or marriage. Then I fucked her—in the best sex of my life, I might add—and when she asked what we were, I told her we were just friends. Now, she's in the hospital, her autoimmune diseases acting up most likely due to the stress of what happened in New Hampshire. I probably sent her into this flare–something I swore to myself I'd never do again.

I'm a complete and total prick.

"Hannah, I..." I want to tell her that she means everything to me. That there is nothing in this world more important to me than her health and happiness. I want to get on my knees and beg her for forgiveness. Tell her that I'll do better. I want to plead for another chance. But she looks so worn out. So defeated. I won't do anything to worry her mind further, so I settle for, "Can I do anything for you?"

When she finally looks at me, her eyes are red-rimmed and puffy. She gives me a sad smile. "Just the divorce."

The word is a dagger to my heart, cutting deeper each time she says it. I suppose she doesn't want me to stay, though I'd happily sleep here all night if it meant she might feel differently in the morning.

"I guess I'll get going, then," I say reluctantly. "I'm glad you're alright. Text me when you get home tomorrow?"

Hannah gives me a stiff nod, her lips pursed as if she's holding back tears. I'm resisting my own.

"Goodbye, Hannah," I say, the words sounding far too final.

It takes all my focus to stifle the sobs that want to burst from my throat as I walk away from the hospital. The hospital where Hannah is. The hospital where Matty died. It was nearly impossible to get myself through those front doors in the first place. My feet felt like they were made of lead as I headed across the parking lot—a walk I made so many times while Matty was sick. But I did it for Hannah.

Because I love her.

The realization strikes me like a blow to the head. I love her. Regardless of the labels, or lack thereof, we've put on our relationship, I've fallen for her. Despite all my reservations, all my resistance, I did the one thing I told myself I'd never do. Fall in love.

The tears I've been holding back begin to flow freely as soon as I climb into my car. I just walked away from the woman I love because I was too block-headed to realize how I truly felt until it was too late.

And that's just what it is. Too late.

The last time I heard from Hannah was last week when she sent me a single text: *Home safe.* She hasn't been in contact since, but I've texted Rhia every day to check up on her. She says Hannah is doing fine. She's resting through this flare, and her new blood pressure medication has been balanced out.

I miss her so much my chest literally aches. In the really bad moments, I torture myself by looking back at photos of us together, mostly from Heather's wedding. In our efforts to convince my family we were a couple, we took lots of photos where we were touching and kissing. Those ones hurt the most. They show me what our future could have looked like if I hadn't screwed everything up.

After a week of no direct contact with Hannah, I'm disproportionately excited to receive a letter from her in the mail. At first, I'm surprised she chose snail mail, but I don't know. I guess there's something romantic about it. At least, that's what I think until I tear open the envelope and see what's inside.

Divorce papers.

Hannah's already signed them, and there's a sticky note attached telling me what I have to do in order for them to be finalized. Every fiber of my being shouts at me not to sign them, implores me to try and change her mind. I know in the deepest caverns of my heart that we belong together. That she's it for me. She wormed her way beneath my deeply rooted walls, taking a roundabout route instead of trying to scale them like every other woman who's ever tried to get close to me has.

Who knew a fake relationship and secret marriage would be the key to finally opening my heart?

I grab a pen and place the divorce papers on the counter. My hand shakes with the pen in my grip. This doesn't feel right. But this is what Hannah wants, so this is what she'll get.

Now, I just need to figure out how I'm going to get her back.

CHAPTER 36
HANNAH

The opening notes of "In Your Eyes" by Peter Gabriel float through my slightly cracked window. It's October, but the crisp air feels refreshing. Someone must be playing music out on a balcony nearby or something. I'm lying on my couch beneath a fuzzy blanket, watching trash television because it's about all my mind can handle these days.

I hear a little *plunk*. Then another and another. The music gets louder, and while I love this song because it's from my favorite scene of one of my favorite movies, it's kind of ruining my current chill vibe. When the music only continues to increase in volume, I finally wrench myself up off the couch to find out what's going on.

It only takes a moment to spot him once I get to my window. Standing down on the sidewalk is Caleb, wearing black jeans, a white t-shirt, and a light-brown hoodie—likely his best recreation of John Cusack's outfit in the boombox scene in *Say Anything*. He's holding up a small Bluetooth speaker that is now blasting the 1980's classic.

I shove my window up higher so I can get a better look. Caleb's lips tip up when he sees me, and he holds the speaker up as high as he can, delivering the heartfelt message of the song straight into my ears. Lyrics about following your instincts, dropping a grand façade, and setting aside pride to reach out to someone settle into my mind.

"What are you doing?" I yell over the music.

He opens his mouth to respond but is cut off by a shout from an apartment across the street.

"Keep it down out there!" shouts an old woman with a wicked Boston accent.

Caleb lowers the speaker and presses a button that instantly cuts off the music. "Sorry!" he calls back, holding up a hand in apology. He turns back to my window and cups a hand beside his mouth. "Can I come up?"

"Sure!" I shout, if only to save him from the wrath of my cantankerous neighbor.

As soon as Caleb disappears from sight, I begin pacing the length of space from the window to my door, anxiously awaiting his arrival. Despite my anticipation, I still jump when I hear the knock. He caught me back at the beginning of my pacing cycle by the window, so I rush to the door and pull it open.

"Hi," I breathe, instantly relaxed by his presence. As annoyed as I am at him for wielding his title as my husband to get special privileges—on top of my annoyance with him for talking me into our absurd deal in the first place—my body can't help but melt a little when he's around. It's like it knows just at the sight of him that I'm safe.

"Hi," Caleb replies, his espresso eyes drinking me in. He shoves a packet of papers in my direction. "I signed the divorce papers like you asked." He hands them over to me. "But before you file them, I need to tell you that I don't want a divorce."

My stomach plummets. Why can't he just make this easy?

Caleb continues, his expression earnest. "I want us to be together. For real. I want to try and make this work. I know the last few weeks have been hectic, but I've also learned a lot about myself in that time, and I think I can do better. Talking to my parents made me realize that what happened between them wasn't a lack of love. It was a painful decision made after facing an unimaginable obstacle. And despite everything that happened, they both still believe love is worth it, even if it's complicated. I guess you were right all along when you kept telling me there was nothing simple about this," he cracks with an impish smile. Then his expression turns serious again. "Relationships aren't easy. I get that. My parents chose to end theirs, but that doesn't mean every relationship is doomed to fail. I'm not giving up on us, Hannah. I'm all in."

I stand there stunned for a moment, the divorce papers hanging limply in my hand. I can hardly believe the monologue Caleb just delivered. It's everything I wanted to hear weeks ago. If he'd only had this realization then, we could have avoided all this heartache. Now, it feels like it could be too late.

When I don't respond right away, Caleb takes a deep, shaky breath. "I love you, Hannah," he says, piercing the crevice that's been growing in my heart and cracking it wide open. "I'm sorry I wasn't able to admit it to myself until now. I hate that I was so dense. I hate that I hurt you. I'm pissed at myself, and I'll do anything to make it up to you."

"Caleb," I murmur, taking his cheek in my hand and rubbing my thumb over his jaw, which is tense with worry. He's been through so many emotional ups and downs over the past few weeks, and I can't stand to see him so upset. "Please don't beat yourself up."

He leans into my touch, covering my hand with his own. "I'll spend the rest of my life proving that I'm worthy if you'll give me another chance. You're it for me."

I run my finger over his lips, savoring his words. He's clearly done the emotional work he needed to do, or at least started it. I'm not sure what more I can ask of him, and I can't deny my feelings any longer. I told Caleb I didn't want to fake anything anymore, and I won't pretend I don't feel the same way he does.

"I love you, Caleb," I say, and his eyes light up like I've just told him he won the lottery. "But I still want a divorce." His eyes instantly shutter, so I quickly go on. "*Not* because I don't want to be with you, but because I want to be with you for real. No more secrets. No more lies. Just you and me. All in."

Caleb presses his forehead to mine, our lips lingering just inches apart. "All in," he repeats, his tone edged with wonder. "Divorced and dating," he adds with a chuckle.

"Yes," I reply with a grin. "It goes with our theme of unconventionality, don't you think?"

He nods, our foreheads rubbing together. "I'd rather be unconventional with you than conventional with anyone else."

I brush my fingers through his long hair. "I couldn't agree more."

Caleb sweeps my lips up with his, backing up his declaration of love with a long, lingering kiss. When we finally pull apart for air, he hugs me in tight, wrapping his arms around me like he'll never let me go. We stand there for long minutes, soaking each other in.

"I need to find a job," I eventually mutter against his chest as my brain starts to form logical thoughts again.

Caleb leans back, taking my elbows in his hands. "I thought about that too. And I actually had a plan B in case you told me you wanted to divorce me after all."

I purse my lips at his sardonic look. "What's the plan B?"

"My meeting in New York went well," he replies. "We scored a huge investment for Meet Your Match, and we're going to be able to launch it early next year. That means we're going to need to start marketing. My boss put together a job description for a social media manager, and I asked him to hold off on posting it until I could talk to you. The job is yours if you want it. I already showed my boss your blog and social media pages. He thinks you'd be a perfect fit, and it would mean you'd get the same free health insurance I do. The hours are flexible, and most of it can be done from home. You could still have your blog, but you wouldn't have to rely on it for income anymore. You could stop dealing with those draining messages. And you'd be making a difference with this job too. You'd be helping people potentially find love, which I'm learning is one of the most amazing experiences ever."

As Caleb lists off point after positive point, my eyes fill with tears for the umpteenth time this week. The way he's thought this all through—from my health needs to my need to help others—shows just how much he truly wants to make this work.

"It sounds amazing," I say, wiping a tear from my cheek. "I'm definitely interested. Let me think about it for a day or two, okay?"

"Of course." He uses his thumb to catch another happy tear. "Anything for you."

This time, it's my turn to capture his lips in a kiss. I stand on my tiptoes to reach his mouth and wrap my arms around his neck, tugging at the ends of his hair as I devour him. My thoughtful man. When he says he would do anything for me, I know he means it.

And all I want from him right now is an orgasm.

Caleb takes control of the kiss, backing me up against the wall and capturing my cheeks to tilt my head to the angle he wants it at. His mouth lowers to my neck, pressing kisses all over. I relish the friction of his beard against the sensitive skin there.

"I love you," he murmurs into my neck.

"Take me to bed," I reply, giving his hair a hard pull.

When Caleb pulls back, his eyes are darker than ever. He scoops me into his arms and makes a beeline for my bedroom, placing me gently on my bed.

"Where do you keep the lube?" he asks as he strips off his shirt.

I point to the drawer of my bedside table before removing my own top. Once it's cleared my head, I find Caleb holding *not* the tube of lube I keep in there, but the suction toy that lives with it.

"What's this?" he asks with a saucy smile, turning the toy

around in his hands. He presses the power button, and the toy whirs to life, vibrating at whatever setting I left it on last time I used it.

I try to snatch it from his hands, but he pulls it out of my reach. "You know damn well what that is," I snip. "When you go as many years without a partner as I have, you need a little help."

Caleb's brow spikes. "And this little thing helps you? You like it?"

I nod as my cheeks heat.

He inspects the toy for another moment, then fastens his gaze to mine. "Show me."

CHAPTER 37
HANNAH

"What?" I squeak, totally not expecting that. I figured Caleb would give me the typical *you won't be needing this anymore now that you have me* bullshit. But no. He doesn't see the toy as an adversary. He welcomes it.

Caleb finally hands me the toy and tugs at the waistband of my leggings. "Take these off and show me how you use it."

I lift my hips and pull my leggings off, unnerved by the intensity of his gaze. "You wouldn't rather just use your mouth?" I ask.

He licks his lips. "Trust me, I'll have plenty of opportunities to use my mouth on you, and I look forward to each and every one. Right now, though, I want to see what you like to do with this toy so I can use it on you too."

The images that crash into my mind are downright filthy. As shy as I suddenly feel, I can't deny that I want to see what ideas Caleb will come up with, and if it means I have to put on a little show first, so be it.

"Fine." I lie back against the pillow, bend my knees, and open my legs.

Caleb doesn't take his eyes off me as he slides off the bed to remove his jeans.

"Lube?" I request, putting out my free hand. He hands me the tube, and I apply a little circle around the opening before lowering the toy to my clit. I turn it on and lower it to the second or third setting then settle into the familiar vibrations.

"You don't like it too strong?" Caleb asks, tracking my every move as he sits back on the bed.

I swallow any shred of modesty I have left. "I like to increase the speed as I go."

He nods as if I'm some sort of master teacher, and he's hanging on to my every word.

"And you don't move it around or anything? You just keep it right there?"

"Mhmm," I reply as my hips start drifting up and down to grind against the toy. This is the point where I'd usually start to up the speed and really get into it, but I'm robbed of the pleasure when Caleb grabs the toy out of my hand.

"I think I've got the hang of it," he says. "I'll take it from here."

I let out a surly grumble. My little toy and I can do just fine on our own, but if he thinks he can do better, I'll let him try.

Caleb's tongue shoots out to wet his lips as he surveys my body. He runs a hand up my thigh then keeps going higher, tracing a line up my side all the way to my breast. He takes my nipple gently between his thumb and forefinger. "Do you ever use it here?"

I shake my head as he latches the toy onto one nipple while continuing to play with the other.

"I n-never thought of th-that," I stammer as he increases the speed of the suction vibrator. My back arches involuntarily. Part of me still wishes it was his mouth on me, but another part knows a human could never achieve this same sensation.

"Does that feel good?" Caleb asks, his wicked smile telling me he already knows the answer to that.

I nod, and he moves the toy to my other breast. He leans down to steal a kiss then nuzzles next to my ear. "Imagine how good it will feel on your clit while I'm inside you," he whispers with a light nip on my earlobe.

A moan rips from my throat. "Do it," I encourage, reaching blindly until I find his groin, giving the bulge in his boxers a squeeze. The suction on my nipple halts. Caleb places the toy on the bed and tears his boxers off. He rolls on a condom he pulled from his jeans' pocket then gets back on the bed.

"Hannah," he whispers as he settles over me, brushing my hair from my face and placing a reverent kiss on my forehead.

I give his ass a little squeeze. "I love you," I reply.

He smirks down at me then gathers me into his arms and rolls us over until I'm on top. "This will work better if you're riding me," he says.

I scramble to sit up and get another dollop of lube, spreading it over my palm then taking Caleb's cock in my fist. A few strokes has him both lubricated and panting. He grips my hips as I line myself up over him. I sink down onto him, sighing as he fills me up so well.

"Fuck, Hannah, you feel perfect," he mutters, his fingers biting into my flesh.

I ride him up and down leisurely a few times as I acclimate to his size. Then, we fall into a good rhythm. I lift my hips at a steady rate as he shifts his hands farther back to help guide me.

I fight disappointment when his hands fall away, but I quickly regroup when I realize he was just reaching for the suction toy. My rhythm falters as I think of what's coming. Caleb's whispered promise.

"Don't stop," he warns as he applies lube to the toy just like I did.

I focus on my movements while my heart and mind race with anticipation. My body jolts when Caleb presses the toy to my clit at the higher setting he worked it up to on my nipples. He quickly lowers the speed, and I hiss as it hits just right. He holds the toy steady while I grind on him, my eyes closing as I zero in on the onslaught of sensations.

"Shit, that feels good," I tell him. Reaching back, I press my palms into his thick thighs and arch my back, pushing my chest out in invitation. With his free hand, Caleb manages to toy with my sensitized nipples. I move faster, and Caleb ups the speed of the toy.

"Caleb," I moan as I really hit my stride. I'm swiveling my hips, arching into his touch and the suction of the toy. It feels so, so good, and I can feel myself about to fall apart.

"Keep it up, Hannah," Caleb says, increasing the speed one more bump.

"Caleb I…oh, fuck," I cry as I come hard, head thrown back, stars blurring my vision. Everything in me clenches tight, as if my body is trying to hold onto this feeling and never let it go. I vaguely register the speed of the toy lowering to a simmer, and it feels incredible against my clit as I pulse around Caleb's length. The heat in my belly flares in what is, without a doubt, the longest orgasm of my life.

Somewhere halfway through, Caleb is coming too, the fingers of his free hand digging into the flesh of my left breast as he pours himself into the condom. God bless him, he does not lose his grip on that toy until I've ridden out my entire orgasm. Then, he turns it off and gently sets it aside before pulling me down on top of him.

"That was fun," he says, his voice muffled against my shoulder. "You'll have to show me if you have any other toys. I'm always down for an electronic third in the bedroom."

I chuckle against his chest. "I have a couple more, actually," I say, and I swear I feel him harden slightly beneath me.

"God, yes," he whispers as he drags his tongue over my collarbone.

I roll to the side so I can face him. "The toys really help when I'm having a bad joint pain day and can't…go acoustic," I say, wiggling my fingers.

He smirks at my description but then sobers. "How often do you have days like that?"

My shoulder that's not pressing into the bed lifts with a shrug. "It depends."

"On?"

"If I'm in a flare or not, if I'm eating well, what the weather is outside..."

Caleb's brows pull together with concern. I know how much he worries about me, and I'm not sure how to reassure him. It's not like I can say I'll heal from these diseases. I'll have them for the rest of my life. They'll ebb and flow and likely get worse over time. They increase my risks for all sorts of serious things from kidney failure to non-Hodgkin lymphoma. Any pregnancies I have will be high risk. No one can ever know what will happen in the future, but life with a partner who's chronically ill is especially unpredictable.

"Are you sure you want this?" I ask, because despite all the progress we've made, I need to know that he's really sure. It's not just a relationship—which is already a big jump for Caleb. It's a relationship with someone who will always, *always* have to live with illnesses that limit her life. Illnesses that will cause her to cancel plans and give her anxiety about making them in the first place. Illnesses that will cause new symptoms to pop up periodically and send her to the hospital at times. Illnesses that force her to be a different person than the one she may really want to be. "My illnesses could become a real burden for you," I add.

"Hannah." Caleb cups my cheek in his palm and gazes at me so lovingly I have to look away for a moment so as not to burst into tears. "I wish you could see yourself through my eyes," he says.

I swallow the lump in my throat and look back at him. His eyes are soft, his hair falling messily over his forehead as he strokes my cheek. I could look at him like this forever. Serene, sated, and incredibly sexy.

"What do I look like in your eyes?"

His lips slip into a smile. "You are the most beautiful, most resilient, and strongest woman I've ever known," he says. "You live every day with an unfair amount of pain and fatigue, and you do it with grace. You are not a burden, but you are a person bearing a heavy burden that you don't deserve to carry alone. It would be my honor to carry it with you." Caleb grabs my hand and holds it snugly in his. "Please, let me help carry it, Hannah."

Tears track down my cheeks. I didn't know I could cry more than I have in the past couple of weeks, but perhaps there's a separate well of happy tears that's now just overflowing.

"Okay," I reply, tugging our joined hands to my mouth for a kiss.

EPILOGUE
CALEB

The sound of our loved ones singing "Happy Divorce Day" to the tune of "Happy Birthday" pierces the air of an otherwise quiet morning at Waffee. The divorce was made official today, and Hannah and I threw a little party to celebrate. Rhia, Heather, and Greg are here with us, and we're all gathered around a couple of tables we pushed together in the corner of the café.

Rhia got the barista to write "Happy Divorce!" on a large, waffled skillet cookie, and a mishmash of candles sticks out of it, flames flickering in invitation. When the song is over, Hannah and I blow out the candles together to a chorus of "Make a wish!" shouts.

I thought I might be sad today, since I always harbored a wish in the very back of my heart that Hannah might decide she wanted to stay married, but I'm not. I actually feel relieved. There are no more secrets surrounding us like sharks in the water. Today, we can begin the second part of our relationship: the *real* part. And I plan to woo Hannah as if we're starting from scratch, even though we've been happily together for the past few months.

Heather cuts the huge cookie into five incredibly uneven

slices, and Hannah claims the biggest one when she's given the first shot. I take the next biggest—it's only fair—and we devour our cookie slices before Rhia pulls out a couple of gift bags.

"I brought presents!" she announces. Hannah audibly groans. She told me about Rhia's penchant for giving wacky gifts, so I'm kind of excited to open mine.

I burst out laughing when I see the "I <3 My Ex-Wife" t-shirt wrapped in corgi-adorned tissue paper. Hannah pulls out a matching "I <3 My Ex-Husband" shirt and holds it up in front of her body.

She shakes her head with a grin. "They're perfect," she says to her friend.

Rhia grins, satisfied.

"I have something too." I pull a small, velvet box from my pocket and kneel in front of Hannah's chair. Her eyes go wide, and she puts her hands up as if to say *stop!* I know what she's thinking, which makes this all that much better. I do hope to propose to her for real someday, but I know we need time to just be us—Hannah and Caleb, the *un*married couple—before we take that step.

"Hannah," I begin, and her mouth flops open like she wants to stop me but can't find the words. I crack open the box to reveal the jewelry—*not* a ring—housed inside. It's a pair of gold earring studs shaped like hearts with a small diamond embedded in each one.

"Will you be my girlfriend?" I ask. "For real this time?"

Hannah places a hand on her heart and releases a breath. "Oh my God," she says. "I totally thought that was going in a different direction."

Everyone around us chuckles. I told them my plan so they wouldn't be worried, but if I'm being honest, I kind of wanted to see Hannah squirm for a second.

"Of course I'll be your girlfriend, Caleb," she says with a smile that's as bright as the sun.

I take out the earrings and hand them to her to put on. They look perfect.

"I had them made with your ring," I explain. Hannah returned her ring to me when we filed the divorce papers. I told her she could keep it, but she felt it was rightfully mine since I'd paid for it. I decided I would want to buy a different ring when I propose for real, so there was no reason to keep this one. I still wear my ring around my neck.

Hannah's eyes shine with unshed tears. "I love it," she whispers as she looks down at the charm then back up at me. "I love you."

"And I love you," I reply as I gaze fondly at the woman who will always be perfect in my eyes.

THE END

If you enjoyed this book, I sincerely hope you'll consider leaving a review on Amazon, Bookbub, Goodreads, or another platform. This makes such a huge impact for indie authors!

Watch Rhiannon find her happily ever after in *In Another Life*, coming October 2o, 2025!

Sign up for my newsletter at www.mollymccarthybooks.com/ newsletter for exclusive updates about upcoming releases, freebies & sales, and more!

Find me on Instagram, Threads, and TikTok as @mollymccarthybooks

AUTHOR'S NOTE

This book is incredibly special to me. Like Hannah, I was diagnosed with an autoimmune disease called Sjogren's in college. It rocked me to my core and impacted every area of my life in a way I could have never prepared for. I had to leave school, lost friends, lost dreams, and, frankly, lost my identity. Eight years later, I look back and laugh at the "five-year plan" I had. It most certainly didn't have writing romance novels on it! While my life doesn't look the way I may have imagined it would, and it may be "smaller" than many of my counterparts', I'm proud to say I'm content with it.

One of my main goals with this book was to highlight some of the many challenges people with chronic illness face—particularly young women. So often, our symptoms are ignored or pushed aside as us overreacting or—worse—"just anxiety." (Newsflash: I had anxiety long before I had Sjogren's. I could tell the difference). Diagnosis often takes years, and we have to advocate for ourselves because no one else will. These universal challenges call for a systemic change in medicine and patient care. All patients and their symptoms deserve to be taken seriously and treated with the respect that one would treat someone with a visible injury.

I am also immensely proud of this book because I wrote it during a particularly tumultuous time in my life. This story saw me through chronic illness flares, major mental health struggles, and leaving a toxic job. It took me much longer than anticipated to write, but I believe this book was worth the wait, and I hope you do too!

My deepest wish is that other chronically ill folks feel seen and validated in Hannah's story. I hope they realize that they are worthy of love, caring, and satisfaction in life. Chronic illness does not make you a burden. It *is* a burden, and you shouldn't have to carry it alone.

Love,

Molly

ACKNOWLEDGMENTS

First off, thank you, reader, for picking up this book. I'll never get over the fact that people care about the stories living inside my head. Whether it's your first or last book of mine, or (hopefully) one of many, I am so grateful.

Thank you to Alyssa and Laura, as always, for your helpful feedback and encouragement. I'm so grateful we've connected not only over having chronic illnesses but over our shared love of literature. Life is so weird and wonderful sometimes.

Thank you to my mom, or Mama Bear, who advocated for me when I was too lost to do it myself. And to my dad, brother, and the rest of my family, as well as Lori, Robyn, and Miranda, who have stayed by my side and supported me through it all.

Thank you to the doctors who believed me and treated me with the care and respect every patient deserves. And thank you to organizations like the Sjogren's Foundation—keep doing the important work.

I am also endlessly grateful to the chronic illness community online for showing me that I'm not alone and that there is a beautiful life to be lived even when your body is fighting against itself.

To my own hole-in-the-wall café, where I spent hours upon hours in the first few years after diagnosis (and where I am currently writing this), thank you for providing the space and sustenance—in the form of food as well as friendship—I needed to carry me through that time.

Finally, to the friends I lost, the college administrators who screwed me over, and the doctor who told me, when I asked how to go on living with this illness, "There are CEOs of companies with Lupus. They just do it," I forgive you. Chronic illness is complicated. I hope you never have to experience it, and if you do, I hope you receive more compassion than you gave me.

ABOUT THE AUTHOR

Molly McCarthy is an avid romance reader and writer living just outside Boston, MA. She can often be found typing away in a café, drinking a latte, and dreaming of happily ever afters. Keep up with Molly on Instagram @mollymccarthybooks.

ALSO BY MOLLY MCCARTHY

The McNally Men

Beauty In The Details

A New Beau

More Beautiful Than Before

Chronically In Love

In Another Life